I drop the vest in the backseat and let my mouth hover closer, closer to his. "Forget the academy rules for tonight. Go back to being the Grim Reaper tomorrow."

"One night," he rasps. "You think that's all this would be?"

"I don't know." I brush his mouth with mine. "How many nights do you need to get me out of your system?"

Something about my question upsets him. His eyebrows draw together, his grip tightening anew on my wrist. "Get back in your goddamn seat."

"No." Whew. I must be out of my mind. Anyone with working brain cells can see he's about to get tough with me. Reject me. Hurt my feelings out of necessity. But something tells me I'll never get another chance to see under his exterior if I don't rip it down right now. So before he can open his mouth and deliver whatever lie he's thinking, I kiss him.

And we go up in flames.

By Tessa Bailey

The Academy Series
DISORDERLY CONDUCT • INDECENT EXPOSURE
DISTURBING HIS PEACE

Romancing the Clarksons
TOO HOT TO HANDLE • TOO WILD TO TAME
TOO HARD TO FORGET • TOO CLOSE TO CALL (novella)
TOO BEAUTIFUL TO BREAK

Made in Jersey Series
CRASHED OUT • ROUGH RHYTHM
THROWN DOWN • WORKED UP • WOUND TIGHT

Broke and Beautiful Series
CHASE ME • NEED ME • MAKE ME

Crossing the Line Series
RISKING IT ALL • UP IN SMOKE
BOILING POINT • RAW REDEMPTION

Line of Duty Series
PROTECTING WHAT'S HIS
PROTECTING WHAT'S THEIRS (novella)
HIS RISK TO TAKE • OFFICER OFF LIMITS
ASKING FOR TROUBLE • STAKING HIS CLAIM

Serve Series
OWNED BY FATE • EXPOSED BY FATE
DRIVEN BY FATE

Standalone Books
UNFIXABLE
BAITING THE MAID OF HONOR • OFF BASE

ATTENTION: ORGANIZATIONS AND CORPORATIONS
HarperCollins books may be purchased for educational, business, or sales promotional use. For information, please e-mail the Special Markets Department at SPsales@harpercollins.com.

TESSA BAILEY

Disturbing HIS PEACE

THE ACADEMY

AVONBOOKS

An Imprint of HarperCollinsPublishers

This is a work of fiction. Names, characters, places, and incidents are products of the author's imagination or are used fictitiously and are not to be construed as real. Any resemblance to actual events, locales, organizations, or persons, living or dead, is entirely coincidental.

DISTURBING HIS PEACE. Copyright © 2018 by Tessa Bailey. All rights reserved. Printed in the United States of America. No part of this book may be used or reproduced in any manner whatsoever without written permission except in the case of brief quotations embodied in critical articles and reviews. For information, address HarperCollins Publishers, 195 Broadway, New York, NY 10007.

First Avon Books mass market printing: May 2018

Print Edition ISBN: 978-0-06-246712-6
Digital Edition ISBN: 978-0-06-246713-3

Cover design by Nadine Badalaty
Cover photographs, Front: © Michael Frost Photography (man);
© Stanisic Vladimir/Shutterstock (background); © SFIO CRACHO/
Shutterstock (desk, window); © Nikelser/Shutterstock (kiss); Spine:
© IIIerlok_Xolms/Shutterstock (kiss)

Avon, Avon & logo, and Avon Books & logo are registered trademarks of HarperCollins Publishers in the United States of America and other countries.

HarperCollins is a registered trademark of HarperCollins Publishers in the United States of America and other countries.

FIRST EDITION

HB 09.12.2023

If you purchased this book without a cover, you should be aware that this book is stolen property. It was reported as "unsold and destroyed" to the publisher, and neither the author nor the publisher has received any payment for this "stripped book."

ACKNOWLEDGMENTS

Thank you so much for reading this book, guys. I know. I always seem to leave that one couple on the back burner, letting them simmer until they're just right—thank you for waiting and being excited for them along with me. Greer and Danika have a big, spacious home in my heart. Right now, they're totally getting their cuddle on and Greer is saying words with his mouth, but in his head, he's thanking fate on an endless loop for giving him Danika. She's doing the same.

Thank you to my editor, Nicole Fischer, for helping me shape this story and series up to the final moment—what an awesome, stress-free working relationship we have. Let's never change. Thank you to my husband and daughter for getting out of the house so I can work in silence—sometimes that's all it takes! Thank you to my Bailey's Babes

Facebook group for being spectacular and inappropriate. And a huge thank you to the bloggers and readers who review my books at the expense of their own time or come to see me at signings. It does not go unappreciated.

I love you all! x

Disturbing
HIS PEACE

CHAPTER 1
— *Danika* —

The ground rumbles when he walks in.

Weird how I'm the only one that seems to notice.

Okay, not the *only* one. There's a trio of other female recruits parked up against the gymnasium wall that zero in on Lieutenant Greer Burns's shifting butt muscles, shaking their heads as if they're mad at it. The dudes stretching around me on the mat are a different story. They live and die by the lieutenant's whistle, but until he blows it, they're still lost in their world of women, baseball and ball scratching.

Ahh, the academy. Never change.

There's this sliver of time, twice a week, that I love to hate. When Greer is scheduled to whip our future police officer backsides into shape, I'm treated with—cursed with—a window of five seconds before he blows the whistle for inspection. During that handful of ticks, he slowly inserts that whistle between a pair of lips that make grandmothers wish for time machines. He tucks it *right* in there. And he looks at me. One cool sweep of those twin glaciers that begins at the tip of my sneakers and ends at my ponytail.

That's around the time I tell him with my eyes to *go fuck himself.*

It's a complicated dynamic.

Anyone else would get suspended for showing the lieutenant a hint of the fire I pack into my morning look. Why does he let me get away with it?

Even more annoying, why do I look forward to it?

Greer hasn't quite made it to the front of the gymnasium yet, but there's a jet stream of anticipation whipping through my blood in hot revolutions. My spine straightens and I firm my jaw, telling myself this time I won't meet his eyes. I'm distracted from my mental preparations when a male recruit drops down on the mat beside me, blocking my view of the approaching lieutenant. His timing is either terrible or perfect. My body is too confused these days to decide.

"Hey, Silva."

"Levi." I flash a tight smile at our resident easy-going, golden boy who's never without a smile or a compliment. "What's up?"

Over his shoulder, I catch the eye of my best friend, Jack, who lets his tongue loll out of his mouth like a lovesick idiot. His impression of Levi, I'm guessing, who has been flirting with me since we started at the academy, but has yet to pull the trigger and ask me out.

To which I would say . . . what? No freaking clue.

"What did you think about COBRA training yesterday?" Levi asks, grabbing his elbow above his head and stretching. "Heavy stuff, right?"

He's referring to the Chemical Ordinance, Biological and Radiological Awareness training we spent the last few days completing. "Yeah." I tear my attention away from Jack, who is now pretending to make out with himself. "There's no cute way to rock a hazmat suit, I guess."

"Oh, I don't know." Levi cuts me a look. "I think you did a damn good job."

Impressive. Ten points to Levi. See, I should be asking *him* out. He's the definition of my type. Growing up around my uncles and boy cousins meant I was always one of the guys. They didn't pull any punches while playing football in the park or critiquing my homecoming dresses with sarcasm. My mother was—*is*—amazing at making me feel girly when necessary, but there was no escaping the men in my family. As a result, I'm drawn to softer-spoken artistic types that treat me like a lady. Which is the number one reason I shouldn't be so . . . affected by the sight of the lieutenant sliding a whistle between his lips. There's *nothing* soft about him.

When Levi chuckles, I realize I've been staring into space. *Way to take a compliment, Danika.* "Uh. Thanks. You . . ." I give him a soft punch in the shoulder. "Did it justice, too."

I'm saved from having to bask in the aftermath of my awkward attempt at flirting when Jack pokes his head in between us and makes a buzzer noise. "Snooze you lose, Levi. Gave you a good two minutes to close the deal. More than enough time." He winks at me, letting me know I owe him one for his intervention. "Danika has plans for the night, anyway. She's cake tasting."

My stomach groans, reminding me I skipped breakfast. "I am?"

Jack nods. "Pays to know the lady who is catering our graduation."

I don't know what's flowing through the drinking fountains at the academy, but in the months since we started, both of my roommates, Jack and Charlie, have been brought to heel by the almighty L word. And I'm not talking the fizzy stomach bubbles, let's share a soda pop kind of love. I'm talking all-out, devoted, want their women to have their babies kind of love. It's a little daunting when I have zero romantic prospects of my own and I can hear the proof of their affection through the thin walls of our apartment. Nightly. My suffering has all become worth it, though, with the utterance of the words *cake tasting.* "I'll be there—"

The whistle blows. *Loud.*

All two-hundred recruits jump to their feet and form rows. Backs go ramrod straight, *chests* puff out. Inspection is always twice as intense when Greer is here, because he doesn't just take roll. He scrutinizes each of us for imperfections. Legend has it, he once made a recruit walk home from 20th Street to the Bronx to retrieve his forgotten uniform gym shorts. And that recruit was never seen or heard from again.

Out of the corner of my eye, I watch the lieutenant approach, my attention traveling down to perform their own inspection on the object of my reluctant obsession. The thighs that—against my will—changed my type from artistic, easygoing guys to big, rough-hewn enforcers. They demand to be taken seriously, as does their owner, by doing nothing more than existing. Through stiff, navy blue uniform pants, sinew creeps from hips to knee, muscles sculpted by a diamond cutter. In weak moments, I find myself wondering if they're hairy or smooth. Or ticklish? Could the man have such a silly weakness as being ticklish?

No. Not a chance.

Lieutenant Greer Burns doesn't have weaknesses. As he strides past the inspection line, the humming halogens overhead paint shadows on his face, darkness settling in the always present frown lines between his eyebrows. When his eyes land on me, his jaw bunches. When is it *not* bunched? It tics and flexes like he's trying to suck the copper off a penny. That tension must be the reason my eyes are drawn to his brutal lips, harsh and full all at once.

He leaves my line of vision, his boots making the mat groan as he weaves behind me, and I'm not—*definitely* not—disappointed that I missed my five second stare-down with Greer today. I'm not annoyed at Levi and Jack for distracting me either. Nope. Uh-uh.

Greer is right behind me when he says, "I'll be demonstrating a new takedown this morning." I feel his gaze on my neck, heating the flesh above my collar. "Any volunteers?"

My hand goes up. It always does, even though he never picks me. Ever. I tell myself it's stupid to think he's afraid to touch me.

My theory is further disproven a second later.

"Silva. To the front."

Greer

What the hell are you doing?

I can't even *think* of the girl without getting wood. Now I'm going to wrestle her onto the mat in front of two hundred recruits?

Silva's head turns slowly, hitting me with the full force of her surprise. And not for the first time, I'm caught between wanting to lick her, head to toe . . . and telling her the gray academy T-shirt really brings out her eyes.

Idiot. You fucking idiot.

This wouldn't be happening if she'd just kept our arrangement. It's very simple. Before I blow the whistle for inspection and become her instructor, she gives me a few seconds of her undivided attention. Obviously we never made this agreement out loud. How would that conversation even start? But it's the one thing I look forward to lately.

Even if she does hate me.

Why wouldn't she? My default mode is insufferable asshole. This is my city and I've been tasked with whipping this group of young people into effective members of law enforcement. I take that responsibility seriously. So why do I like letting Silva get away with that open disdain *so damn much*? I can't tell her that she's . . . important. Special. Even if those words cram into my throat when she's around, twisting my stomach up like a pretzel. So I satisfy the urge by letting those heated looks slide and hope she doesn't sense this pointless infatuation of mine.

She's definitely going to catch on when I pin her to the floor and my cock salutes the tight, sexy shape of her. God, what is she going to *feel* like under me?

Silva isn't the only one shocked that I picked her for the demonstration. My brother, Charlie, is giving me jerky *bad idea, bad idea* head shakes, making me wonder if he's caught me staring like a fool at his roommate. If so, I need to be more careful. Recruits are off-limits. I've never had a problem adhering to that rule in the past. Not even close. They were all just uniforms with varying skill levels until she showed up.

Some jackass two rows back whispers about how *he* wouldn't mind pinning Silva, and the comment brings my focus roaring back. Jesus, it's that shithead who always wears aviator sunglasses again. He goes white when I turn and narrow my eyes on him. "I hope you don't mind staying an hour late today and wiping down the mats, because that's how you'll be spending your evening," I snap. "Try and locate some respect while you're down there."

"Yes, sir."

Christ, on top of being sex-starved for an off-limits girl, I'm now a hypocrite. Didn't I choose Danika for the demonstration because I *hated* watching her flirt with someone else? Because *I* wouldn't mind pinning her, to put it mildly. Yes. *Hell* yes. And that moment of weakness is going to cost me big-time because in a few minutes, her curves are going to be pressed to mine. I'm going to have her beneath me. She's the only one inside these four walls that could shake my professionalism with something as routine as a takedown—and I've damned myself with my jealousy.

"Was I somehow unclear?" Self-disgust makes my voice hard as I pivot to face Silva again. "To the *front*."

The way she jerks on a gasp stabs me in the gut. For a split second, right before I shouted at her, there was wonder, maybe even appreciation, in the way she looked at me. Because I stood up for her? The possibility makes me wish I'd suspended the recruit who made the comment. Or sent him on a walk to Montauk. How would she have looked at me then?

Doesn't matter now, because I ruined it.

Just like I'm about to ruin myself.

Following in Silva's wake to the front of the room, I can't help but suck in the fresh grapefruit scent that follows her. I don't know for sure, but I think it comes from her shampoo. Perfect, now I'm trying not to think of her in the shower, soaping all those black, wavy curls she keeps up in her ponytail. Trying not to think of steam clinging to her full, sarcastic lips and taut skin. Good thoughts to be having when I'm about to wrestle her in front of a crowd.

There is total silence, apart from the lights buzzing overhead and the occasional cough. In my head, though, there's a riot taking place. Will I ever be satisfied with five seconds of eye contact ever again once I've had her beneath me? Of course not. Hell, I'm not satisfied *now*.

"As you know, an officer never wants to end up on the ground. Your weapon becomes accessible to someone other than yourself. There's a lack of mobility and a potential to be assaulted by a perp. In other words, this is a worst-case scenario."

I'm about halfway through the beginning of my speech when it dawns on me that a guard escape is probably the most intimate move I could have chosen. It's not something I did intentionally after selecting Silva as my volunteer, it was on the morning agenda—and now it's too late to change course.

Silva is beside me, trying to look fresh out of fucks, but I can see the pulse going wild in her neck, the eagerness to learn in her brown eyes. It starts my own pulse hammering, that determination in her. That bravery. Just some of the reasons I can't seem to make it through an hour of the day without thinking about her.

"The goal of a guard escape is to gain back control of the situation and get your perp cuffed, as fast as possible, before you can be subdued or worse. Understood?" I wait for the chorus of *yes sirs* before lying on my back. They've seen me down here countless times, demonstrating moves—it's a vital part of their training—and I try and fail to focus on the familiarity of teaching. How can I when Silva is staring down at me, her mouth in a little O. "Feign an attack, Silva."

"On . . . you?" she whispers.

"Yes." She's nervous. Before I can make a conscious decision, the need to reassure her takes over. "This is it. Your chance has finally arrived."

Laughter ripples through the recruits and it seems to ground her. But I'm the furthest thing from grounded when Silva drops down on her knees between my bent legs. Her tits are still jiggling when she wets her lips, and I'm the furthest thing from fucked. My balls are suddenly five pounds each, pressing in around the base of my dick. *Christ.* This is already torture, but I have no choice but to get even closer. Any other time, I would continue my lecture from the ground, but I can't. I have to get this over with as fast as possible.

Her cheeks are fire-engine red as she leans over me, her dukes up, punching at the air. And with a final, hard swallow, I lock my legs around her waist, bringing her head down safely into the crook of my neck to stop the supposed attack. Then I drop a foot to the outside of her planted knee and use the ground as leverage to flip her over.

It's the sound that comes out of her mouth that well and truly screws me.

That—and the way her eyes roll back, swollen lips popping open to let it out.

It's a moan. It's pleasure and excitement and need, all rolled into one little, choked noise that will probably haunt my every waking moment going forward.

Does she *like* being pinned down?

For a few seconds, all I can do is stare down at her flushed face, her body trapped between my thighs, and wish we were alone so I could—

So I could *what*?

I don't get involved with women. For very good reasons. It's a rule that has served me well. *All* the rules serve me well, and I'm breaking them right now by keeping my hips planted on top of Danika's stomach far longer than necessary.

"Find a partner and practice," I call to the room, still unable to stop staring down at Silva. "I'll come around and—inevitably—correct you."

The room breaks into motion, and so does Silva, sliding backwards up the mat and rolling to her feet. I stand, too, facing her. My pulse is pounding in my ears as she hesitates, words poised on her lips, fingers twisting in her T-shirt. But she doesn't say anything, turning instead and jogging away to partner up with one of the girls. It's a good thing my brother approaches, nudging me with his elbow. Otherwise, I might have gone after her and apologized. Or asked to pin her down again. Jesus, what *is* it about this girl?

Her moan goes off in my head, and I grit my teeth as I turn to Charlie. *"What?"*

Nothing can knock the humor off Charlie's face. Not even me. "Nothing. Just . . . you really decided to *make your move* in a literal sense." Before I can respond, he holds up his hands. "Forget I said that. Nothing was said. I'm just here to issue an invitation."

He might as well have handed me a bouquet of flowers. "A *what* now?"

"You're making this so easy." Charlie scratches the back of his neck. "Ever is baking sample cakes tonight and we're taste testing." I say nothing. "Ever is my girlfriend . . . she's the chef who's catering our graduation . . ."

My sigh cuts him off. "I know who she is and what she does."

"Considering this invite was her idea, she'll be thrilled."

That gives me pause. And an irritating tug in the region of my chest. "Tonight. Where is it and who is going?"

"Brooklyn. I can text you the address. It's me, Jack, Danika . . ."

I don't hear the rest of the names. I'm out. It's hard enough to be around Silva at the academy. Seeing her outside of these walls in regular clothes, without the visible, concrete reminder of my position as her instructor to keep me away? Bad idea.

But even as Charlie walks off to go join the other recruits, I'm looking for every excuse to drive over the bridge later.

CHAPTER 2
Danika

Nothing like baked goods to soothe the sting of humiliation.

Thank God none of my friends have mentioned the moan heard around the world. The moan that came from me, while beneath Lieutenant Greer Burns. I'm having a hard enough time wrapping my mind around what happened without having to explain. There *is* no explanation for the wicked click that took place inside me when Greer pressed me back into the mat. I can't even chalk it up to my romantic dry spell, because I've been practicing moves with other male recruits for months. I've had their sweaty balls way too close to my face and smelled things no woman

should have to smell. I'm convinced nasal forti-
tude is part of the training.

I'm not supposed to get turned on. Especially
by a man I can't stand.

Greer is like a pair of distressed leather boots in
a shop window. I can admire them and hate them
a little for drawing my eye, but I'm definitely not
supposed to try them on. This afternoon, I was
dragged from the street into the shop and pinned
down on top of the cash register. Because *cha-
ching*. I liked that show of strength way too much.

Galling is what it is. Especially because I'm a
certified control freak. Ask my family. I'd rather
run errands, until I'm in a stupor, than delegate.
I *love* being the person my family relies on. It's
the reason I became a cop. That satisfaction I get
from others relying on me, multiplied by a whole
city? That's what I want out of life.

That momentary theft of my control today? I
didn't like it. I . . . loved it. As soon as I got home
from the academy, I buried myself under my
comforter and used the highest setting on my
LELO. Picturing Greer and those caveman
thighs despite my brain's protests. Should I be
scared that the lieutenant inspired a need to explore something new and exciting I've never felt
before? Probably. But is that going to stop me?

Greer hasn't become the object of my scorn
merely because he's a world-class tool to the re-

cruits. Or because he doles out positive reinforcement like it's *literally* killing him. Oh no. I've got a long memory. Long enough to stretch back to the afternoon he showed his true colors, saying something awful about Jack. I overheard. Now, any time my admiration for his sterling police record makes me want to soften, I force myself to remember he claimed to have no respect for my best friend.

I'm not sure where my ability to carry long-standing grudges came from, because my mother is a forgiving Catholic to the bone and my father falls on the who-gives-a-shit end of the spectrum. But here I am. And I don't forget. Thankfully, I make up for being a grudge holder in other ways. For my friends and family, I will march up into their business and straighten out whatever is broken, free of charge. Being the boss is my thing. If anyone looks at them sideways, I want to be the one on speed dial.

For both of these reasons, I still haven't forgiven Lieutenant Greer Burns.

Getting him out of my head—especially after today—however, is proving annoyingly difficult.

My erstwhile thoughts are interrupted by the slamming of a steel oven door.

"Strap on your taste buds. It's game time, kids!" Across the massive kitchen, Charlie's girlfriend, Ever, executes a perfect pirouette, balancing a baking pan in each hand. She sets them down with a flourish, eliciting oohs and ahhs from the group, which also includes Jack and his newly minted girlfriend, Katie.

That's right, I'm the fifth wheel. As soon as graduation from the police academy rolls around, I plan to fix the universe's little oversight and find myself a man. Greer will be out of sight, out of mind, and I'll go back to cruising sensitive dudes. With regular-sized thighs.

Charlie rubs his hands together, a wolfish smile on his face. "Tell us what we've got to choose from here, cutie."

"My answer is already both," Jack says, his arm wrapped around Katie. "You're going to be feeding a bunch of recruits who've been living on pizza for months. You should probably worry less about flavors and more about inciting a riot for seconds."

Ever's start-up catering company, Hot Damn Caterers, has an off-site facility in Williamsburg, which is where we've come tonight to play taste testers. A privilege that totally makes up for having to be the fifth wheel. "Jack is right." I pick up a knife and slice off a small portion of the carrot cake sitting in the center of the table, alongside a red velvet one. "You're more likely to have your arm gnawed off while serving than to get any complaints."

"Any gripes can be forwarded directly to me." Charlie saws off a giant portion of the red velvet, throwing Ever a wink. "As if there will be any."

Picking up a wooden spoon, Ever leans in to kiss her boyfriend's cheek before going back to the stove where other concoctions are bubbling and sizzling. "You heathens aren't the only ones eating. Charlie's father will be there, along with other NYPD brass. Parents. A bunch of New York One news anchors . . ."

Katie gasps. "I love New York One. Especially when they tell you what happened on this day in history. Last week, it was the mob execution of Blue Eyes Duffy." She accepts the bite of carrot cake Jack pops into her mouth, chewing a moment. "They repeat the same hour of news all morning long, but I watch it anyway."

"That's because I won't let you out of bed long enough to find the remote," Jack drawls. "You have no choice."

"That's not the only reason," Katie whispered in her melodic Irish accent, cheeks flushing red. "The repetition is soothing. And . . . I like knowing the weather."

Jack shrugs a single shoulder. "Whatever the weather, it's always warm in our bed."

I ball up a napkin and toss it at Jack's head. "Not if you keep torturing the poor girl."

Okay, true story. I love Katie. Not only be-

cause she's honest, hardworking and sweet—
not to mention, a badass weapons trainer—but
she saved my best friend when my help wasn't
enough. Jack is making progress every day in his
battle with alcoholism. It's his fight. But he never
wanted to fight before Katie. So she has me in her
corner for life.

Everyone in this kitchen is family now. Family is
everything to me. My parents, aunts and cousins,
all of whom still live in Hell's Kitchen, rely on
me for a lot. Not a day passes where my phone
isn't ringing, someone asking for a favor, advice
or help out of a jam—be it with the landlord or
an in-law. Does it stress me out sometimes, having so many balls up in the air? Having so much
responsibility? Yes. But how will I know for sure
a problem will be handled the right way, unless
I see to it myself?

"My vote is for red velvet," Charlie announces.
"No, wait. Carrot. Wait . . ."

"I'm stuck, too," Katie says. "They're both
lovely."

Jack puts up both hands in surrender. "I'm a
hung . . . jury."

My sigh is exaggerated. It usually is. "Oh,
fine, leave it up to me." I tap the fork against my
pursed lips. "I'll go with—"

I don't get chance to finish, because the rusted
side door leading into the kitchen space opens

slowly, revealing an outline I know too well after today's training session. It fills up the frame a lot like it fills my mind. My pulse starts to hammer, remembering that rough grind of his hips down onto mine, those seconds where I couldn't move, because his weight was an unmovable force on top of me. *Stop thinking about it.* What is he doing here?

"Hey, big brother," Charlie calls, good-natured as usual. "Wasn't sure you'd show."

It's news to me that Charlie invited his brother, but it probably shouldn't be. Charlie has been bending over backwards in the last month, trying to improve his relationship with Greer and his father, a big-time NYPD bureau chief. Their family is a law enforcement dynasty, heavy on work ethic, low on affection. Watching my roommate spin his wheels and get barely anything in return from Greer is yet another reason I'd like to deliver a right cross to his smug, all-knowing face. It's not the main one, though.

My job isn't to single out bright shiny stars. My job is to conform these men into team players. Groom them for something larger than themselves. Lone wolves get their fellow officers killed, the way my partner was killed, and that's exactly what Jack Garrett is. A lone wolf with no respect. And I have no respect for him.

Before I walked in on that meeting between Greer and Katie last week, I already disliked the lieutenant, but those words effectively sealed the deal. Sure, Greer helped Katie out with the work visa that allowed her to remain in New York with Jack. He's also taken an interest in Jack and stopped treating my childhood friend as if he's a waste of space.

But like I said, I have a long memory. My mother would say to turn the other cheek, but when Lieutenant Burns saunters up to the table and surveys the two cakes like they're some paltry offering being presented to a king, I turn both cheeks in his direction, tilting my head back to meet bored, flinty eyes.

"If I'd known you were coming," I say for his ears alone, "I would have suggested a devil's food cake."

CHAPTER 3

Greer

It's obvious I didn't knock loose any of Silva's hatred when I flipped her over on the mat today. Good. I *certainly* wasn't hoping for anything different.

The way she's looking at me now, one might think I imagined that husky moan and the flutter of her eyelashes this afternoon. The spasming of her thigh muscles. No. My mind sure as hell didn't fabricate those things. And I've spent way too much time over the last few hours wondering what they meant. One answer is clear: They didn't soften her toward me.

Refusing to acknowledge the stab of disappointment, I mentally repeat what I told myself on the drive over. My job is to train this scrappy, little brat into a decent police officer. After that, my association with her will be over. No more passing her in the hallway or watching a bunch of twenty-something assholes eagerly volunteer to be her training partner. Perhaps I've never been so anxious for a class of recruits to graduate, but can anyone blame me? They've challenged my patience and my sanity at every damn turn.

First, Charlie loses his shit over the blonde chef who's currently fussing over a bowl of pink frosting, turns into a wounded beast and almost blemishes his fledgling police record. Next, Irish Annie Oakley shows up and makes me care a little too much about how I've classified Jack Garrett. I was only ironing out a few misgivings about him when Danika walked into my office uninvited last week. Now, I've got a pissed-off recruit plotting my death from behind the most . . . incredible brown eyes I've ever seen.

That slippery thought makes me grunt, and Silva narrows said eyes, clearly waiting for me to respond to her barb. Devil's food cake. Not bad. Although I've been called worse things than Satan by perps and colleagues alike. No one likes the dick who keeps everyone accountable, and I'm good with that. I'm just fine being alone.

In my thirty years, I've never given a second thought to another person's opinion of me. Or my teaching style—unless you count my father, who

taught me about police work. Why I should consider . . . *adjusting* to make this short-tempered . . .
beautiful, passionate girl happy—

Dammit.

For some reason, Silva's pleasure seems to be
infinitely more desirable than her disappointment. It's why I've tried to make up for what I
said about Jack in that meeting, by checking on
his progress in treatment, as often as I can. And
there's no sense in pretending she didn't bring
me all the way out into Brooklyn tonight.

I tried to convince myself that by showing up,
I'd be humoring Charlie into thinking our family
has a hope in hell of being functional. Whatever
my version of love is, I have that for Charlie. The
kid is nothing like me. He's optimistic, for one.
He has the ability to make everyone around him
feel included. He talked a bunch of hard-assed
cops into a flash mob to win back Pink Frosting
Girl, for chrissakes.

In my gut, though, I know I came tonight because I wanted to see Silva. Assure myself she
was safe. Working in Manhattan, I don't have
any firsthand knowledge of the neighborhood
where this kitchen is located, so I came to check
it out. Now that I've seen for myself there's no
machete-wielding maniacs in the vicinity, I
should probably go.

But, my feet stay right where they are, inches

from the tips of Silva's boots. Those kind that stop at a woman's ankle and make her legs look even better than they do in gym shorts. The fact that she has some kind of control over my usually ironclad will stirs impatience in my belly. Impatience and the need to gain back the upper hand. Without a sound, I let her scent slide into my senses and give her a nice, long once-over, like I usually do when she's lined up for morning inspection. If I can't inspire pleasure from Silva, I'll settle for riling her up.

"Someone should have baked you an angel food cake," I say, my voice cracking from disuse. Twin blooms of color appear in her cheeks on the heels of a little intake of breath. Across the scant distance between us, my body feels hers soften and does the opposite. A grudging invitation for . . . something. Just like today on the mat. I like her response so much that I have to go and ruin it. "Maybe it would make you lighter on your feet, since you were dragging ass during drills today."

"Ohh," she breathes. "If I was dragging ass, it's because your lecture failed to motivate me, Lieutenant." Her smile is deceptively sweet. "Might want to work on your oral skills."

She slaps both hands over her face, groaning over her slipup, and I have the strangest urge to laugh. To peel her hands away and witness the damage underneath. Our stolen moments before inspection have become the highlight of my week, but we've never taken it further than those blistering seconds of eye contact. I've never made so much as a suggestive comment. Ever. I'm her instructor and I will not abuse my authority.

So temporary insanity or the way she melted beneath me today must be the culprit for what I say next, my voice at a low murmur. "Are you volunteering to help me practice?"

Silva shoots backward and knocks into the table, sending forks clattering in every direction. The other four people in the room, who either heard nothing or have better poker faces than I gave them credit for, reach out to steady her, but I beat them to it. My hand is wrapped around her elbow, keeping her from falling, and the physical contact sends heat slicking up my spine. My tongue grows heavy. All I want to do is haul her close. Take a fist full of her hair and rub it against my open mouth. Down my neck and chest. Jesus.

She jerks her arm away, and I command myself to regain control. Not for the first time, I ask myself what the hell is it about this girl? Ever since she walked into the academy, my eyes follow her everywhere, my head full of her when I give in to my needs at night. When I tuck an eager hand into my briefs, roll onto my stomach and fuck myself. If it was just sexual interest, I could wait out the next four weeks, no problem. She'll be gone and the infatuation will fade.

But here I am in Brooklyn, worried for her safety.

Caring what she thinks.

Hating the fact that she heard me say something shitty and is now mad at me.

I need a run. A good run will make these stupid feelings manageable. Until tomorrow.

"Uh yeah . . ." Charlie's voice trickles into my awareness. "So we're testing out two Ever cakes here, and Danika was getting ready to woman-up and make the final judgment."

I manage to tear my eyes off Danika, who's clearly still shocked over what I said. Join the club, baby. Baby? "What is your choice, Silva?"

"The, um . . ."

She needs a nudge out of her apparent stupor, so I provide one. "Today, please."

I sense her lift a boot, like she's going to stomp on my foot, and I almost hope she does, because I'd be required to touch her again. But she gives a cool answer, instead. "Red velvet."

Picking up a fork, I sample the two cakes and have to admit they're good. I've been wondering if my brother's bragging over his girlfriend's culinary skills was a product of his pussy-whipped status, but he didn't exaggerate. "I'll go with carrot."

Four sets of eyes ping-pong over to Silva, who looks like she's concentrating on not stabbing me with her fork, but Ever speaks up before Silva gets a chance. "It's settled then," she says, too brightly. "We'll go with both—"

"This calls for a tie breaker," Silva interrupts, lifting her chin. "Wouldn't you say, Lieutenant?"

The saucy way she pronounces my title makes me insane. What would she say if she only knew? She moans that title in my dreams, along with my name. Loud and nightly. "Did you have something in mind?"

"Yes. Always."

"Let's hear it."

"Since you're so underwhelmed by my performance today . . ." She shrugs, but I glimpse her nerves peeking through. "Quiz me on radio codes. Five of them. If I get them all right, we go with red velvet. Anything else and you can have your fuddy-duddy carrot. No offense, Ever. I'm just not big on vegetables."

"Fair enough," murmurs the cook.

I don't like Silva having the misconception that she underwhelmed me. She never does. She's one of the more impressive recruits at the academy, male or female. She's focused, doesn't complain when she's exhausted and improves every day. Of course, I can't tell her that. If she softened too much—or hell, at all—toward me, I'd never be able to stay away. It's imperative that I do. The only thing permanent in this life is my job. Friends, women . . . hell, even family, comes and goes.

People lose people every single day. Parents, children, spouses. I see it constantly in my profession. Betrayal, abandonment, death. It all ends in one thing: solitude, with the added gem of knowing what love and togetherness once felt like. I stay beholden to myself and the city of New York, because we're substantial. We can't quit on one another, the way people quit on their loved ones all the time. At least I got that lesson out of the way early in life, so I could avoid having to face it again and again, like some fucked-up *Groundhog Day*.

Speaking of groundhogs, I've gone down a dark hole while Silva's gauntlet still lies between us. "You're on," I finally answer, codes filtering through my mind in neon green ribbons. "Ten-fifty-two F."

"Dispute with a firearm."

I'm doing my best to appear bored, but I'm suddenly having fun. It might have something to do with the fact that she's smiling at me. It's a cocky smile, too. According to the flickering of my pulse, it's my favorite smile of hers. "Correct. Ten-eighty-four."

"Arrived at scene."

"Yes. Ten-eighteen."

That one gets her stuck for a second, and I find myself willing the answer into her brain. "Warrant check . . . active warrant."

My nod is brisk. "Ten-ten S."

"Possible crime. Shots fired."

Last one. Jesus, this is beginning to make my dick hard. She's looking at me like she wants a challenge, so I give her one. "Ten-fifty-nine N."

Her smile wobbles and drops. I look around the table to judge if anyone recognizes the code, but only Charlie stares back at me with knowledge in his eyes. And he's telling me without words that throwing this code—active brush fire in progress—at Silva makes me an asshole. There hasn't been a brush fire in Manhattan since the inception of the NYPD, and thus, it isn't part of the assigned study material. I can't take my question back, though. It's out there, and she's chewing it over like a piece of tough steak.

"Uh . . ." She rolls around on the balls of her feet. "Second call for ambulance."

Fuck. I open my mouth to tell her she's wrong. Instead, I say, "Guess we'll be eating red velvet cake at graduation."

The girls start cheering, Charlie's eyebrows shoot sky high and Silva slumps with a release of breath. A little satisfied smile plays around the edges of her mouth, sending the dumb-ass organ in my chest traveling in a ricochet pattern. I like seeing her happy way too much. I like even more that I'm the one who made her that way, even at the cost of being wrong. About police work. My life.

Bad. Very bad.

I turn for the exit. "I'll leave you all to it."

"Oh, wait," Ever calls, elbowing Charlie, who's still watching me with obnoxious fascination. "You don't want to weigh in on frosting?"

"Anything but pink." I wrench open the door and barely resist one last look at Silva. "You have drills in the morning. It's your choice whether you come in early and set an example or show up smelling like cake and bring everyone down to your level."

"There's the lieutenant I know," Charlie drones.

Silva huffs a laugh. "Did he ever leave?"

Yeah, for a second there I had left. Became someone who cared about feelings . . . about someone . . . over being right. I can't let it happen again.

The door slams behind me.

CHAPTER 4
Danika

I'm walking home from a typically brutal day at the academy when a red light gives me the chance to lean down and massage my throbbing calf muscles as traffic races past.

Coming in early to set an example for the other recruits has its drawbacks.

Number one being the nod of approval from the lieutenant, as if I'd shown twenty minutes before inspection just to make his king-of-the-universe ass proud. Even more vexing was the tug of satisfaction as he noted something on his clipboard when I walked into the gym. It's not such a crazy concept for a recruit to be happy when met with their instructor's—albeit meager—praise. But I don't want him to have

that control over me. After months of his con-
descending style of teaching and what he said
about Jack, he shouldn't have such a lofty position in my mind.

Yet, he does. Winning that bet last night made
me run a little faster today, listen harder, take the
guys to the mat with more dedication. More heart.

The academy is a lot of hard work. It's exciting,
knowing we'll be employing the skills we're
learning in the field someday, but the day-to-day
grind can get repetitive. My radio codes pop quiz
victory last night reminded me why I want to be
a cop so bad. Making my family proud. Sometimes achieving that means always having the
right answer. The solution.

I'm the oldest of my cousins. I've always been
the one to lead by example, which is probably
why Greer's parting shot last night had me setting my alarm to go off early this morning. My
mother always teases me, claiming I was born a
mother, not a daughter, and I suppose that's true.
Look at how I bullied Jack through junior college
and into the academy.

You're welcome.

My parents came to New York from Colombia
in the eighties, and their siblings slowly followed, once my parents put down roots. I'm the
first of this new generation. Before my cousins
were born, the expectations of my family were

concentrated only on me. What would I do? How fast could I do it? Those pressures stuck and I got used to them. Now my family comes to me with their problems more and more. When my mother needs to schedule a repair with the super, or have something straightened out at the bank? She calls me. When one of my cousins needs homework help? I'm their girl. And I love having that responsibility, even if sometimes I take the lead when I haven't—technically—been asked. If I don't fix things when they're broken, who will?

Which leads me to the second drawback of showing early: occupying my time with lunges and extra running, thus turning me into a hobbling invalid waddling down the sidewalk. As soon as I get home, I'm commandeering the bathroom and taking a shower hot enough to melt off a layer of skin. Then I'm scarfing whatever is handy in the fridge and passing out. Tomorrow I'm showing up on time, not early, and Lieutenant Burns can deal with it.

Even as I make that vow to myself, I know deep down I'm going to break it.

When my cell rings in my hoodie pocket, I take it out, frowning down at the screen. My cousin's name—Robbie—fades in and out. "Hey," I answer, laughing. "I was just thinking about you. How's the job?"

Robbie is a senior in high school and the

youngest cousin on my father's side. A couple weeks ago, I helped him fill out a job application for the frozen yogurt shop down the street from his building—and I was super proud of him for nailing the interview and getting hired.

This kid usually talks a blue streak, and he's currently taking measured breaths, pacing footsteps in the background. It takes me the space of three seconds to detect something is wrong.

"What's going on?"

"Danny, I didn't . . . I promise this wasn't my idea . . ."

I stop short and turn, jogging back toward the avenue I just crossed, scoping for available cabs. "What wasn't your idea?"

His sigh is shaky. "A couple of guys at school found out I got this job, and they started asking me all these questions. You know? Like, what time do we close? Have I had any annoying customers? You know, normal stuff." The panic is making his voice a higher pitch than usual. "Then yesterday, they asked if I work alone. If the manager is always around. I knew something was wrong, but these guys, everyone knows they're wannabe gangsters."

It's rush hour, and it seems like every damn cab has their lights off, but I finally catch one letting out passengers and spring in that direction. "Did you answer those questions?"

"Yeah," he groans. "They're not easy to ignore, and I couldn't just lie to them, you know? What if they found out I lied, then took it out on me?"

"Fifty-Second and Ninth," I call through the cab partition, praying that by some miracle cross-town traffic won't be a bitch for once.

"You . . . you can't come here, Danny."

"Just keep talking." Still working my calm voice. "What happened after you answered their questions?"

It takes a long time for him to continue. So long that I have to check the connection, but the call time is still ticking upward. "They told me they were coming in to see me tonight. They said I should just go along with whatever happens . . . and they would cut me in." I can hear his gulping swallow through the phone. "I told them I didn't want to be cut in, but they just laughed."

No. Not happening. A couple of punks are not going to pull my cousin into an inside job and get him into trouble. Robbie works hard in school, wants to study abroad when he gets to college. See the world outside Manhattan. I'm not letting some neighborhood kids looking for some spending money rip those dreams away. And after all the studying I've been doing and horror stories passed around the gym and locker room, I know how badly a black mark on a permanent record can block every single avenue of opportunity.

Greer could handle this.

Some instinct I wasn't aware of before pipes up, telling me he would drop everything to meet me at the yogurt shop. He'd put the fear of God into those kids about robbing the yogurt shop and screwing with my cousin. The lieutenant might be a jerk, but he's on the side of justice. Like a superhero whose power is being a prize dickwad.

If I call him, though . . . if I ask for his help, I'll owe him. Probably forever, because in what world would the invincible lieutenant need a return favor from me?

Dammit. The sides of my stomach grind together. Pride sits on one shoulder, filing her nails. On the other side, the Scared Face emoji screams, hands slapped to her cheeks.

"Danny?" Robbie's voice pulls me back to the present. "I really don't think you should be involved in this. You're going to be a cop. Maybe I should have called my dad—"

"No. No, I got this." I swallow any remaining reservations and focus on making this right for my cousin. Like I always do. Aren't I spending every single day training to handle issues like this? Until I get there, it's imperative to keep my cousin calm, so he doesn't do something irrational or dangerous. "Look, I went to school with kids like these. They're not as big and bad as they think."

The cab flies through a yellow light, and I judge we're about three minutes away. If I call the police, it would be Robbie's word against two guys. They could corroborate one another's story about Robbie being involved—and my cousin had already ruined any chance of looking innocent by answering their questions about when the manager is around. Sure, he could claim he'd had a change of heart, but there would still be suspicion. He'd probably lose his job, possibly have an arrest on his record. Not good. I'll have to judge the situation when I get there. It'll be easier to call on my training when I'm not going at this blind.

As soon as the cab pulls up outside the yogurt shop, I throw a twenty through the opening in the partition and jog to the entrance, the pain in my quads forgotten.

My cousin is standing behind the counter, and I'm relieved to see there are no customers in sight. "Did they say when they're coming?"

"Like around five-thirty, six." Robbie plows both hands through his dark hair. "I can't believe this is happening. I never should have told anyone I got this job."

"We'll talk about it later. Right now, you need to stay behind the counter, ready to call 911 if they try to go through with it."

"Are you serious? I can't call the police on these

guys. It's bad enough I called you. They'll make my life hell, Danny. Yours, too." He moans up at the ceiling. "I can't believe this."

"I'll handle it." How often in my life have I said those words? "Please calm down and do what I tell you."

He nods and follows my directions, but he's not happy about it. Only about two minutes have passed since I walked into the store when two kids—probably seventeen or eighteen—shoulder their way into the shop, hands stuffed into their pockets. One has his hood pulled down low over his forehead, but I get a pretty decent look at the other. Chapped lips, dirty blonde hair, nervous eyes. They take a seat near the entrance, faces turned away, shoulders hunched, obviously waiting for me to leave. So they can rob my cousin. And this won't be the last time. Oh no. They'll want to do it again next week.

I start to approach them when I see it. A flash of steel in one of their pockets. Gun. Immediately I divert to a nearby table, trying to appear as casual as possible. But with my heart slamming in my throat, I pull out my phone and text my cousin to call the police. Now.

He disappears into the back room and both kids sit up straighter, exchanging a look. They don't like Robbie being out of sight. The tension burns in the air. And slowly, one of them turns around to face me, probably noticing the family resemblance between Robbie and me.

"Hey, girl—"

Flashing lights appear to my left, tires screeching to a stop at the curb. NYPD vehicles. Three of them. Too fast, though. Right? That can't be the cops Robbie called, can it? Impossible. So who called them?

Two uniforms exit the closest car and approach the yogurt shop, weapons drawn, and I don't think, I just put my hands up. Oh God. Oh Jesus Christ. This is not good. No, this is terrible.

"Robbie," I shout, keeping my eyes trained on the officers, hoping to pass on some kind of message. *I'm one of the good guys.* "Set down your phone. Put your hands up and walk out. No phone in your hand, okay?"

When my cousin walks out and sees the police, arms lifted above his head, he looks so scared that I want to get sick. Apparently that conversation about being careful won't be necessary. He's going to be scarred for life.

More officers have joined the original two on the sidewalk. Between the flashing lights and intimidating numbers, the would-be robbers have finally gotten wise and put up their hands, too. One of the officers enters the yogurt shop, followed by his partner, screaming at everyone to get down on the ground, and there's no hesitation from any of us. We hit the deck, cheeks to the floor, and when the handcuffs slap closed around my wrists, I start to shake.

CHAPTER 5
Greer

Wings are flapping in my ears. Loud. Sounds that I normally find soothing—tapping keys, filing cabinets sliding open—are attacking my eardrums like needles, turning them into pincushions. On a regular day, people seem to move interminably slow when I'm trying to get shit done. Right now, though, while I'm waiting to be taken to a back room at Central Booking, such lethargy is fucking unacceptable.

"I don't need an escort," I say though my teeth at the pencil dick manning the front desk. Upon arriving, I showed him my lieutenant's badge and he almost pissed himself, calling for a superior to act as my tour guide, as if I need one. I've made it my business to know every nuance of protocol, and I can walk through any door I choose, if I deem it necessary.

And that's exactly what I need to do right now. Get through the door to the place where Silva is being held. So I can demand an explanation, then shout at her no matter how reasonable it turns out to be.

"Call again. I'm in a hurry."

He fumbles with the intercom. "Yes, sir."

Half an hour ago, I was sitting at my desk completing case paperwork when my phone buzzed. A courtesy call from another precinct informing me that one cocky, beautiful—damn me for noticing—recruit is in custody requesting my presence as soon as possible. That's when the flapping in my ears started and it hasn't stopped, merely growing more deafening during my drive downtown. God, as soon as I see her, I'm going to . . .

Make sure she's okay.

Yeah, man. That ought to teach her a lesson.

A vision of my hands roaming over her back is interrupted when a stiff-lipped officer arrives, putting his hand out for a shake. "Lieutenant Burns. Sorry for the wait. Follow me."

We move through a series of hallways, each one dimmer and smellier than the last. The farther we get into the bowels of Central, the more anxious I get for the sight of Silva. She better be pissed off or flippant about this whole situation, because I'm not sure I can handle anything but her usual cocky attitude. Not when she's spent the last couple hours caged inside these walls.

A growl builds in my throat. "Fill me in."

"Yes, sir." The officer takes another turn, leading to another hallway, and now I'm starting to get really irritated. "Couple of teenagers in Hell's Kitchen had plans to hold up a yogurt shop. Might have pulled it off if they hadn't alluded to their plans on Facebook. Posted pictures of themselves in masks, like a couple of Grade-A jackasses."

"Jesus Christ."

"You said it. One of their mothers called the closest precinct and tipped them off. Officers followed the perps to the location. They probably wouldn't have called in backup and made any arrests if they hadn't seen one of the kids with a weapon. Confiscated a twenty-two pistol. Belongs to the kid's father, but it's not registered."

If the officer notices the hitch in my step, he doesn't comment. How the hell did Silva end up in a situation where her safety was in jeopardy? I need answers now, or I'm going to start breathing actual fire. But I want those answers from her.

"Same mother who called in the tip is now complaining about how long it's taking to bail out Heckle and Jeckle, if you're a fan of irony." He pushed out a sigh. "Meanwhile, the girl seemed like an innocent bystander. Probably would have been questioned and released at the scene, but she wouldn't leave her cousin."

"Cousin?"

"Yeah. Kid worked behind the counter at the shop. She kicked up kind of a fuss when we arrived at The Tombs and separated them."

"Funny, that doesn't sound like her," I mutter. We stop outside a locked door, and I bite the inside of my cheek while the officer moves in slow motion, unlocking it with a loaded down key chain. "I'll sign the paperwork for their immediate release. Have it ready for me as soon as possible."

"Yes, sir."

He pushes the door open and there's Silva, swallowed up by the cold, gray room. As soon as she sees me, she shoots to attention at her feet, then hates herself for it. But not as much as she usually would, because she's . . . upset. Her bottom lip is red from being worried by her teeth, there's a crumpled tissue in her hand. Goddammit. Just like that, I'm transported to no-man's-land. A land populated by sad girls who speak a different language.

Realizing I've been quiet too long, I clear my throat. "Thank you. I'll take it from here."

That almost sounded convincing.

The silence that reigns in the wake of the door closing is solid. Brutally so. I expect Silva to launch into an explanation, but she doesn't. Just stands there, across the room, balancing on the balls of her feet, mutilating that tissue. This could have been so much worse. I know that lesson well. It's inked on my insides in permanent marker. I want to shout it at her until my voice gets hoarse, but instead, I find myself moving toward her cautiously. Maybe I'll get that coveted chance to yell later, but that image of my hands stroking her back won't leave me.

I get within a couple feet, and she turns her face away, giving me the quiet dignity of her profile, a front row seat to the little hairs curling behind her ear. Which unfortunately brings me another step closer. Another. Until her body heat is mingling with mine. We're not touching, but her breath fans my neck, our fingertips come dangerously close to brushing.

"You're . . . unhurt?"

"Yes," she whispers. "Thanks. For coming."

My gaze drops to her mouth, the lift of her upper lip, the dip in the center of the lower one. I have this insane urge to run my palm over that mouth, curve my fingers around her chin. Trail them down her neck. Then snag her elbow and yank her up against me with all my might.

I've never been a man given to dominating

women, although being the aggressor is a given. It's in my blood to lead. And ever since I dropped Silva to the mat and heard that goddamn moan, felt that spike of awareness that she somehow *needs* that intensity, my fantasies of her have changed shape, texture. They were indecent and filthy before, but now I'm . . . consuming her. The hunger to bring those fantasies to life forces me to step back, but the loss of her heat is too sudden. Horrible. "You better have a good explanation for being at the scene of an attempted armed robbery, Silva."

"I do, Lieutenant." She faces me, all traces of her upset going up in smoke. "It was hard enough calling you for help. Please don't make it worse by talking down to me. Just this once."

It was hard for her to call me for help? I don't like that shit. At all. "Why was it hard?"

"I—" Her mouth opens and snaps shut. "Because you've arrived to rescue the damsel in distress, and now you're going to lord it over me." She scrutinizes me for a beat. "Aren't you?"

"No."

"Really?"

My nasty grunt is nothing short of elegant, but I'm feeling very . . . perturbed. Not like my usual irritable condition, either. This is hitting me lower, like I ran full force into a stuck turnstile. "There might be some form of consequences for what happened today, but after you give me an explanation, we'll never speak about it again. Does that meet with your approval, recruit?"

Maybe I'm the one speaking a foreign language. That's how she's staring at me. "Why would you do that?"

Because somewhere underneath the panic I've been experiencing since I got the phone call . . . there's satisfaction that she requested me. That she chose to depend on me in a time of need. "Why? So you don't do something else stupid and allow your pride to keep you locked in a dungeon, instead of calling me. That's why."

Her eyes fire off twin flares. "I don't make a habit of being stupid. But either way, you're not my designated get-out-of-jail-free card."

"I don't see anyone else here."

"Well . . ." Her chin wobbles, firms. "Lucky me, huh?"

She almost apologizes for the sarcastic comment, but I shake my head to let her know it isn't necessary. Not when her chin is wobbling. "What were you doing in the yogurt shop?" I'd supervised drills that morning, but left the recruits in another instructor's hands for the afternoon. "You couldn't have been dismissed for twenty minutes when shit hit the fan."

"I took a cab across town." She leans back against the metal table. "My cousin Robbie works at the yogurt shop. He told me what was going down. He was scared."

"Was he in on the robbery?"

"No. Not intentionally. These kids pestered him for the information they needed. Before he knew it, he was aiding them, but Greer—" We both freeze at her use of my first name, for the first time ever. God help my cock tonight. I'm going to stroke myself blind to the memory of her saying it. When Silva . . . when Danika continues, her tone has quieted some. "I mean, Lieutenant. He's a great kid. Good grades. A future."

"One of the perps' mothers called the police. Did you?"

"Not at first." Her eyes slam shut. "I thought I could handle some stupid neighborhood kids. I didn't want them to lie and drag my cousin down with them."

My blood heats to a boiling point, fast and furious. Every muscle in my body is screaming to gather her up, push my mouth against her ear and list the potential consequences of her actions. Every grisly detail, until she never tries to brave a dangerous situation alone ever again. God help me, my hands ache to connect with her backside. Rough, no nonsense slaps, five times on each side. Not only to punish her for being reckless, but to . . . soothe her afterward. Both of us. Her body is tense, as is mine, and some new intuition is whispering the fix in my ear. But I'm not sure I can trust it. Not when Danika makes me question every rule I've lived by for so long. Have I completely overinflated what happened during that takedown exercise? Am I insane to think she could be turned on by the images in my head?

"You don't have to lecture me. I know I made a really dangerous decision." Lecture her? I almost have to laugh at how tame she assumes my thoughts to be. I've been masturbating to her for months. "If I need to take the blame for this, on Robbie's behalf, so be it."

"You're not taking the blame for anything," I snap. Out of sexual frustration. Over the fact that she's being noble, which makes me like her even more. Or maybe I'm still ticked she was in danger, especially when she didn't need to be. All of the above. "They're getting the paperwork ready now. You'll both be released within the hour. I'll make sure this doesn't end up blackening either of your records."

"Really?" Danika straightens, gratitude blooming on her face. "Thank you, Lieutenant."

I could leave the situation as is and bask in the fact that she's grateful to me. I could. But I won't. It's not how I'm built. "Don't thank me yet."

"Uh-oh."

A hum vibrates in my throat as I pace to the opposite end of the room. "There's a reason the recruits call me Lieutenant Hard-Ass when they think I can't hear." I wait for her to deny it, but only get a slight coloring of her cheeks. "The nickname fits."

She cocks a hip. "Are you going to punish me?"

A growl rumbles in my chest, my fingers flexing of their own accord. God, this interest in swatting her ass builds by the second into a sharp longing. A need to . . . assert myself. Make her aware of how insane she makes me. It doesn't seem to conflict with this overwhelming need to make her pleased with me, though. No, these two desires intersect right in the middle. "You might consider it a punishment, but I suggest you view it as a learning experience."

"Definitely a punishment."

I sigh. "I have the power to sweep this all under the rug. Favors are traded in this department more than I care to admit. No one would question me. But I don't do favors. Not without consequences. If everyone faced real consequences for every decision, they'd think twice before acting. And as your instructor, I'm doubly responsible for making sure you make a better call next time. Same goes for your cousin."

Her lips move as she processes that. "What are you going to do?"

"Your cousin is going to do some community service in my precinct." Taking out my notepad, I jot a quick note to hook Danika's cousin up with our community liaison. "Graffiti removal, helping little old ladies cross the street. We'll think of something. The goal is to make him understand cause and effect. That's my condition for making this go away."

"Fine. I agree with you," she surprises me by saying. "I would have settled for nagging him on the phone every day until he leaves for college, but your plan is better."

My mouth twitches at the word *nagging*. What would it be like to get a phone call from this girl? Nice. Reassuring. Provoking. All of the above. "As for you, Silva . . ." I flip my notebook shut. "Until graduation, you're on probation."

Her chin drops. "Probation?" She searches the room for answers. "How will that work?"

"You'll continue training. Nothing will change. But on days when I'm not instructing at the academy, you'll report to me. In person, if I'm available. Over the phone, if I'm tied up with work." Thoughts stream behind her eyes. Is she wondering what it'll be like to call me, too? "I'll arrange for a couple ride alongs. With me."

It hits me that I'm forcing us into constant interaction. Am I out of my mind? My mouth is apparently making decisions without consulting my brain. Is the ache in my pants in control? Or even the knocking organ in my chest? Unacceptable. No, probation is the only way I can justify swinging my weight around to keep their records clean. That's all it is.

"That kid today could have opened fire at the police. The police might have fired back. You or your cousin could have been a casualty." It takes me a moment to loosen my constricted throat muscles and continue. "I want to be confident when I pin that badge on you. I want you to be confident in the department you're joining, too, so that next time, you don't strike out on your own and take unnecessary risks. Checking in with me will keep what happened today fresh. And maybe you'll learn a thing or two when I take you out on duty." Again, I question my sanity. I'll never get the scent or memory of her in my passenger seat out of my head. Where will that leave me when probation is over and she graduates? "Are we in agreement?"

She's looking for a way out, and I don't blame her. I'm an asshole in small doses, and now I'm going to be a fixture in her life. After a moment, though, she nods, and the knots in my chest untie themselves. "Yes, but . . ."

"But what?"

Her eyes flash at my sharp tone. "I don't have your number."

"Oh. Right." I take my notebook out again, scrawling my number and handing over the ripped sheet. "We'll start tomorrow." She stares down at the piece of paper, making me . . . self-conscious? Is that what this is? Fuck. I head for the door and yank it open. "I'll go check on your release."

"Lieutenant."

Setting my features to bored, I turn back around. "Yeah?"

She seems about to say one thing, but settles on another. Sliding the slip of paper into her back pocket, she gives me a cocky shrug. "Lieutenant Hard-Ass isn't your only nickname at the academy." A touch of a smile, before she turns away. "Personally, I prefer the Grim Reaper."

It takes a conscious effort not to smile as I return to the front desk.

Until I remember the torture I've just signed on to endure.

CHAPTER 6
— *Danika* —

D ammit, I'm early again.

At least Greer isn't scheduled as our instructor today. Not that I can avoid him after the deal I made with the devil yesterday, but I'll ride this wave of avoidance as long as possible. Whether out of nerves or . . . curiosity, I couldn't stop myself from rehearsing our first phone call in the shower this morning. In the beginning, I was dead set on launching straight into an explanation of my whereabouts, followed by a quick assurance that I'm staying out of trouble—kind of like I have been for twenty-six years—after which I would hang up without waiting for a response.

That's what the lieutenant expects from me, right?

Around the time the water began to run cold, though, I decided I don't want to be predictable. As soon as I'm dismissed for the day, I'm going to march into his precinct and shock the smug expression right off his face.

Yeah.

There really should be a sense of victory at the thought of giving him a jolt. And there is. After all, I humbled myself in front of the man, admitted I made a mistake and asked for his help, taking several blows to my pride in the process. It wasn't easy for me and he knew it. Instead of cutting me some slack, he made himself my babysitter for the next month. Reporting my movements to my über-demanding instructor during my free hours is *so* not on my bucket list.

But. I kind of brought this on myself, didn't I? Thus curbing my satisfaction over ruffling his feathers. A lot of the things he said yesterday were . . . reasonable. I almost got the impression it was important to him that I understand his methods. His code. I've always assumed he was just a natural born asshole, but I spent the night tossing in my bed, wondering if I overlooked something.

Not only in Greer, but in myself. It was all gravy when I could chalk my reluctant fascination with the lieutenant up to his He-Man thighs. But I've been replaying that demonstration in my head with alarming frequency and seeing ... *feeling* ... other things. I liked the way it felt having him look down at me, that hard jaw bunched up to match his shoulders. I liked my back smacking the mat and knowing he would let me up when he was good and ready. That until then, I didn't have to be proactive or in control of anything.

That's not me. Is it?

Bottom line: the sooner these four weeks are over, the better.

The only sound in the academy hallway is my footsteps walking toward the locker room. I'm one of about a dozen female recruits, and none of them have arrived yet, so I'm alone among the interesting smells and dripping faucets. Quickly and efficiently, I change into gray yoga pants and my white uniform shirt, don my sneakers. The slam of my locker is still ringing in the air when I wheel back into the hallway and jog to the gymnasium entrance.

I come to a quick stop just inside the door. Leaning against a stack of mats, Greer is studying the clipboard in his hands with a frown. He looks up at my entrance, his gaze ticking down for a split second to my legs, before rising again.

"Lieutenant." I hide a wince at the breathless quality of my voice. "I was jogging. That's why I sounded like that. So."

He just stares at me.

"You're not supposed to be here."

"Yes, I'm aware of that, Silva. The other instructor is sick." His tongue slides along the corner of his mouth, distracting me. Too much. "Thank you for staying on top of my schedule."

And just like that, we're back on familiar ground. Only, we're not *really*. He witnessed me in a desperate moment and bailed me out. It wouldn't kill me to make a tiny effort to show my appreciation. In my own unique way, of course. "Why so cranky? They didn't have the right ingredients for your protein shake this morning?"

"I make my own." He hugs the clipboard to the side of his thigh. "Smart-ass."

The laugh bursts out of me before I can wrangle it. He seems taken aback by the sound, like it's an offensive, winged creature flying past his face. "So you come in early even when I'm not here."

"That's right." I pull my right ankle up to my butt, groaning as the move stretches my sore quad. "I come early for myself. Not for those little notes you make on your clipboard." Am I imagining things or does he look disappointed? "Do you walk around your apartment with that thing?" I lower my voice and attempt to mimic his low rasp. "Minus two arbitrary points, dust bunnies. Better form next time."

That corner of his mouth—the corner he

licked—hops up. "You assume there's never any living, breathing humans in my apartment to judge."

I don't see it coming. That has to be why jealousy hits my stomach like a spiked volleyball. Greer and women. Women and Greer. How many are there? How frequently? Are any of them serious? All of a sudden, it's an effort to make words. "I didn't . . . I wasn't asking—"

"Book club." The two words are delivered on a sigh, like he's already bored with the conversation. But his eyes are on me like a hawk. "Sometimes my book club comes over."

The jealousy doesn't subside right away, hanging around like hot pins stuck into my shoulders and neck, but . . . it ebbs the more I process what he's telling me. "You're a member of a book club?" He goes back to making notes on his clipboard, just a brick shit-house cop with flexing cannons for biceps who has a book club. "Is it just an excuse to drink wine, like my mother's book club? Or do you actually have discussions?"

"Picture me drinking wine, Silva."

"You're right, that was a stretch. Beer?"

A tight nod. "Only if I'm not working the next morning."

"Of course," I say with exaggerated gravity. "I wouldn't expect anything less."

"Good. You shouldn't."

Dammit, the jealousy is still prickly. Have to purge it. No choice. "What kind of people belong to this club? Just men, or . . ."

He's quiet a moment, simply studying me. "We should work on your interrogation technique while you're on probation." Shit. I had that coming. A moment later, I'm relieved right down to my toes when he doesn't probe for the reason I asked. Like *I* even know the answer to that? "Yes, we have discussions. Usually about whatever thriller we've just read. Or in my case, listened to." His tone deepens. "It's cops, mostly. Active and retired." A pause. "Just men, Danika."

I suck in a breath and look down at the mat, trying to play it cool that he called me by my first name. But there's nothing cool about the sensitivity of my nipples, how they pucker inside my sports bra, as if the lieutenant did way more than just say my name. That can't be all it takes for him to make me . . . horny. Okay, Jesus, yes. I'm horny for the lieutenant. All because he said my first name, the way I said his yesterday. Like we're trading an inside joke that isn't meant to be funny at all. Or maybe it's how I can feel him staring at me right now, deep blue eyes reaching up beneath my clothes and making me uncomfortably hot.

The gymnasium door blows open, and two recruits walk in, distracting me from my mental strip show. One is a determined-looking Levi, and, yeah, my burgeoning cop sense tells me I'm not going to escape being asked out today. There's a sour gurgle in my stomach at the idea of Greer watching it happen, which is *ridiculous*, so I shake it off. Behind Levi is his friend Nick, who never really says much, but likes to hang out in Levi's shadow. Not easy, considering he's twice as heavyset and several inches taller.

"Hey there," Levi says, crashing down on the mat beside me. "Exactly how early do we need to get here to stop you from making us look bad?"

I'm still hyperaware of Greer within earshot. Why? So he called me by my first name. That doesn't mean I should avoid talking to other guys. Or that he even wants me to. This new awareness I have of him needs to bounce or it's going to be an awkward few weeks. "I could tell you, but then I'd have to kill you," I respond. "Or lap you again during cardio. I haven't decided."

"Ouch. Don't pull any punches," Levi teases, flirting with me. Again. Why do I mind so much? Before Lieutenant Sinewy Thighs was introduced into my life, I would have jumped all over Levi's attention. He's got a good sense of humor and that Disney Prince smile. Heck, *he smiles*. Period. "Today is the day, Silva," Levi continues, dragging me back to reality. "You're finally going to give in to my out-of-control charms and agree to go out with me."

Behind Levi, Nick shakes his head. "Shakespeare is spinning in his grave."

Levi kicks his friend in the shin, and Nick seems to fight off a smile. "Come on, Silva," Levi drawls, giving me a slow wink. "Put me out of my misery."

I'm preparing to turn him down when recruits start to pile into the gym, cranking the volume level to ear-piercing. Levi's temporary distraction allows me to sneak a peek at Greer, but the intensity he was leveling at me before is nowhere to be found. Did I imagine it?

Yes. Of course I did.

So he called me Danika. We're going to be spending a lot of time together. He probably just figured it was time to graduate to a first-name basis. I live with his brother, for God's sake.

The return of the lieutenant's aloofness shouldn't disappoint me like this. I'm nursing an infatuation with someone who isn't available. Someone who isn't interested in me as a friend, let alone an . . . other.

The fact that I'm even considering Greer's interest level panics me into accepting the date. "Sure. Yeah," I finally respond to Levi. "Let's do it Saturday. Pizza or something."

"Really?" He clears his throat. "I mean . . . cool. I was totally prepared for that answer."

Jack fills my vision, followed by Charlie. They resemble two big hunting dogs who've just cornered a duck. "Did you just agree to a date?"

I punch my best friend in the shoulder, checking the urge to look for Greer again. "Say it a little louder. They didn't hear you in Germany."

He cups his hands around his mouth, obviously preparing to shout my evening plans into the stratosphere, but the whistle blows. Hard and punctuated. We're on our feet and in line for inspection within seconds, slaves to muscle memory.

I definitely imagine Greer taking twice as long with his inspection of Levi.

Definitely.

CHAPTER 7
Greer

Hot water scalds my neck and I let it. I don't usually shower in the academy locker room, but I don't have time to run home before I'm due at the precinct. This is the final few minutes of relative silence I'll have before my twelve-hour shift begins. Once I walk through the front doors of the precinct, every officer in the vicinity will magically forget how to make decisions by themselves. My cell phone won't stop buzzing—hell, it buzzes incessantly when I'm not on shift, doesn't it? The life of a lieutenant. Tonight I'll beg the fates for a shift without violence, but it won't happen. There's already a robbery in progress or a pedestrian struck by a vehicle. Domestic disputes. A weird smell coming from someone's apartment.

Back before I was assigned a partner, I attacked these issues with cool focus. There was a process for everything. A protocol. My job was to follow that protocol, then file the corresponding paperwork. No gray areas for me in police work. Just black and white. Right and wrong. My partner, Griffin, forced me to let go of those scruples, just a little. But for me, that loosening of my iron fist on the rule book was huge.

Once I went back to working alone, the easiest way to cope was by throwing myself back into those original habits. Forgetting the person I'd started to become and vowing never to let my guard down again. When the rules are flouted, bad things happen. Following the law to the letter is the only way to be a successful cop. One that stays alive.

But recently, that level of concentration is getting hard to maintain. I'm not able to stay cold and stick to the script. I'm more affected than I used to be when I'm called to a crime scene. The faces, the sounds . . . they stay with me longer. My words, the spiel I've given seven thousand times seems to ring hollow. The tap of a gong. Words spoken into the wind.

Is it Danika? Am I losing the ability to shut myself off, because I spend so much time . . . on? Whenever she's around, it's impossible to keep myself closed off from the chaos she kicks up inside me. It's making me feel *more* in all areas of my life. Specifically, my job. And that's no good. Not in my line of work where taking home the shit with you spells disaster. Shaking off a bad day is becoming more and more impossible.

There's a term for this. Burnout. No one would suspect me of falling prey to such cliché bullshit— and no one ever will. If I admit I'm fallible, just like every other burnout that came before me, I might as well hand in my badge, because I'll lose the respect I've earned. In this profession, respect is lifeblood. Without it, I'm dead.

Because it's all I have. I built this solitude for myself to keep others away, so I don't have what other cops covet like gold. Family. Someone to warm them up when the cold of this city gets into their bones. Even Charlie has someone now, despite my father's warnings every day of our youth about the distraction relationships cause.

When our mother took off without warning another lifetime ago, she left a silent void behind. One that was never filled or even spoken about. Charlie managed to overcome the memory of that feeling. Of being left.

But he doesn't know what I know about my mother's life after New York. Or the pain of losing a partner you've sworn to protect. I hope he never experiences such a thing, either, but I can't keep him from it. I can only hope I'm the only brother who shoulders that burden.

That almost contact I had with Danika yesterday at Central Booking is the closest I've come to touching another person in a non-teaching capacity, apart from obligatory handshakes or wrestling with a perp, since she walked through the gymnasium doors at Academy orientation. Before that, there was the occasional meaningless hookup, and I was fine with that.

Fine.

Last night, I went to the grocery store and bought candy bars. Explain that. I dropped them into my cutlery drawer like they were on fire and slammed it shut. This ridiculous notion keeps occurring to me. What if Charlie stops by with his friends? There's little chance of that, considering my brother has been to my place a grand total of twice, but . . . what if? What would I give them? Give her. Everything circles back to my smart-mouth recruit. She's the reason I threw those Snickers bars on the conveyer belt, then added Reese's Peanut Butter Cups as an afterthought.

Idiot. I can still hear her flirting in the gym, accepting that date for Saturday night. The candy is going in the trash as soon as I get home in the morning, along with whatever ideas I've been having lately. Is my apartment boring? Who the fuck cares?

Resolve locked and loaded, I punch the silver shower button, cutting off the spray. My towel is hanging over the tile wall, so I turn to retrieve it—and stop dead as the locker room door opens. I have fast hands, faster than anyone, but I make no move to snatch the towel. To wrap it around my waist. Instead, I watch with fascination as Danika takes two steps into the room and skids to a halt, her startled brown eyes dropping to my naked cock.

"Shit," Danika squeaks, whirling back around. "I—I didn't think anyone was in here."

No help for my blood running south. None at all. I never took myself for a flasher, but hell if my dick doesn't lift and swell, wanting more of her attention. God knows I'm a rule follower, but conflict wages in my chest. She's a recruit—and a woman—so I should cover my junk and pretend this never happened. But I meant what I said yesterday about cause and effect. She's in an area where she shouldn't be, once again flouting the rules like they don't apply to her. So I leave the towel right where it is.

"Do you need something?"

She peeks back over her shoulder, probably assuming I'm decent by now, her eyes shooting wide when I'm not. "I stayed a little late to run, since tomorrow is a classroom day and I wanted to feel good about sitting on my butt or whatever. But I left my towel at home, so I was just going to use paper towels to dry off after my shower, but there weren't any in the girls' locker room, so . . ."

I've never heard her ramble before, but knowing she's nervous does nothing to ease the sting of my jealousy. In fact, having her near makes it more fresh. Makes everything fresh. The self-disgust over creating a candy stash for my apartment. The amount of time I've spent imagining how her body heat felt yesterday. How it made me feel connected to someone, just for a few seconds. Ever since she showed up with her cocky attitude, challenging looks and big brown eyes, I've been less and less content. How dare she?

"You came in here for paper towels?"

Her back stiffens, hands curling at her sides. "Yeah."

I settle my hands on my hips. "Go get them, then."

Without seeing her face, I know she's analyzing her route to the bathroom. She'll have to bypass the shower where I'm standing naked, refusing to put on a towel. Honestly, I have no idea what the fuck is wrong with me. This is such a fantastic fucking breach of protocol. But I'm so exhausted and angry with myself—angry with her—because down to my very deepest layer, all I really want is her body heat again.

"Do you mind putting on a towel?"

If I didn't loathe the idea of her being fearful of me, I would continue to refuse out of principle—this is the men's locker room and she's the intruder. But I won't sacrifice her trust to teach her a lesson.

Except now I'm thinking about *that* lesson. The one that ended with her flattened beneath me, her sex a few inches from mine. Close enough that I could have rocked into that notch and felt the shape of her pussy. I'm suddenly aching to prove I didn't imagine what happened that morning. That I didn't misread her body's appreciation of me being rough. Can I do that without scaring her? I'd die before doing that. But I think I'd die if another minute passes without being near her, too.

When the towel is secure, I grunt to let her know the coast is clear. She peeks back and wets her lips, then moves like lightning toward the bathroom. Before she can reach it, though, I'm in front of her, caging her in against the lockers.

She makes that damn sound. The one I've been replaying in my dreams. It's halfway between a moan and a cry. It's so throaty and honest, I feel every note of it in my belly. "What are you doing?"

Absorbing as much of your heat as I can before I'm put back out into the cold.

"Technically, going into the men's locker room is a violation of your probation." My hands are flat on the lockers, our bodies separated by an inch and a prayer. "You're not authorized to be in here."

I expect her to argue or shove me. If she pushes me away, I'll go. But she passes me a wobbly smirk, instead. "And yet you seemed so happy to see me."

Lust tears through me like a mobbing crowd, pouring into every corner, sharpening my senses and turning up the volume of my frustration. Just having her acknowledge me in a sexual way is making me hurt. With that blessed body heat of hers, I want nothing more right now than some hint that I'm not alone. That I'm not just some crazy man who buys candy bars, travels to Brooklyn and breaks speed limits to Central Booking for a girl who sees me as nothing more than her instructor.

That acknowledgment is dangerous, but god-dammit, I want it.

"Are you happy to see me, too, Danika? Like this?" I ease back just a little, giving her a better view of my torso, naked from the waist up. I bite back a groan while watching her run curious eyes down my pecs, lower to my stomach . . . down to the erection tenting my towel. "Maybe we should examine the facts, since you don't seem inclined to answer."

Her pulse tic-tic-tics at the base of her neck. "H-how?"

Is that an encouragement? She's still studying my body from beneath hooded eyelids, and Jesus . . . maybe I'm not alone in this fixation. "Let's see." For the first time, I let my attention descend from her face, raking it over her tits, which seem to rise under my scrutiny. As if she couldn't help arching her back. The little peaks in the center betray her excitement, and the rod between my thighs grows in response. "Hard nipples are a key piece of evidence."

"It's cold in here," she rasps.

It's sweltering—at least in our heated bubble—and the flicker in her gaze tells me she's aware of her lie. "Would you like to be warmed up?"

There's that sound again. It shoots past her lips, half sob, half moan. We're still not touching, but I can sense her trembling. Still, her chin is lifted in that brave way that keeps me awake at night. Keeps my focus glued to her whenever we're in the same room. "What do you mean by . . . warmed up?" she whispers, her tone suggesting she can't believe she's asking.

That makes two of us. But her encouragement to keep going, to keep talking like this to her, has my hunger surging to an eleven. There's something keeping me from touching her, like some mental fail-safe put in place for self-preservation, but I'm so not cold right now. My skin is buzzing, head to toe. I want to wrap myself up in her and lie down, but the talking, the knowing I'm not alone . . . it'll have to be enough. I'm forcing it to be.

What the hell would I do with more?

I allow my mouth to brush those curls at her ears, the sensation dropping my voice to a scrape of sound. "I'm talking about fucking you, baby. You know I am." My tongue must have a mind of its own, because it licks along the rim of her ear, my memory collecting the whimper she makes and locking it away in a safe. "Tucked back in the showers, your legs open for my thrusts, blood running down my back from where your nails are digging in. Bet that would warm you right the hell up."

With a rough intake of air, she dips, legs losing power, and I surge forward on autopilot, my body and mind conditioned to save her from falling. The no-touching rule is no longer a possibility. We're flush from the neck down, my hips pinning her belly, our thighs bumping, my hands gripping her hips to keep her balanced. Jesus. Fucking. Christ. Her mouth up close might as well be a billboard for forbidden fruit. It's puffy, parted and glossy from her tongue. I can't, I can't. Kissing her will be like jumping off a cliff, no idea what the ground below looks like.

"Greer . . ."

The shaky way she murmurs my name turns my hands to fists, punishing the material of the thin, gray pants she's been taunting me with all day. "We could take these off. Gather that final piece of evidence that you're just as happy to see me as I am you." Just a touch, just a little, I tug down the cotton, stopping just beneath her hip-bones. Her answering moan, the tipping back of her head, entices me into pulling them down one more inch. Just one more. "I've got a hard dick and you've got a ready pussy. It's been getting wetter and wetter since you walked in here. Isn't that the truth?"

"Yes," she gasps, writhing in my grip. "Okay? Yes."

The way she answers zaps me out of my trance. Because it's exactly the tone, the manner, almost the exact *words* she used when making a date with that recruit this morning. Like she's appeasing me. Impatient to get what's happening over with. There's a chance she wants me to shut up and touch her more, but now I can only focus on one thing. She's going on a date with someone else. She made that date right in front of me.

The intimacy of the locker room, our pressing bodies, vanishes. My jealousy spills over, bleeding my lust through with green. My stupidity for thinking we made a connection this morning, only to have my mistake stare me in the face for the rest of the day. I'm the only one who thinks what's happening is special. "Better go get those paper towels, then."

I regret the words the second they're out of my mouth. But it's too late to snatch them back. Danika flinches hard, the desire I stoked clearing from her eyes, giving way to . . . embarrassment. Fuck. Not that. Robbing this girl of her pride is unforgiveable.

"Danika—"

She shoves me back and I go, putting my hands up, forcing myself not to stare like a lecher at her still-aroused body. "You're an asshole," she breathes. She doesn't wait for a response before turning and jogging out of the locker room. Without the paper towels.

Regret weighs me down as I dress and prepare to go back out into the cold.

CHAPTER 8
— *Danika* —

I balance a grocery bag on my hip, smacking the door of my parents' apartment with my free hand. Inside, the television is muted long enough for my father to yell at my mother to go open the door. My straining biceps are not impressed.

Honestly, my parents are the best. They gave me a safe, happy childhood with limited means. They encourage me and make me laugh. I love them. I really do. But I'm not even inside yet and I can tell today is going to be one of those days, where I'm pulled in eighty directions. And I'm right. Minutes after I step over the threshold, I've put away the groceries, called Con Edison to dispute a charge on the electric bill and now I'm sprawled in the middle of the living room floor trying to repair my mother's vacuum.

"How is Jack?" asks my mother from the kitchen. "He never comes to see me anymore. Tell him I'm not happy with him."

"Gladly." I select a screwdriver from the assortment of household tools, which we keep in an old Folgers coffee can. "You've been thrown over for an Irish girl. That must burn."

My mom waves that off. "As long as she treats him good." She assumes a fighter's stance. "Otherwise we're going to have trouble."

A laugh vibrates in my belly, and I'm punched with nostalgia. There's something about lying on your stomach in your childhood living room and giggling that makes you feel as if you never left. There's a million memories trapped within these four walls. Watching movies on rainy days, big bowls of ice cream settled on our knees. Walking out in the morning and finding Jack asleep on the couch and knowing his mother must be entertaining a man upstairs. Just another reason why I love my parents. They gave Jack a key, told him *welcome to the family* and never brought up why his escaping to our apartment was necessary.

For all these reasons and more, I give up Saturdays to help my mother clean. To babysit Robbie's sister's new baby. To schedule my father's physical therapy appointments. Stock the fridge, sort the bills, fix appliances. That's what you do for people you love, right?

I'm totally not throwing extra energy into my visit today to distract myself. I'm not.

But it has been two days since Greer turned my dial from mildly horny millennial to sex-starved kerfuffle of hormones. He hasn't been scheduled to train us at the academy, and since the sick instructor is healthy again, I haven't seen him. Or spoken to him.

He can't honestly expect me to carry on with this probation after what happened, though. We both underwent an unexplainable psychosis in that locker room. There's no other explanation for the lieutenant nearly orgasming me with a few well-placed sentences. Although, there were some well-placed muscles, too. Very well placed. Let's face it.

Then there's the matter of his penis.

It's magnificent. Long and thick with one of those Roman helmet-looking heads. Pretty appropriate since the thing was prepared to march onto a battlefield. Oh my God. I can't close my eyes without seeing it rise, the skin stretching, veins growing more prominent.

For me. The invincible lieutenant was turned on for *me*.

"Danny, when you're done with that, can you

help me get the ironing board down from the top of my closet?"

"Yeah, Mom."

"And I need stamps to send out the bills."

"Caught her trying to sneak a couple from your collection again," my father says, finally entering the conversation that has been taking place around him for twenty minutes. "Don't worry. I wouldn't let her."

My mom throws up one shoulder like a shield. "I was desperate!"

My father snorts. "Your collection hasn't seen a new addition in a while, Danika. You planning to get the new Elvis stamp? It comes out next week."

Elvis? I'm too focused on the stamps my mother needs to think about some . . . beautiful square piece of heaven featuring the King.

"I, uh . . ." Tension creeps into my shoulders. It usually does when my plate starts to get crowded, but I shrug it off. Sure, I could say no to my mother's requests, that I want to spend Saturday with my friends. Or I could delegate some things to my cousins, but I hate admitting I can't do something. It's just a few errands. No big deal. Sometimes I wonder, though. Would they still want me around if I wasn't doing things for them? "I can run down to the bodega for stamps. The post office is going to be too crazy."

"Thank you, angel." She's quiet a moment, her potato peeler moving in a blur, sending brown debris into the sink. "I might need a police report filed, too."

I drop my screwdriver. "What?"

"Your mother's bike was stolen," says my father. "She didn't lock it up right."

"The bike we got you for your birthday?"

"Yes." My mother's face is pinched. "I put it in the building hallway so I could talk to Pearl across the street. She wanted to show me the dress she knitted her grandbaby."

My father huffs. "She was over there for two hours. Forgot all about the bike."

"I didn't forget, I got sidetracked." She shoos him with a wrist flick. "Watch your sports, old man."

We bought my mother that bike because she was feeling cooped up in the apartment. Ever since she started riding it along the river, I'd noticed more color in her cheeks, more bounce in her step. But I won't be able to afford a replacement any time soon. All my saved money is being used for rent and food. I sigh and pick the screwdriver back up. "I'll file the report. But I'm sorry, Mom. I don't think you'll see it again."

"That's okay," she says quietly. I don't realize she has crossed the room until she stoops down and cups my chin. "You're a good girl, Danny. So responsible."

"Thanks, Mom."

All at once, I feel like an imposter. Am I responsible? I haven't seen or checked in with Greer since Wednesday, when I witnessed him in all his buff, naked glory. Sure, he was a complete jerk in the locker room, but he helped me out of a bind. Not to mention Robbie worked with the NYPD community outreach program yesterday to clean graffiti off a local elementary school. I could tell over the phone how proud he was to do something positive to cover up the negative. To be responsible.

Meaning the Grim Reaper's lesson was working.

But here I am, not living up to my end of the bargain.

I blow out a breath and tighten the final screw, giving the vacuum a quick test. "Mom, let's get down the ironing board. I'll go grab those stamps, then I have to go out for a while." Hopping to my feet, I dust off the back of my jeans. "I'll be back later to babysit, but I can't stay too long. I have a date."

My mother looks like she's just been informed the Pope is coming to dinner. "A date?"

"Kind of." Although it doesn't feel like one at all. More of an obligation. "It's just pizza."

But first? I have a date with the devil.

I'VE NEVER ACTUALLY been inside the Ninth Precinct where Greer is stationed, but I'll admit to crafting my route occasionally so I can walk past the gray stone building. It's arching steel entrance boasts glowing green lights on either side, letting all who pass through the door know that serious shit is going down inside. But I don't really have a grasp on how serious until I step through the entrance, my Vans squeaking on the polished marble floor.

It's not loud or chaotic, but the mood is laser focused. Two cops nearly mow me down as they march through the foyer, accompanying their low conversation with precise, cutting gestures. I've spent a lot of time envisioning myself walking into a precinct and punching a clock, rubbing shoulders with veterans and rookies alike, but it suddenly seems much further in the future.

Shaking off the negative worry, I propel myself toward the front desk, waiting patiently for the female officer to acknowledge me. She assesses me like spots on a drinking glass. "Yes?"

"Hi, I'm here to see Lieutenant Burns."

At least now she looks interested. "What's this pertaining to?"

"Nothing. I'm just . . ." Just what? A recruit on probation? It might be the truth, but I'm still not sure it's appropriate for me to be visiting my instructor on my day off. Definitely should have thought this through a little more. Intending to walk back outside and call Greer on my cell, I start to back toward the exit. "You know, I'll just—"

"Name," she sighs.

Mud. "Silva."

She picks up the phone and hits a few buttons. A few beats pass before she hangs up. "He's still in a briefing. Have a seat."

Her no-nonsense tone gives me zero choice, so I park it on the far end of the waiting room, hands wedged beneath my thighs. When the front desk lady rises a few minutes later and opens the hallway door, Greer's voice drifts—okay, barks—out and my spine goes straight. All I hear are the words pinpointing possible locations before the door closes again. Except now I'm curious. What does the lieutenant look like in action? Are his officers as scared of him as us recruits? What kind of case if he working on?

Judging I have two minutes max before the receptionist returns, I creep toward the hallway door and open it for a peek. About fifteen yards ahead on the left, I can see Greer through an entrance marked Briefing Room, standing in front of a whiteboard. Before we collided in the locker room, I used to feel tingly whenever the lieutenant was around. Aware. Sensitive. But ever since *I'm talking about fucking you, baby*, tingly doesn't quite cover how it feels to see him again.

Those low, intimate muscles between my legs tighten up, my nipples turning to spikes. Inside my shoes, all ten of my toes curl under. And I'm suddenly a mouth breather.

It doesn't help that he's ten times as intimidating when leading a meeting. He's standing, hunched forward over a desk, propped on giant fists. His frown is made of nightmares. Every time he speaks, I jump a little at the ringing intensity, the decisiveness with which he answers every question.

My line of sight trails over his broad, bunched shoulders, down his back to settle on the curve of his butt. Damn. It's not tight, exactly. It's definitely muscular, but there's some meat. I have this sudden vision of Greer checking out his ass in the gym mirror, growling over the extra cushion he can't manage to banish—and it happens. I breathe a giggle.

Blue eyes snap to mine so fast, I freeze like a clumsy moose in a hunter's crosshairs. That's all the reaction I get out of the lieutenant before he resumes the briefing, delegating and indicating things on the whiteboard with a tapping knuckle. Finally, I force myself to close the hallway door and sit back down, only now I'm considering bolting for the street. I can hear him now. *Eavesdropping is technically a violation of your probation.*

But I already have violated it by avoiding my

responsibility for the last two days. That fact, along with my determination to make it right, is the only thing that keeps me glued to the plastic bucket seat.

I strongly rethink those intentions ten minutes later when the lieutenant fills the hallway doorframe like an irritated king and crooks a finger at me to follow.

CHAPTER 9

Greer

When Danika walks into my office behind me, it's as if I'm seeing it for the first time. God, it's fucking boring.

Sure, there are framed pictures of me on the wall shaking hands with the mayor, alongside commendations, degrees and awards. But there's nothing personal. No propped-up family photos or children's finger painting. Little things cops use as reminders that the entire world isn't locked inside the tired gray walls where topics like assault, homicide and suspicious packages are discussed like the weather. There's a paperweight—a birthday gift from Charlie—that says, "I'm not bossy, I just know what you should be doing," but that's it.

Christ, this is ridiculous. I just led a briefing with an audience of jaded, hard-nosed cops regarding an armed assault suspect at large. Now this girl half my size is making my palms sweat. I track to the far side of my desk and gesture for Danika to sit down, wondering how long the smell of her will hang around when she leaves. Maybe it can be my version of a finger painting, just for a while.

"What are you doing here?"

She sits down, brown eyes flicking between me and the pictures on the wall. "I'm checking in, Lieutenant."

I don't allow any surprise to show on my face, but it's expanding in my throat. Since I sent her storming out of the locker room, I haven't let myself harbor an iota of hope she'd voluntarily put herself in my company again. Hell, she shouldn't. I can't even turn off my asshole function when the girl I've been fantasizing about naked gives me permission to do just that. I've been vacillating between congratulating myself for putting a stop to an inappropriate situation and wishing it was possible to kick my own ass. Not a great couple of days.

"I assumed it was clear after . . ." Frowning down at the papers on my desk, I make a big show of shuffling them so I can avoid a replay of the humiliation I caused. "After what happened,

I think it's best to end your probation. You're off the hook."

Her eyebrows draw together. "I don't want to be off the hook."

"Why?" My tone is still hard from the meeting, and I attempt to soften it, reminding myself she's not one of my officers. "I haven't seen you since Wednesday. What changed your mind since then?"

For the first time since she walked in, I realize her hair is down. Have I ever seen it that way? No, it's always in one of those flippy ponytails, bouncing all over the place when she runs. It's wavy today, stopping a few inches past her shoulders. Even with her tits.

Don't think about her tits.

"My mom's bike got stolen," she answers, sweeping back the uneven ends of her hair. "She told me I was so responsible, offering to file the police report for her. It made me feel guilty for taking the easy way out. With you."

"I see." Her honest answer takes me off guard. I expected sarcasm. But I like her being truthful with me. Very much. "There's no reason for you to feel guilty. I didn't behave like a gentleman."

A laugh puffs out of her. "Most men don't these days."

"They should," I bite out. "They better with you."

Dammit, why can't I operate with a clear head around Danika? My mouth acts on its own, right along with my cock. Brow furrowed, she's staring down at the ground now, sneaking curious peeks up at me through her eyelashes, like I'm an alien life form. "I make sure they do, don't worry," she murmurs. "On the rare occasions I have dates. They're like a lunar eclipse."

"You have one tonight," I point out, before thinking better of it. Great. Now I'm not just her weirdly protective—older—instructor with a boring office. I'm also the guy who has a mental calendar of her social schedule.

"Yes." She rolls her lips inward. "It's just pizza."

Is that why she's wearing her hair down? I don't like the style as much as I originally thought. My hands itch to shove the strands through one of those rubber band deals. I expend the extra energy by printing out a stolen property form for her to fill out, and sliding it across the table.

Watching as she plucks a pen out of my cup and begins completing the questionnaire, I can't seem to keep my curiosity at bay. Curiosity? That's hilarious. If I didn't think it would get me locked in a mental ward, I would book an interrogation room to get every detail of the upcoming date out of her. "Are you on your way to this . . . outing now?"

Her eyebrow goes up at the word *outing*. "No, I

have to run back to Hell's Kitchen and babysit my cousin's baby for an hour."

"You were already there once today?"

She nods. "Mom's vacuum was broken. And she needed groceries and stamps—"

"So you came all the way east, just for . . . this? Only to turn right back around?"

"That's right. When something is bothering me, I try to face it right away." She rubs her cheek on her shoulder in a gesture I know well from the academy. She's always doing it during lectures. "I don't want to get away with shirking my responsibilities."

"It sounds like you have a lot of them. Responsibilities." Every once in a while, when interrogating a perp, the cop strikes a nerve. Sometimes that nerve has no connection to their possible crime, but we hit it nonetheless. I've just prodded Danika's sore tooth by pointing out how busy she seems to be on others' behalves. It's my nature to dig deeper, but this time it's because I want to know what makes her tick. No denying that. "I'm aware that Jack Garrett joined the academy thanks to your influence. Your cousin called you when his store was going to be robbed, too. Does everyone depend on you?"

"If they do, I'm glad." She says it too fast, and we both know what that signals. When I raise an eyebrow, the tension seems to leave her neck.

"Maybe sometimes . . . I keep myself available, just in case my family needs me."

"You don't know how to say no."

Signing her name on the form and pushing it back toward me, she smirks. "No."

I see you now, tough girl. Thank God I keep that sentiment in my head, because we're both uncomfortable by how far this conversation has gone. Me, because I genuinely care about her answers and want to help. Her, because she probably thinks revealing her weaknesses to me is a bad thing. Does she have any idea how hard I can relate to her hating the chink in her armor? "All right, Silva. Consider yourself checked in—"

"Is this your book of the week?" Her gentle fingers are combing through the paperwork on my desk. Which is so intimate, she might as well be combing through my chest hair. Finally, she retrieves my copy of *The Lost Order* by Steve Berry and holds it up. "For book club?"

"Yes." I shift in my seat, commanding my hands to stay where they are. "Brought it to read on my lunch break. But I never get one, so I guess the joke is on me. You can put it down now."

Danika tilts her head, setting off sparkles in her eyes. "You don't like people touching your books?"

"The corners get damaged very easily."

"Hmmm." She lays it down carefully. "What are your book club meetings like?"

"Most of the officers are there by recommendation of a department therapist." Sliding the book off my desk, I place it in my top drawer, mentally reciting the page number where I left off, since I never bend pages. Ever. "Officers who've discharged their weapon or dealt with a traumatic event while on duty. Reading is a way to occupy their thoughts and the club keeps them accountable."

"And you lead the group." Her delicious-looking mouth slides into a smile at one end. "Did you . . . create the group?" I give a brisk nod and she falls back into the chair. "Oh."

The urge to explain catches me off guard and I don't suppress it in time. "I was required to attend sessions with the department therapist after . . ." When her smile drops I know she's aware of the reason I had mandated therapy. It's no secret I lost my partner. Ignoring the stab of discomfort in my jugular, I keep going. "I hated it. Figured there were other officers who'd rather drink a quick beer and talk about something besides themselves. So I got it done. There's no tears or hand-holding. It's not a support group, Silva."

"Yes, it is. A really cool one."

My laugh surprises me. "You just called my book club cool?"

Danika shrugs one shoulder, her mouth twisting. It seems like she might say something important, so I hold my breath. "I collect stamps." I'm still holding my breath, but now there's satisfaction burrowing under my skin. "It wasn't supposed to be a serious relationship between stamps and me, but my father used to work as a post office clerk. After school, I'd meet him there and we'd walk home together. Every once in a while, he had a special edition stamp for me. It became a habit to press them into my scrapbook . . . so I kept doing it." She nods in the direction of my drawer. "So there. We're both secret geeks."

Warmth coats my insides. She just shared something with me.

Danika sucks in an excited breath, and my belt begins to feel confining. "There's a collector's edition Elvis stamp coming out next week. It'll probably be gone by the time we're dismissed from drills in the evening, but I'll get to see it online."

"Why don't you ask someone to go get it for you? Your father, or . . ."

She shakes her head. "No, it's fine. It's no big deal."

I see you even more now, tough girl. "So favors for everyone else, but you refuse to ask for your own."

"I asked you for one, didn't I?" We stare across

the desk at one another for a few moments, while I exult in the fact that she did, in fact, ask for my help when she doesn't do it often. With anyone. "I need to get back to the West Side. Are we good here?"

"Yes." I gain my feet, as well. "Thanks for coming in."

"Thanks for organizing that community service for Robbie." She pushes up from the chair. "I think it was good for him."

Her words linger in the air when she leaves the office, along with her scent. I circle the desk in three long strides and close the door, trying to keep it trapped. After a greedy inhale, my eyes stray to the clock. Four more hours on shift. By the time I get home tonight, she'll be on her pizza date with another man. The reminder makes my gut tighten, acid shooting up my throat.

How will I fucking stand it?

CHAPTER 10
— Danika —

Why did I agree to this? I hate dating. This chaotic stretch of island is packed full of people with complex wants and needs. We're all here to pursue something. A dream, an escape, an unknown. Problem is, people don't always know what they're pursuing. They just want something, and they want it fast. Are we all expecting some bell to ding in our heads when we run into the right person? It's such an unrealistic hope for people who don't understand what they want. Or worse, what if what we want is the wrong thing?

For me, dates usually go one of two ways.

One, the man tells me what I want to hear, in the hopes that I'll put out. The irony being, there is literally nothing that could turn me off faster, except a wedding ring. Two, my pending status as a police officer intimidates the man, and he spends the night overcompensating. *Look at the size of this steak! Damn right I'll eat the whole thing! Beer me!*

Levi is a safe choice. He already knows I'm going to be a cop, and he can handle my good-natured ball breaking. Not to mention, if he tries to get me into bed on the first date, he knows I'll probably break his nose.

My cell phone is sitting on the sink, and I check the time. Half an hour until I'm due to leave. The closer my departure looms, the more my stomach starts to tie in knots. Am I nervous about pizza with Levi? Uh, no. I'm nervous because going on a date with one guy feels wrong when I can't stop thinking about another.

Dark blue eyes materialize in my mind, looking me over, head to toe. Observing my knee-high rain boots—in deference to the weather—my black skinny jeans and loose, off the shoulder T-shirt. A red bra strap peeks out, covered only by the ends of my hair. Would Greer think I look sexy? He's never seen me in makeup. I haven't even seen myself in makeup since training began at the academy. Would I be excited if I was meeting him for a date, instead?

I squeeze my thighs together at the mere idea. Of

having his possessive hand on my back, those fingers brushing my neck during dinner. We wouldn't even pretend to make small talk. Maybe we would be like we were today, in his office. Talking about real things that forced me to see him in a different light. If he organized a book club for officers who'd undergone a trauma, is he really the hard-ass I've built up in my head?

One last swipe of my hairbrush and I turn off all the apartment lights, throw my purse over my shoulder. Jack, Charlie, Ever and Katie spent the day at Governor's Island at a concert, but the rain has probably already sent them back to Manhattan. I'd rather be gone when they get home, so I don't have to answer any pre-date questions or overanalyze everyone's reactions to my outfit.

Resolving to walk slowly toward the pizza place, I open the door—

"Oh my God," I gasp, my walloping heart sending me back a step. "What . . ."

Greer is standing in the hallway, watching me with shadows in his eyes.

Rain drips off the folded edges of his NYPD beanie and fingertips. He's so still I almost think my imagination is putting him there, but then he speaks in a clipped tone.

"Cancel it."

My . . . date? Oh yeah. He's talking about my date, and there's no denying the indignation that fires to life inside of me. I don't care if I'm attracted to this man. He doesn't just get to show up and order me around. On a Saturday night, no less. We're not in the academy gym right now— we're on the threshold of my house.

Then why am I so excited? There's a whole gallon of relief pouring down over my head, almost like I'd been subconsciously hoping he'd show up and make this exact demand. Make demands . . . period. The sound of my back hitting the mat, Greer breathing heavy above me, frees itself from my memories. Those incredible seconds I spent having my will tested by someone I trust won't leave me alone. Now he's here to do it again and . . . I have to fight the desire to let him, because his demand is irrational and high-handed. Isn't it? *Yes.* "No way," I breathe. "I'm not canceling."

A muscle leaps in his cheek. His boots thunk twice on the ground, before creaking onto my side of the doorframe. If he thinks I'm going to back up, he has another think coming. My chin lifts so we can maintain eye contact. Dammit, I hate being short. But my lack of height is the last thing on my mind when Greer leans down and almost—*almost*—grazes my lips with his damp ones. "Do you need a little convincing?"

The way he says *convincing* curls fingers of heat below my belly button. It's a scrape of two knives together, and there's no way to misinterpret what kind of methods he'd use to convince me to cancel my date. "H-how?" I ask anyway. "How would you *try* to do that?"

"Yes or no. Do you want to be convinced?" Finally, just a hint of his lips brush mine, and the answering, down-low clench is so intense, I almost hit the deck. "Understand this. I'm going to do it my way, Danika. And I'm only figuring out what this way is now—with you—because I think you love it. Need it." A single blunt finger lifts and traces my right hip, moving up my rib cage and detouring toward my breasts, raking over each hard nipple slowly. "Think you'd love some rough goddamn convincing, wouldn't you, baby? Yes or no?"

This new need he stirred to life isn't my secret. He's known. "Yes."

Without warning, he throws me over his shoulder. "Which bedroom is yours?"

It happens so fast, my thoughts are upside down, along with the room. "I—I . . . what?"

"Never mind, it's the one closest to the bathroom." He strides in the correct direction, steps purposeful. "You would have fought the boys for the best location."

My room is dark when he walks inside, and my heart starts to hammer in heavy, furious beats. I'm in my bedroom with Lieutenant Greer Burns, and he's made the demand for me to cancel my date. *I'm going to do it my way.* What does that entail? Does this mean that he cares? My thoughts are sent in a tumble again when I'm lifted off his shoulder and settled on the edge of my bed. I stare up at his imposing figure in the darkness, my breath traveling in and out in labored puffs.

God. God. He's massive, his shoulders blocking out the streetlamp framed by my window. He looks even larger somehow when he carefully removes his wet jacket, laying it neatly across the top of my Ikea desk. His beanie follows, along with his gun belt. Methodical, confident. Sexy. Shouldn't I be questioning his timely arrival instead of noticing how the material of his button-down shirt stretches across his pecs?

I've just about gathered enough presence of mind to form sentences when his coarse fingers lift my chin, turning my head side to side, like he's examining me.

And then he's gone, striding from the room. What the hell?

In my periphery, I register the bathroom light being turned on, the water running. Without him in the room, my common sense tries to roar back. A man has shown up at my apartment and demanded I change my plans. I'm an independent, badass future policewoman, and this shouldn't be working for me in any way, shape or form. I *should* use this opportunity to grab my purse and make a break for it. But I don't. I sit there like a moron, anticipation rising like a tide inside me. Still, when he strides back into the room and kicks the door shut behind him, I notice he's carrying a washcloth, so I shoot to my feet. There has to be a line he can't cross, right? Why do I want him to toe that line so hard? "What are you doing?"

"Most times, I would think this stuff on your face looks pretty." He backs me up until I have no choice but to fall back down onto the bed's edge. "Tonight is not one of those times."

The warm washcloth swipes gently across my mouth, left to right. Back again. It glides up to my cheeks and over one eye. My common sense is screaming at me to fight, to call him an over-bearing jackass—and I'm just about to, when he presses a kiss to my hair. His thumb traces the curve of my jaw, my lower lip. Reverently enough that I forget what he's doing. At least until he throws the wet washcloth across the room, which carries twenty minutes of work in the bathroom mirror along with it. "Cancel it."

His abrupt change in demeanor makes me sputter. "You don't think I'm stubborn enough to walk out of here looking like a drowned rac-coon?"

"Oh, I know you are." Outside, the rain picks

up intensity, moisture attacking the ancient window. "Time for you to find out how deep my stubborn runs, though, Danika. Isn't that why you planned this little . . . date?"

My nipples turn to points when he bites out that last word. I feel every ounce of my femininity with him looming over me so determined. So frustrated. I'd never admit to being fragile, but if this man has a will to press on me? Yes. I'm fragile. He outmatches not just me, but most of the population, in every physical way. But more so because there's a not-so-secret part of me that needs him to press that will. I want to know exactly how big and bad he is. Is he right? Did I agree to this date to goad him? "I'm not canceling it, Lieutenant, so get to stepping."

"You will." He slides a finger beneath my red bra strap, and I don't dare breathe as he slides that digit back and forth. "So help me God, you better not have the matching panties on."

My stomach muscles draw in tight, just hearing a delicate word like panties on lips made of carved granite. "Wouldn't you like to know?"

His finger stops moving. "Last chance to cancel it."

I can't lose this opportunity to find out why he came. Is this just physical or something more? "You haven't even told me why. Why should I cancel it, Greer?"

The dark bedroom zings with the fact that I said his first name. Blue eyes track sideways from my shoulder to settle on my mouth. And I want to take back the question, because the answer scares me more than a little. This is not a man to be managed. Or played with. He might not even be knowable. There are so many mysteries locked up behind that carefully honed, cold exterior, who knows what might be lurking?

"I don't have the words for an explanation," he rasps, going down on his knees. I'm so glued to what he's saying, I don't even resist as he yanks off my rain boots, letting them thud on the ground. One. Two. "I only know if you go on that date, any date, I'm not going to get rid of the cold that comes with it. You're not supposed to go on dates."

If he didn't sound so lost, I could've kept my final, tenuous shred of indignation alive. He does, though. Now I'm lost, too. I'm going to be lost until I find him, I think. Oh, Jesus, that's scary. Since orientation day at the academy, gravity has pulled me toward this man, and now I'm caught. What happens next? "What should I be doing instead?" I whisper. "Of dates."

Warm hands close around my feet, climbing the backs of my calves, before sliding around to my knees. Thighs. Higher and higher, until his gaze lifts to mine. Hunger, a man's hunger, bleeds from those eyes with so much force, I go soft and wet between my legs. Simple and damning biology, woman preparing to please and be pleased. "I want like hell to say you should be with me, but I don't know if that's true." He growls a curse, those huge hands kneading my thighs. "Danika."

That's it. All he says is my name, three syllables packed with warning and need, before he prowls onto the bed, knocking me onto my back. A sob wracks my body, my senses already overwhelmed with his innate dominance, when he's barely even touched me. His bulk hovers an inch above mine, the capable strength of his arms keeping him elevated.

Finally, he drops his mouth to the air above mine, loitering there so long, I almost scream. "Cancel it," he rasps. "Now."

Or what, is on the tip of my tongue, but I can't find it in me to challenge him. Not when he's looking at me like a . . . gift. One he's afraid to play with, but can't help it. "If I cancel it, will you kiss me already?"

He nods, his eyelids weighed down with anticipation. "By the time I'm done fucking that smart-ass mouth with my tongue, you're going to know what real stubborn tastes like."

I don't even command my legs to part, they just do it. As if that filthy promise was the magic words my hormones had been waiting for. Unfortunately, Greer is still holding himself above me, probably refusing to press down until I cancel with . . . who is the date with again? Oh, right. Levi. "M-my phone is in my—"

Greer cuts me off with a grunt, tipping his head toward the purse, which I hadn't noticed in my periphery, nor can I remember how it got onto my bed. It only takes me a few seconds to dig out the device and pull up Levi's number, hitting CALL.

"Making this call with you listening is so wrong," I mutter. "On every level."

The lieutenant drops his hips, just enough to ride his thick erection up the valley of my parted legs, pressing down on my clit. Staying there. "There's your motivation."

CHAPTER 11
Greer

Am I a sick bastard to gain satisfaction out of Danika canceling this date while I'm pinning her hips to the bed? Probably. But I'm too worked up and jealous to give a fuck. I've had all afternoon to convince myself I have no claim on this girl, but none of my mental tricks or distractions worked. I could no more go back to my silent, sterile apartment and let her go out with someone else than I could survive without water. Sitting at my desk was like being in the electric chair, set to go off when the date started. I couldn't work, couldn't *think*. Now, my police vehicle is parked at a hydrant down the block, probably crooked, but I can't remember anything but throwing the damn thing into Park and storming her building.

"I don't even want you on the phone with him," I whisper against her parted mouth. "So make it fast."

She's freaking out a little bit, probably because I'm coming on so strong. Shit, maybe too strong? I made the decision to trust my intuition that we both need these . . . roles. Me on top, in control. And God, it feels really fucking right having her hand me the reins. Still, last week, we only communicated with our eyes, or exchanged words about academy business. Now I'm in her bedroom, commanding her to cancel her evening plans. If her reactions weren't making it obvious that this is definitely what she needs, I'd question her more first. But her breaths are shallow, almost wheezing. The hand holding the phone to her ear is white-knuckled. Her hips can't keep completely still, and as soon as she cancels with him, I'm going to give in and buck. Anticipation has my muscles straining, my hands holding so tight to the yellow comforter, it could tear any second.

After what seems like forever, the encroaching shithead answers. "You're canceling."

Danika winces. "I'm sorry. J-just not feeling well."

"Whoa. Sounds like it. Rain check?"

I shake my head no.

"Sure," Danika answers. "Have to go. I'll see you Monday."

She hangs up and drops the phone like it's on fire, shooting resentment at me from the depths of her brown eyes. "You better be a good kisser—"

Goddamn euphoria. Her lips open under the insistence of mine, my tongue sliding home, and I have no clue, no fucking clue if I'm a good kisser or not. I just need so bad. A whimper cuts off in her throat, then continues in fits and starts, like Morse code. Can't put all my weight on her, can I? But I do, because she grabs my face between her hands and my arms give out. So good. She's holding my face and letting me kiss her, and it's amazing. I'm crushing her, and that feels good, feels right, too. My mouth is a punishing force on hers, but she's taking me, handling me, letting my tongue stroke hers, play with it, lick at it.

Her lips. God, her lips. If her body heat was enough to sustain me, the soft submission of her mouth could power me through the next life. Submission. Yeah. I'm intoxicated on how pliant she is, her fucking incredible body letting mine . . . fuck her. I'm so high on her mouth, I don't realize at first that I'm dry humping the shit out of her, grinding down on her pussy, my hips rearing back, then returning for more. More.

"Jesus Christ," I roar, ripping my mouth away,

suctioning it to her neck. "Am I making you feel good? Do you like this?"

"I'm . . . Oh my God, I'm going to come." Her fingers slide into my uniform pants, right over the bare flesh of my ass, digging her nails in. If possible, my cock hardens even more, straining inside my pants. "Please."

No. Not yet. My own denial confuses me, because I want Danika to be satisfied. I need that to happen. But since the beginning, she's woken up this part of me that demands control. With her. Just . . . her. And I have a vicious need to dictate when and how she comes. She sure as shit isn't coming from some sloppy dry hump I was barely aware of until a minute ago.

"Your mouth distracted me," I slur into her neck, unable to stop the punctuated roll of my hips. "It does that a lot. I see it and I want it working for me. Want it to talk to me, want to kiss it. Use it. I think about that last part when my dick is in my hand."

Even with my weight pressing her down, she manages to arch her back. Her thighs are jerking around my waist, little broken moans shooting past her lips. Christ, she's so damn gorgeous. I could watch her all day. "Greer . . . Greer."

As usual, my first name in her mouth sends out a ripple of satisfaction, starting in my belly, reverberating all the way up in my head. "We're not done here yet, Danika." I still my hips, and she wails, trying to urge me back into moving. But I'm already dragging my mouth down between her tits, giving each stiff nipple a graze of teeth. "We're going to find out about those matching panties now, aren't we?"

I push up the hem of her shirt, like I've fantasized about doing so many times. Her belly shudders up and down, begging for me to cage it between my hands and hold it still. And I might have if the impulse to mark up that smooth, flawless skin wasn't stronger. I drag my stubbled chin and cheeks across her belly button, leaving redness behind, recording her shocked sobs to be replayed later. My fingers work the fly of her skintight pants, my impatience rearing its head until I'm jerking down the zipper, ripping the pants down her legs. Just want to get to her pussy. Want my tongue in it now.

She's wearing the red panties.

"Tomorrow is laundry day. That's all." Her fingers skim along my jawline, but I can't process how nice it feels over the ringing in my skull. "No one would have seen them if you hadn't shown up, Greer. I . . ." Her voice drops to a scrap of sound, but I'm beyond hearing. "I think I only said yes to the date to make you d-do something like this. And—"

I flip her over onto her stomach, cutting off whatever else she was going to say. This possessiveness I've only ever felt for Danika is raw. Unrefined. What I want, the visions that have my hands shaking with wild lust, haven't been explored. Hell, maybe I repressed them too long, watching her from a distance. Whatever the reason, I move out of necessity, gripping her hips and yanking them up, leaving Danika on hands and knees. Her beautiful ass is covered in the hated red silk, but my groan breaks loose nonetheless at the sight of her. "Look at you. Fuck."

My dick is so swollen, I'm almost dizzy, but I've been miserable so long with needing to fuck Danika, it doesn't even occur to me to take it out of my pants. There's only one thought that keeps circling around in my head.

"You were going to wear these out with someone else."

"I told you, it's . . ." She trails off as I lower her panties, leaving them stretched around her knees. "What are you going to do?"

The jealousy must have left a shred of decency behind, because I can't bring myself to punish her if I'm not positive she wants it. "I want to take my hand to these cheeks." I gather a grip of flesh, molding it, gritting my teeth when the parting of her backside shows off her pussy. Wet. So wet and beautiful. Needing the same relief I'm hot to give.

"Do it," she says in a husky whisper, pushing her ass up. "I want you to."

"Why?"

"Because it'll make us both feel good." She looks back at me over her shoulder. Her eyes are excited, but cautious. "At least . . . I hope it will."

My hand won't wait any longer, it rears back and lowers the first slap. *Whap.* The sound wraps my brain in clarity, and I'm suddenly so present, so in tune with Danika's reactions, her breathing, I wonder where the fuck I was before. Shit, I was almost incoherent after we first started kissing. Is it because I needed a direction? A plan? "Well?" I bite out.

"Oh my God." Her slight sides heave in and out. "Again."

Yes. This time, there's more bite in the glancing blow of my palm. Her tight ass shivers with a quick vibration, before stilling. Three more, I decide. My blood is burning, I'm so fucking horny, but I'm laser-focused on her. Danika. Her moans fill the room. She crowds everything else out of the stadium of my mind. She's made me feel out of control since I met her, but now she's giving it back to me, in this incredible way I didn't know existed. Maybe because it was designed for her.

By the fifth spank, her ass has turned bright pink and something about that color, knowing I've been given the privilege of painting it on, makes me desperate to return the favor. I needed her, now she needs me. With that truth ringing in my head, I push her sweet cheeks apart and bend down, licking her pussy from behind.

"Oh." Her upper half drops onto the bed, elevating her bottom even more. "Oh, please don't stop this time."

"Move your knees apart," I growl, pushing my middle finger inside her, pumping it a few times, as she follows the order. Then a few more times, because I can't believe the tightness waiting for me. "This has been mine for months, hasn't it?"

Her choked cry, the tilt of her hips, is the only answer I need.

"It's a good thing I didn't know, baby, or I wouldn't have been able to help myself. All those times you showed up early would have been spent in my office, riding my cock."

"Greer," she moans, her thighs starting to tremble. "I need—"

"I damn well know what you need. I'm the one who gives it." I untuck my finger from the warmth of her pussy and push my tongue through the slick sweetness of her folds. When my tongue hits that tiny nub, I keep it there, lapping at her until broken renditions of my name start to leave her. She moves her hips like an ocean wave, each sexy movement rubbing her against my working tongue. When she hits her peak, I grip my cock and squeeze hard, but it's not for pleasure. It's a gesture of pride. Pride in myself for making Danika come.

Jesus, the shaking she does, the light sheen of sweat on her forehead when she flops down and rolls over . . . it's the most incredible thing I've ever seen. She is.

"Oh . . ." She shakes her head and I swear, her eyes cross a little. "Whoa. I mean, just, whoa." Her eyes track down below my waistband, a soft exclamation appearing on her lips. "Come here."

That same need for control rises in me, swift and not taking any bullshit. She must sense it, because the excitement flickers back in her drowsy eyes. Will she let me decide what happens after I finally unzip my pants?

The way she lets her cupped hands fall to her sides, the awareness in her expression, tells me yes. "Tell me what you want," she murmurs. "Please."

There's a roaring in my head, a certainty that I've found my place—

But it's cut off when a door slams and the apartment fills with voices.

IT'S NOT THE intrusion that breaks me from my trance. It's the way Danika jackknifes on the bed, pulling her panties back into place with clumsy hands. Hiding her pussy away so fast, I have to tamp down the urge to rip the silk back off. She doesn't want to get caught with me. Of course she doesn't. I'm the asshole instructor everyone calls Lieutenant Hard-Ass behind his back. I know my brother and his friends will keep their mouths shut, but I don't rely on secrecy.

Cause and effect. Consequences. Those things are supposed to be black and white to me, even when I'm on the receiving end. I should be worried about being caught in a compromising position with one of my recruits. But I'll be damned before I hide in her closet like some pansy-ass high school kid.

"You home, D?" Jack Garrett shouts through the door. "There's soggy pizza out here."

"They'll probably come in and check if I'm here," Danika whispers, buttoning her pants. "If you don't want to be found, I would—"

"You would what?"

She breathes into the silence. "Why are you snapping at me? I wish they hadn't shown up, but they did. You really want to explain what you're doing in my bedroom?"

Her logic is unwelcome when my dick is throbbing like a motherfucker, she looks like pure temptation in the darkness and there is no clear, concise definition of the situation. What is going on between us? I don't have enough experience speaking about these kinds of matters with women, nor do we have time for me to make an attempt. "How would you explain it?" I asked anyway, already cursing myself.

"I don't know." Watching me closely, she draws her knees up to her chest. Is she self-conscious? "If you want to walk out there with me and eat soggy pizza, I'll tell them all to mind their own business. Like, i-if that's what you want."

Now her eyes are on the ceiling, leaving me to drift. But I don't just drift, I blast right out of this warm, dark, rain-stained bedroom back to reality. Walk out into the kitchen and eat pizza? Like some kind of triple date? No. No, that's not a possibility. What would happen next? I spend the night, spooned around one of my recruits? Wake up in the morning and make plans for the next night? And the next?

I banish the torturous rise of yearning and get up from the bed. While I replace my beanie, gun belt and jacket, she's so still on the bed. Too still. What the hell was I thinking coming here? She could be out right now with some fresh-faced kid who isn't burned out at age thirty. Someone who doesn't see the horrors of his job every time his eyes close. Most of all, she could have a real chance with a guy who isn't so fucking crippled by potential loss, he can't share any real part of himself.

Knowing all that, I would still come here and

demand she cancel her date, if I could do tonight all over again. How big of a bastard does that make me?

I pause with my hand on the doorknob. "You'll check in with me tomorrow."

Her nod is jerky. "Yeah."

She needs kissing and holding—even I can see that—but I can't give those things to her without falling down a rabbit hole. Chancing more and more, until I'm in too deep. So I suck up the regret and walk out the door, closing it softly behind me.

Everyone freezes, slices of pizza halting in midair. If I was capable of laughing right now, I would. At least until the shock on Charlie's and Jack's faces turns into something else. Something with the potential to turn me into a snarling beast, if I let it. They're defensive. Protective over the girl I just left alone in her bedroom.

The realization that I just fucked my chances of making her protection my job burns my esophagus. "You have something to say?"

I'm not sure I've ever seen Jack angry, but he's there now, sliding off the kitchen stool. Katie's hand is on his chest, but he kisses it and sets it aside, without taking his eyes off me. "Out in the hallway."

Ever nudges my brother. "Paging Charlie for mediation services."

"On it," Charlie mutters, throwing down his napkin.

We all move toward the door at the same time, but when I notice the girls floating in the opposite direction to Danika's room, I pause on the threshold. Does she . . . need checking on? She's always so tough and irreverent. Maybe she's not always that way?

My throat fills with cement, my hands feeling useless as I follow my brother and his roommate into the hallway. Charlie, ever the voice of reason, closes the door and steps between me and Jack. "Okay, look. We all saw this coming."

That catches me off guard. "What?"

Jack throws up his hands. "You couldn't have been more obvious with a rose clamped between your teeth, man."

There's an unwanted image. Even if Jack speaks the truth, though, they wouldn't have seen anything coming unless Danika was obvious in her interest, too, right? "Did she . . . say anything about me?" Their mouths fall open around the same time I hear myself. "Forget I asked that."

"I'm really going to try," Charlie says, looking at me like I just spoke Dutch. "Jack, I think the important thing to remember here is Danika is a grown-up. She doesn't need us to interfere."

"She's getting it anyway," Jack shoots back,

pointing a finger at me. "You hurt my best friend and—"

"You'll what?" My jaw tightens to a near-shattering point. "Watch what you say to me."

"Deep breaths, men," interjects Charlie.

Amazingly enough, Jack follows my brother's advice, taking a moment. "Listen. You helped me keep Katie in New York and you're taking me seriously at the academy now. I don't want you to think I take those things for granted. But I'd be drunk on a dock somewhere if Danika hadn't befriended my worthless ass. I owe it to her to make sure she isn't hurt." He pauses for a breath. "Just tell me it's more. Tell me you're going to do right by her, and I'll shut my mouth."

Fuck, I want to. I want to storm back into the apartment and wrap her up in a bear hug. When I think about the way she offered to walk out of the bedroom with me, my chest can barely withstand the pounding inside of it. It wasn't easy for her to make that gesture. To put herself out there. And I rejected it. Her.

At same time, I look at Charlie and Jack, their whole world this shiny, new bundle of possibilities, and my mind tells me I did the right thing. They think it's so simple. Find the girl of your dreams and give her everything. My everything is nothing, though. As a rookie cop, I was just like them, but strips have been taken off me, one by one. Losing a parent for what felt like the second time, losing a partner just when that wound was beginning to scab over. Daily tragedy followed by solitude. I won't offer Danika a sad shell of what used to be human.

"Greer," Charlie urges me in a low voice, his expression already one of disappointment. "Answer him."

The words won't come.

Jack goes back into the apartment, leaving a curse hanging in the air. I start to leave, too, but Charlie calls out to me, stopping my progress toward the stairs.

"Hold up." He shoves his hands into his pockets. "I know getting advice from your younger brother is your equivalent of naked hang gliding, but just listen for a second?"

That's not true. I love being around my brother. I'm so fucking proud of him, how hard he trains, his ingrained need to help people he cares about. Because he wants to, not because he's obligated. If he didn't serve as a constant reminder of what I could be without all the hideous shit in my head, I'd probably be a better brother. Spend more time doing things that don't revolve around our career paths. "What is it?"

He comes forward a few steps. "You like her. A lot. I knew it for sure when you let her win that bet in Brooklyn." I don't say anything and he doesn't expect me to. "Brace yourself, because here comes something shitty. If you can't offer her anything, leave her alone. I tried to keep Ever as a friend with benefits, and it blew up in my face. I could have lost her. And that would have been the end of me, okay? I never would have been the same."

"You and me are different people, Charlie."

"I hurt her." He braces a hand on the wall. "The whole time I was trying to fit Ever into a space where I was comfortable, I was hurting her. Bad. Times I didn't even realize it." A beat passes. "I know you don't want to do that to Danika."

My stomach roils at the memory of her so still on the bed. If that's what pursuing whatever this is leads to, I have to stay away. "No. God no."

I don't realize Charlie has gone back into the apartment until the door clicks shut, leaving me to return to my car alone in the rain.

CHAPTER 12
Greer

Double-parking is a huge problem in this city. I've made more than my share of enemies on the force by ticketing department vehicles that linger too long, blocking bike lanes and congesting the avenues. At noon on Monday, there isn't a damn spot in sight outside the post office—the fourth one I've driven to today. And I should really take that as a hint to stop searching for Elvis stamps, return to the precinct and do my fucking job. Yet here I am.

Gritting my teeth, I circle the block one more time, looking for somewhere appropriate to leave my car that won't disrupt the flow of traffic. It's amazing in a city so huge that one damn car can screw things up for miles. An artery blockage on wheels. Sort of like how I've felt since Saturday night. Blocked. My blood is the traffic, and the fact that I might have hurt Danika is stuck right in the center of my vein, dividing me in two.

I'm an idiot for thinking stamps are going to help. In fact, they'll probably make things worse, because she might read something into it. What? Like, *the truth,* maybe? That kissing her Saturday night made me feel like everything was going to get better? Until I left, that is. Nothing has gotten better since then. I was sick to my stomach until I remembered Elvis, and that's all I've been able to focus on. Now if the United States Postal Service would cooperate and make the damn things available, I could go back to being miserable at my desk, thank you very much.

I'm waiting at a red light, trying to massage the headache from my head with punishing fingers when my cell phone rings. Being that it has been ringing nonstop since I set out on this fool's mission for square adhesives, I almost answer without looking at the screen.

Silva, Danika (your recruit, asshole) flashes in white, digital letters.

I sit up straighter in the driver's seat. She called me to check in yesterday and I missed it, because I was watching a suspect interrogation. It turned out to be a good thing, though, because she left a voice mail that I listened to more than once.

Probably an unhealthy amount of times, actually, but who's counting?

Lieutenant Burns, this is Danika Silva calling to check in. So . . . ch-ch-check. You're writing on that clipboard right this very second, aren't you? Knew it.

The memory makes my mouth edge up at the corner as the light turns green. But the ghost of a smile disappears when I remember how fast she talked, like she'd had to work up the courage to call me. The phone stops ringing by the time the post office comes into view again, forcing me to coast to a stop so I can listen. Right there on the avenue. Jesus, she has turned me into a double-parker.

Hiiii, no it's fine, don't bother answering. You, uh, never really specified what I'm supposed to say during these check-ins, but Charlie marked your birthday on our community kitchen calendar, so you're getting your horoscope.

She's talking fast again and that bothers me because it's my fault. But I can't help but feel a tug in my chest. She looked up my birthday? How many pages did she have to flip to find it?

Pisces, cautious Saturn is in your money corner, so it will throw the penalty flag if you consider that impulse buy. Retail therapy is not your friend, so before you hand over that plastic, think hard. Do you need those nude pumps? Food for thought, Lieutenant. Byeeeee.

Oh Christ, how cute was that? I can't even hear the passing traffic over the ricochet of my heart off my rib cage. How mad or disappointed can she reasonably be if she's reading me my horoscope? Either she has decided me showing up unannounced to give her head was no big deal, or she's just putting on a brave face to hide her real feelings.

I have extreme dislike for either option.

And I'll go to another hundred post offices to get the stupid stamp, if necessary.

Ignoring the eye rolls from passing motorists, I slam the car door and enter the post office. Everyone is attempting to mail shit or score money orders on their lunch break, so *of course*, the line circles the interior. Twice. If I get in the back of the line, there's every chance Elvis will have left the building by the time I reach the window. Nope. Not happening.

With a sigh, I take out my badge and hold it up, approaching the first postal worker with an opening. But an elderly woman moving with the assistance of a walker beats me there, as if I haven't taken enough punishment today. "I'll take a book of the Elvis collector's edition stamps, please," she says. Because why not, universe?

The teller hits a few buttons on his computer screen. "You're in luck. It's our last one."

Oh, so this is really happening. Incredible.

They both notice me at the same time. "Can I help you, sir?" asks the teller, looking nervous. Probably because I look ready to grab the stamps from an old lady and run.

"I'm going to need those stamps, ma'am." My badge is attached to my wallet, so I flip it over and open the money pocket. "How much is it going to cost me?"

"Nothing. They're not for sale."

"We have Marilyn Monroe," supplies the teller. "Or Spock."

I shut him up with a withering side glance. When I come back at the woman, she has already squirreled away the Elvis booklet and put on her game face. Apparently I've met my match. "Hundred bucks."

"Nope."

"Three hundred."

She sniffs, taking me in with a sweeping look. "You don't strike me as a collector."

I clear my throat and make sure there's no one else within earshot. "They're for a girl who's mad at me. She's the collector."

Perfect. Now she's smiling. What is it about women that they love to see one of their kind bring a man to his knees? And I realize that's where I'm willing to go. One taste of Silva and I've lost my damn mind.

"Are you useful around the house?" Stamp Stealer asks me.

"I have no idea."

"Lord. Can you at least change some light bulbs?" She gathers herself up, like she's getting ready to lay into someone. Hopefully not me. "My landlord won't change them because of some liability nonsense, and my son lives in Texas."

I weigh the mountain of paperwork on my desk against becoming a handyman for an hour and finally getting those stamps. It's no contest. "My car is outside. Let's go."

She waits until I open the passenger side door for her to ask, "How about litter boxes? Mind changing a couple of those, too?"

Christ.

CHAPTER 13

—— *Danika* ——

Who's got two thumbs and doesn't let some man get her down?

This girl.

One of my fellow lady recruits holds the door for me on the way into the locker room, and we exchange a fist bump. It's going to be a great Wednesday. Even if Greer is on the schedule for the first time this week and I'll finally be coming face-to-face with him again. No big deal. I'm even wearing the red panties again for an extra boost of confidence, maybe even a sassy, secret middle finger to the lieutenant.

There is absolutely nothing that can break my stride.

Except maybe an envelope taped to my locker.

I frown at the white rectangle and carefully remove it, settling it in my lap as I plop down onto the bench. Making sure there is no one looking, I lift the fold out . . . and a book of collector's edition Elvis stamps slides out into my palm.

Mayday, mayday. Stride broken.

Oh my God. They're so beautiful. Crisp, scalloped edges. Bright, vivid pinks and oranges. The King is crooning into an old-fashioned microphone with a stray, black hair dangling over his forehead. My fingers are already itching to add them to my book.

Greer is the only one who knew I even wanted these stamps, which means . . . he left them here for me. An apology? Or did he buy them out of guilt?

My muscles seize up and I can't move, which is much the same condition I was left in Saturday night. Oh, I played off my humiliation when Ever and Katie came to check on me after Greer left. Putting on a smile and joining the crew for a slice of pizza made me wonder if I should look into working undercover, because I put on quite a performance. I think I fooled everyone but Jack into believing I was fine. Thank God no one asked me directly what happened or I might have cracked.

What *did* happen? Nothing like a man barreling into a girl's apartment, wiping off her makeup, spanking her, giving her a monumental orgasm, then leaving. Nothing confusing about that at all, right?

I made the decision to follow through with the probation, though, and nothing is going to stop me from fulfilling my end of the deal. If I want to make my family proud, setting an example for my cousins and their children that come after? That example is going to be authentic. Unfortunately, Greer hasn't been answering his phone, so I've been leaving messages like a clingy one-time hookup who won't take a hint.

Yesterday's was the most ridiculous so far. *Do you have book club merch? Asking for a friend. If not, she was thinking you should look into bookmarks. That way you don't have to remember the page number. That is what you've been doing, isn't it? Okay, bye.*

Funny enough, leaving messages has made me feel a lot better. Him walking out on me when I was vulnerable might have hurt—more than I will ever admit—but making light of the whole situation helped me take back power. Suggesting Greer stay and eat pizza was stupid. Seriously stupid. For a minute there, I even thought I wanted him to accept the offer. To what? Be my kind of boyfriend? No wonder he legged it. What happened in my bedroom was a hookup that got cut unfortunately short and won't be happening again.

Only . . . now I have stamps. What do they mean?

A whistle blows out in the gym, rousing me from my stupor. I'm alone in the locker room? My glaze flies to the clock and I'm late. Shit. How long have I been sitting here? Time seems to slow down as I change into my academy T-shirt and a pair of black yoga pants, hopping on one foot while tying my sneakers. I almost wipe out minutes later as I skid around the corner into the brightly lit gym, finding everyone already lined up for inspection.

Every head turns in my direction, including Greer's, and I want to stab him with his pencil when he makes a notation on the clipboard. I take the walk of shame to the end of a line, ignoring questioning looks from Jack and Charlie. They're probably wondering how I left the apartment before them and somehow showed up late.

Well, you see, fellas, I was mooning over some stamps.

Every time Greer does inspection, walking down the line of recruits to mark us present and presentable, I have to think about something gross to keep my nipples from getting hard. Usually I think of eating snails or birds regurgitating food to their young, and it does the trick. But today, the closer he gets to me, the harder I find it to concentrate on keeping my body neutral. My backside hasn't been tender since around Monday, but the skin he slapped wakes up and tingles now, like it wants more. Those tingles travel on little lightning clouds up and around to my breasts—and I'm in major trouble now. He's only about two people away, and my buds are beginning to strain underneath my T-shirt. There isn't a sports bra on the planet with enough thickness to keep them hidden . . . and I witness the moment Greer sees them.

Hard for him.

He drops his head forward, that pencil scratching across his clipboard, but I see him. He's watching me though eyelashes I never noticed before. How does he make them look so masculine? Every part of him is. That ripped chest and those stupid, incredible thighs. Was this man really in my bed?

"Break up into three groups." Greer's voice booms, confident and full, but I notice the dark rings around his eyes. Darker than usual. "A through J, you're downstairs in the firing range. Garrett, you're leading the session. Think you can handle it?" My blastoff to Planet Horny is aborted, pride plowing into my stomach. I look over in time to find Jack's mouth curl into a hesitant smile before leading his group toward the stairwell. "K through S, you're with me for drills. Everyone else, head to the track. Go."

A blow of his whistle sends everyone running, faster than we move for any other instructor. I don't have far to go since I'm staying with Greer for drills, which, let's face it, is going to be awkward. It was uncomfortable *before* he woke up this new desire inside me to be manhandled, because I've wanted a ride on the Thigh Express since day one. Saturday night was a game changer, however . . . and I should be feeling more exposed here. Why don't I?

It's the stamps. The fact that he listened and realized they were important to me. It's the fact that he just built Jack up in front of the whole room of recruits. And while I know my best friend deserves that recognition for his recent hard work, Greer is also trying to make up for what I overheard in that meeting. So *he's* the one who's exposed. Because that hard-ass lieutenant image is chipping away with each little gesture he can't seem to help making.

Damn. This is a real inconvenient time for my resentment toward him to take a nosedive. He walked out on me and hasn't answered a phone call since. I can recognize his efforts to be a better guy as much as I want. It doesn't change the fact that he's not interested in anything serious. Saturday was nothing more than temporary insanity.

My resolve to continue on like I'm completely

unaffected by what happened Saturday night re-affirms itself. The alternative is to let Greer think he has the power to upset me, and I don't want that. If I face him now, pretending I'm made of Teflon where he's concerned will get easier each time, until it's finally true.

Instead of joining the rest of my group at the mats, I stay where I am and wait for Greer to draw even with me. "Can I help you with something, Silva?"

Hearing him use my last name crams my belly with disappointment, but I ignore the feeling. What did I expect? Him to call me *baby* again? "Buying me stamps really takes the sting out of your dickhead act."

"It's not an act." Hard blue eyes flick to mine. "I think we established that on Saturday."

"Maybe." My voice is threadbare, because I didn't expect him to bring it up. The fact that he did throws me off. "We definitely established you're a giver, not a taker."

Wow. God, that was bold, even for me. What am I doing? My goal was to act like Saturday was no big deal, sure, but I didn't plan on invit-ing a conversation about it. Or making it sound as though I'm hoping for more. Without taking his focus off the clipboard, he speaks to me in a sharp tone. "That mouth is going to land you in trouble again."

His warning makes me think of slapping sounds, followed by groans of satisfaction. Wetness lands between my thighs, and I pull my T-shirt down on reflex. He notices, a muscle beginning to tic in his jaw. I want to push him further, to ask what kind of trouble he means. But we've been speaking privately long enough to draw attention to ourselves, so I go a different direction. "I've been staying out of trouble. You have the voice mails to prove it."

It might be my imagination, but warmth seems to wink in his eyes before they go cold again. "That I do. You're taking the commitment seriously."

"Guess that makes one of us."

That got his undivided attention. The suggestion that he's not doing his job correctly brings one eyebrow shooting up the surface of his forehead. "Excuse me?"

Courage, young one. "You said ride alongs were part of my probation." I shrug. "Maybe you didn't mean it."

His unwavering stare might send a smarter person sprinting for cover, but I force myself to remain unblinking in the line of fire. "Be outside the Ninth at six tonight."

Shoot. "Can we make it six-thirty? I have to run to the West Side to bring a prescription to my dad after we're dismissed."

"Send me the address." His chin is set. "I'll pick you up there."

"At my parents' place?"

Has a sigh ever been more withering? "I'm not coming for Sunday dinner. I'll wait for you outside."

What would that be like? Walking out of my parents' building and having Greer waiting for me at the curb. I guess I'm going to find out. "Done."

"Don't be late," he grunts.

"You either, Grim Reaper," I let sail over my shoulder on the way to join the group.

It's a challenge not to turn a cartwheel on my way to the mat. Although, I have no idea if I've won a victory with the lieutenant . . . or set myself up for more disappointment.

CHAPTER 14

Greer

G ridlock on 23rd Street made me late. And fuck, she's going to make it sting.

When I pull my police vehicle into the fire hydrant space outside the building, I expect Danika to be waiting at the curb with a smirk on her face, but she's not. This is going to be my penance, huh? Going upstairs and picking her up like this is some kind of date?

Fine. I throw the car into Park and hesitate a second before reaching for the glove compartment and removing a tin of Altoids. I'm only popping a breath mint because I had tuna fish for lunch. No other reason. If I check out my mug in the rearview and grimace over three days' worth of five o'clock shadow, it doesn't mean anything. So why am I still sitting here?

There's absolutely no way a fishing hook should be tugging on my gut right now. Since when do I care about making a good impression on a girl's parents? I bought the Elvis stamps so I wouldn't have to rely on words to make up for being an asshole to Danika. And I accomplished the mission—end of story. The sparkle was back in her eye when she spoke to me in the gym this afternoon. But nothing is going to come from what happened in her bedroom Saturday evening. Nothing except a lot of inappropriate fantasizing about it happening again, day and fucking night. Enough that my dick is rubbed raw and I've had to change my bed sheets twice.

Throwing myself into work Sunday through Tuesday helped occupy my mind, but seeing her today at the academy brought it all back with interest. The taste of her mouth, her pussy, her voice in the dark. The half-fascinated, half-ferocious way she frowned at me when I cleaned off her makeup. That stubborn tilt of her chin, teamed up with vulnerable eyes. Her invitation to stay, followed by her quiet embarrassment when I turned her down.

The fishing hook in my gut pulls hard.

Enough. My brother might be young, but he

made a lot of sense. *If you can't offer her anything, leave her alone.* That's what I have to do.

My eyes are drawn to the small photo taped to the right of my two-way radio. Griffin used to hate that picture. Which is obviously why I taped it up in the first place—to torture him. That was how my partner and I rolled. In the snapshot, he's posed in his uniform with a mean expression. Since I'm the one who took the picture, I know Griffin laughed immediately afterward. He wasn't a serious person, except when it came to the badge. That was the only thing he and I had in common. We just took it seriously in different ways. I did everything by the book, while Griffin rode his impulses like a wild horse. He didn't want to be a quiet hero, he'd wanted to be a loud one.

When we went through the academy together, everyone called him "Cowboy," and the nickname had stuck. He'd been paired with me, his exact opposite, in an attempt to rein him in. After a rocky feeling-out period, though, we'd become best friends. We remained that way right up until his pressing need to be the big hero had gotten him killed.

My attention swings from Griffin's photograph to the building where I'll be meeting Danika. And for the first time, something occurs to me. Danika has a little cowboy inside her, too. Or cowgirl, as the case may be. The way she flouts the rules by breezing into the men's locker room, her cockiness, her fierce need for independence, that stunt she'd pulled at the yogurt shop by not calling the police. Cowgirl. Getting involved with someone who's twice as likely to find trouble or tragedy would be mental suicide. Even if this job wasn't my life, I'm not leaving myself open again to being the last one standing.

What am I thinking even doing this ride along? Every second I spend close to her, the harder it is to stay away.

If you can't offer her anything, leave her alone.

And I don't have anything. Right? Besides sex, my protection, the respectability of my career and a few candy bars, what would I offer? The occasional booklet of stamps? She deserves more than that. No, I can't be anything more than her instructor. Her friend's brother.

Before I climb out of the car, my gaze strays back to Griffin. When I met him, I didn't know how to have a friend. I didn't want a friend. My youth was all about preparing for the job, and I'd already seen firsthand how easily someone who claimed to love you could leave you in the dust. What it was like to eat breakfast with a parent—the person who should be the most committed to you in the world—and find their closet empty that same afternoon. If a mother wouldn't stick around for me, what hope did I have making friends? Someone who had other options? But Griffin had been relentless, hammering away at my shell bit by bit.

I will not allow myself to forget the days, months, years following Griffin's death. How much I regret letting my guard down around him, only to be left with no exterior and a shit-load of guilt and pain. That's why I leave the photo taped up. It'll be a good reminder while Danika—a cowgirl in the making if I ever met one—is in the car with me. Maybe I should include a picture of my mother beside it for good measure.

I'm the fucking picture of resolute walking into the building. One ride along. A couple of hours, then I'm dropping her off and going about my night. No mooning over the light brown shade of her eyes or complimenting her on the impressive effort she put into drills today. Nothing that might give her the impression that I'm interested in a repeat of Saturday.

My chafed dick mocks me from inside my briefs.

Someone has left the building door propped open with a phone book, but I kick it back into the foyer, making a mental note to speak with Danika about the safety of her parents' building. I check the buzzers for the name Silva and head to the second floor. Outside the apartment door, I pause, my hand poised to knock.

Danika is laughing on the other side, these great big, gulping laughs.

I've never heard her let loose with that kind of sound before. It hits my chest like a brick. She's usually smirking or concentrating. Never this happy. What's making her that way? There are other people in the apartment . . . men yelling at a televised game, it sounds like. The smell of meat sails through the door and reminds me I haven't eaten dinner. It's a home inside that apartment, and I suddenly feel like a mannequin compared to the life happening over the threshold.

I'm turning to leave when the door opens.

"You crazy people are making me late for my meeting with the—"

Danika cuts herself off when she sees me standing in the hallway.

"Devil?" I supply. "Grim Reaper."

To her credit, she recovers fast. "I was going to say lieutenant."

"You're a bad liar."

She raises an eyebrow. "Thank you."

Already, the resolve I walked into the building with is losing steam. She's still dressed in those tight pants she had on at the academy, but she's wearing a fresh white T-shirt that lets me see the outline of her bra. It's not a sports one, either. It pushes her tits up into a V, which might as well be a fucking arrow pointing right at her rack.

An older woman's voice comes through the doorway. "Danika, who's there?"

We must have been quietly staring for a while, because we both seem to shake ourselves. "Uh, it's Lieutenant Burns, Ma."

"The devil?"

Danika winces, making a laugh build in my belly. But I don't let it out. "Are you ready to go? I've been waiting outside since six-thirty. You're late."

"Now who's the bad liar? I can see the curb from the kitchen window."

Shit. If that slip isn't proof this girl throws me off my game, nothing is. "Then why didn't you come down when I pulled up?"

"I was fixing the leaky faucet, then my mother made me eat—"

"Made you eat?" A woman comes up behind Danika and pokes her in the rib with a manicured finger. "You had two helpings."

While Danika groans and shrugs on a light denim jacket, I greet the woman with a nod. "Mrs. Silva. Is the door of your building always propped open with a phone book?"

"Yes."

"Why?"

She smiles up at me. "Because I put it there, so I don't have to dig for my keys."

"That's why your bike got stolen," calls a man from the living room.

"Just watch your damn game," she shouts back before grabbing me by the elbow. "Come inside and have something to eat. We have plenty."

"That won't be necessary—"

"Don't fight it," Danika says, taking her jacket back off. "It's hopeless, even for you."

I've been inside plenty of New York City apartments. Being that we're in a pre-war in Hell's Kitchen, I think I know what to expect. Worn, wooden floors. Basic white Sheetrock and maybe one or two exposed brick walls. Lots of belongings crammed into limited space, which is the hallmark of the city. But it's . . . amazing. Every wall seems to be a different color and theme. Family pictures cover one wall, while a bookshelf takes up another. The furniture is dark-colored and plush, but the kitchen is the reverse. It's bright, open. Dried flowers hang down from strings, held there by clothespins. Some sort of raspberry smell drifts in the air, like maybe there's a cheesecake in the oven.

"Nice, right?" Danika catches my attention beside me. "Makes you wonder why I choose to live with two smelly boys."

"Danika is the one who makes it nice," calls her mother from the kitchen. "Always coming to fix things or paint. Bringing me stuff she finds at stoop sales."

"There's a lot of stoops on my weekend walks crosstown." She seems self-conscious, shoulders up around her ears. "Makes it easy."

"Hear that?" She winks at her daughter. "So humble, my Danika."

I can't help but choke a little at that. "Are we talking about the same girl?"

"How would you describe her?"

That question comes from a man who has just joined us from the living room. I know with one glance he's Danika's father. They have the same stubborn chin. A handshake is in order here—I think—but he doesn't seem inclined. And it doesn't surprise me one bit that it only took me thirty seconds to fuck up this introduction with her parents. When they see me again at graduation, Danika's mother will lean in and whisper to her husband, *That's the asshole that came to our apartment once. Remember?*

My stomach lines itself with lead thinking about it.

"Yes," the mother chimes in with a sniff, the skillet in her hand suddenly taking on the dimensions of a weapon. "How would you describe our girl?"

Danika might have looked self-conscious before, but she now appears to be enjoying herself quite a bit. She takes her time sitting down and crossing her legs. "Be careful how you answer, Grim Reaper." Her voice drops to a dramatic whisper that makes me think things I shouldn't be thinking in front of her mommy and daddy. "The best fried chicken of your life hangs in the balance."

If I'm being honest, I want that goddamn fried chicken. Charlie brought me leftovers a week ago; some concoction from Ever. But apart from that, I haven't eaten a home-cooked meal in years. Unless you count the slop I throw together in fifteen seconds and label dinner. Even more than the chicken, though, I want to be better than some asshole that spent a few uncomfortable minutes in their apartment. When they see me at graduation presenting their daughter with her diploma, I want them to know she isn't just a face in the sea of uniforms.

"She stands out." The compliment emerges rusty, so I clear my throat. Danika's head comes up, too, her brown eyes flashing up at me from beneath dark lashes. "When I implied she wasn't humble, I didn't mean it as a bad thing. Someday when she makes detective, she'll be one people want assigned to their case, because she'll annoy everyone until it gets solved. If she can learn to be cautious and trust her fellow officers, she'll be important to the department." Silence. "She's important."

No one says anything. Are they waiting for me to say more? That's the most I've spoken without a break outside of a lecture in a long damn while. That's all they're going to get. I'm seconds from excusing myself and going back down to wait in the car, but Danika's parents converge on her so fast, I'm forced to step back. They throw their arms around her in a hug, one that is brief, but fierce. Danika is frowning at me over her father's shoulder, but there's a smile playing around her lips. It starts my pulse thrumming heavy in my ears.

Her mother steps back, swiping at her eyes. "He gets dessert, too."

CHAPTER 15
— Danika —

Dude. This is intense.

I'm in the passenger side of Greer's un-marked car. He's a lieutenant, so he doesn't use one of the standard NYPD Ford Fusion Hybrids, although most people would recognize the killer black sedan with tinted windows as a law enforcement ride. I feel like we're phantoms, bobbing and weaving in and out of traffic, by-passing gridlock in the bus lanes, flying down the avenues surrounded by the rumbling purr of the engine.

His air-conditioning is set to a reasonable level. No music is playing. When he started the car, he even adjusted his mirrors for optimum visibility. He drives with two hands, because of course he does. Ten and two. That's the rule and he's a by-the-book man.

Never mind that he turned to an unfamiliar page in my parents' apartment. Lieutenant Greer Burns thinks I'm important. He wouldn't say it unless it was true. Unless he really believes it. And there must have been a little part of me that hadn't believed in myself before he'd said those words, because my first reaction was relief.

Some days, walking into my parents' apartment in a navy blue uniform feels like nothing more than a dream. As if I'm a little girl who wants to be an astronaut. Everyone tells her she can do anything if she simply tries hard, but they don't really believe she'll make it to space. Right now, I think I could strap into a rocket and make it to the moon.

Am I a tiny bit resentful that it takes so little from this man to reaffirm my commitment to being a good cop? My confidence in myself should be enough, right? However, I'm starting to think this probation is actually teaching me a lesson. Two people being confident in me is better than one. Being accountable to someone other than myself is a good thing, because I can't save the world alone, like I tried to do at the yogurt shop. Argh. I landed myself in Central Booking for ignoring what I've been taught. So I'm not going to do that again. If some positive reinforcement can have such a profound effect on me, there's my proof that I can't become a good police officer on my own. I need other people. I need to trust.

Needing and doing are two different things, but admitting I'm not strongest alone is the first step, isn't it?

"So . . ." I trail off, but Greer grunts for me to continue, never taking his focus off the road. "Most lieutenants act as the coordinator at a crime scene or direct arrest processing, but they spend a lot of their day at the precinct doing paperwork, right? Like more of a delegator. You don't like doing that?"

"No." I swear he's going to leave it at that, but he keeps going once we're stopped at a red light. "I have no choice but to delegate and complete a lot of forms, but I have to get out. Seeing the city. If I'm not familiar with what's happening and changing on the ground, I can't do my job from inside four walls."

I cast a glance outside my window at the familiar sidewalks, bodegas, diners and nail salons of the East Side. It looks exactly the same as it always appears to me. "What are you seeing now?"

"For one," he says, tipping his head forward and to the right. "That van has out-of-state plates, and it has been there since the last time I drove past, this morning. No tickets. So someone has been feeding the meter every two hours all day.

On a weekday. That's unusual. In Manhattan, a van usually means deliveries or somebody is moving. Neither of which would take this long."

While he picks up his radio and calls in the plate number, I try not to watch him and marvel. That was some impressive observation though. A lot of recruits bitch about the lieutenant, claiming he probably made it to such a high rank so quickly because his father is a legendary bureau chief. I never believed that, mostly because Charlie tells us stories about Greer's brilliance and dedication. Seeing it firsthand makes me glad I never bought into that nonsense. He might be an unholy jerk on occasion, but he's great at his job. Isn't that what matters?

When he hangs up the radio, my eyes are drawn to the picture taped up beside it. I don't recognize the person in the photo. "Who is that?"

He's quiet a moment. "Griffin Bates. My ex-partner."

Way to step in it. It's common knowledge that Greer's partner died a few years ago, although I don't know the details. I should probably back away from the subject slowly with my hands up, but . . . some intuition stops me. If he still has the picture taped up, maybe he wants to talk about Griffin. Maybe he doesn't want to avoid talking about him. "I can't imagine you with a partner," I say, wading in slowly. "What was that like?"

His right hand slips to three o'clock, then shoots back to two. "We hated each other when they assigned us. He knew the department wanted me to babysit him. I just wanted him to stop talking."

"What did he talk about?"

"His girlfriend. Video games. The Yankees." He's shaking his head. "Whatever new Apple product was being released. Cattle."

"Cattle?"

"If he ever won the lottery, he was going to buy a ranch."

"Huh." I should stop there, but I'm too busy imagining him in a *Starsky and Hutch*–type situation, him and his polar opposite partner hunting down bad guys while wearing cool shades and uttering catch phrases. "Did you talk back?"

"Not at first." He shifts a little and looks over at me. "I had to drive out to his place in Queens to get paperwork signed one weekend, and he was having a barbeque. I was only going to stay five minutes, but . . ."

"But you saw him in a different environment, and you realized he wasn't just the annoying guy who takes up space in your car?"

"Yeah. Something like that." His voice is rough. "His girlfriend pretty much chained me to a seat and kept feeding me."

I laugh and the car jolts, as if he hit the brake by accident. "You have a habit of showing up and getting fed, don't you?" Is it my imagination or does the right corner of his mouth lift? "Anyway, after what you said, you probably have a standing invitation from my mother."

"She could achieve world peace with that fried chicken."

This time, when I laugh, he doesn't almost crash the car. But slowly, he grows more and more tense, his easy demeanor being replaced by the hard one I associate with him. When I replay the conversation in my head, flames lick up the sides of my face. "Relax, Lieutenant. I didn't mean anything by saying my mother would feed you. I'm not actually expecting . . . or hoping . . . for you to show up or anything."

This is now the second time I've accidentally hinted at wanting to spend more time with him. Pizza with the roommates and now my mother's house. What is wrong with me? Is it something I want without realizing it? He's clearly opposed to any association with me that isn't directly related to work and my future career. Unless you count the time he went down on me. Jesus, men are confusing. *This* man is confusing.

I feel Greer looking over at me, but I pretend I don't. "Danika—"

"So how did you manage to snag those stamps?" A muscle in his cheek jumps over the interruption, but I press on, really not wanting another rejection. "You have to be there first thing in the morning, or they sell out. Did you pull some strings?"

He shifts in his seat. "You could say that."

"Ooh. Cryptic." No response. "Well, come on. Don't leave me in suspense. I want some pointers for next time."

"Wear rubber gloves and invest in nose plugs."

"What?"

The radio crackles. "Five fifty-one Second Avenue. Ten-thirty in progress. Suspect is armed . . ."

There's a robbery taking place very close to where we are. Right now. I barely have a chance to process that before Greer whips a U-turn at breakneck pace, squealing the tires. And then we're going seventy miles an hour down the avenue—facing the wrong direction. I watch in awe as Greer very calmly presses the button to turn on his siren and flashing lights. Seriously, his expression doesn't even change, except a slight hardening on his jaw. My jaw? It's on my lap.

"You're not to get out of the car, Silva." We're back to my last name, which is his way of telling me he means business. "Repeat the order."

"You're not to get out of the car, Silva."

Greer looks over at me and . . . okay, he definitely smiled this time. He's smiling right at me, while driving to a robbery. Leave it to my vagina to clench at this totally inappropriate moment, right? There isn't a woman alive that could blame me, though, because he's such a badass, threading traffic needles while responding to the dispatcher in an even, confident voice. He's not my instructor right now, he's this heroic being that can sometimes be the devil and other times, a seemingly tortured man who makes me cancel dates.

We screech to a halt outside what looks to be a Subway shop. "Ten-eighty-four," Greer speaks into the radio, letting the dispatcher know we've arrived at the scene. An NYPD vehicle shows up at the same time, blocking traffic from entering the scene. One officer climbs out and starts to direct civilians out of the area, barking commands and herding them toward the side streets. Some attempt to take cell phone pictures, but most of them run like hell. Greer once again picks up the radio, hits a few buttons and his voice comes over the loudspeaker.

"This is the police. Walk out with your hands in the air."

I hold my breath, watching the entrance to the store. Several vehicles arrive at once, lights flashing, officers jumping out with weapons drawn and crouching down behind their cars. It's so swift, efficient. Incredible. But I'm too focused on the door of the Subway to pay much attention to the process. Come out. Come out.

A man's voice comes over the radio. "I can see one female civilian inside the store. Green shirt. Probably an employee. She appears to be arguing with the subject."

Greer snatches up the two-way. "Get our negotiator on the line. Have him call the location."

"Two calls have been made." The dispatcher again. "Suspect isn't answering."

"Try again—"

The door to the Subway swings open. A man wearing an oversized green jacket fills the doorway with hands raised. No weapon in sight. He looks distraught, rocking back and forth on the balls of his feet. "Approaching suspect," Greer says before hanging up the radio. I don't have a second to react before the lieutenant is drawing his weapon and slowly easing out from behind the open door of the car, keeping his gun leveled on the suspect. "Put your weapon on the ground."

The man doesn't respond. Or maybe he does, but it seems more like he's talking to himself than Greer. His face crumples and kicks the glass door behind him. My heart is rapping against my eardrums, and I can't breathe. Can't swallow. A few minutes ago, we were talking about a barbeque, and now he's walking toward a man who could be armed. Jesus. Watching Greer reassures me, though. His capable form moves slowly, not a single hitch in his step.

"Put your weapon on the ground," Greer shouts once more, this time with bite. Again the man doesn't respond or even acknowledge the lieutenant. Instead, his hands drop down and flatten on the top of his head, his shoulders shaking like he's crying.

"I'm on the other line with the employee now. Suspect is her ex-boyfriend." There's a long pause. "Suspect is still armed—"

Then everyone moves, the series of events blurring together into a couple of terrible slow-motion seconds. The crying man's hands drop to his big pockets, he removes a gun and fires. A second shot is fired closer to me. The suspect's mouth opens in a pained O, he lands on his knees and rolls sideways, clutching his thigh.

When Greer stumbles and falls, I'm positive my eyes are playing tricks on me. He's the lieutenant. Immovable. Capable of making a recruit pee themselves with a well-placed glare. He doesn't get up, though.

He doesn't get up.

And when medical personnel run in his direction, denial goes screaming through my head, drowning out every other sound.

CHAPTER 16

Greer

'␣ve been shot.

Technically.

My Kevlar vest stopped the bullet from penetrating my chest, but I'm on the ground, and I have no idea how I got here. Sure, the impact and shock of being hit by a bullet could have sent me to the asphalt. I should stand up, though. I should stand. The spot underneath where the bullet hit is stinging like a motherfucker, but I've felt much worse pain. In comparison, this is nothing. But I don't get up.

Christ. I knew the suspect had a gun on him. How did he get the drop on me?

I'm tired. I'm so fucking tired lying here, I can't find the right answer. Maybe I don't even have the ability to do that anymore. Have I been sliding into this state of burnout so long, I didn't see I was already there? This situation was so similar to the one where Griffin was shot and killed, maybe my head wasn't in the right place? That day is always there, lurking in the back of my mind, ready to jump out and bite me. Why did I let it happen this time?

Shit. Shit. This is unacceptable.

A paramedic squats down beside me and begins asking me questions. That's when I look up to find Danika standing a few yards away, stunned horror reflected in her eyes. Right where I stood while the paramedics tried to save Griffin. Jesus. I almost laugh because it's like the universe is just trying to prove I've been right all along to stay away from her. To stay away from everyone. I could easily be lying here dead, setting Danika up for the same pain I live with. Or worse. So much worse. She could be lying in my spot, and I could be in her shoes, watching her leave me. That thought rips through me and damages everything in its path.

Shoving off the hands prodding at my chest, I finally stand and direct my anger at the recruit who's wisely already backing toward my vehicle. "I told you to stay in the goddamn car."

My roar sends her tripping over a crack in the asphalt, but she manages to remain on her feet.

The horror hasn't left her eyes yet, though, and it's driving me crazy. Making me want to shake her. Because she seems to care? Because I want her to? I don't have a clue.

As soon as she's back inside the car, I force myself to focus long enough to answer a few questions and assure the paramedics that I don't need medical attention. I oversee the suspect being loaded into an ambulance that will take him to NYU around the corner with a wound in his right leg. My officers are a little shaken up over watching me catch a bullet, so I spare a few minutes to give orders for securing the scene. To remind them I'm invincible and I do my job, no matter the circumstance. Even though I'm feeling the furthest thing from invincible right now. I feel the opposite and I resent it. Hate it.

When I get back into the car, Danika stares straight ahead and doesn't say a word. "I'm sorry I shouted at you."

My own apology catches me off guard. I don't know why I issue it, I only know that shit feels shaky enough and I don't need her pissed off at me on top of everything. "If you want to apologize," she says, her voice husky, "apologize for lying on the ground longer than you needed to. I could kill you myself. Why didn't you just get up?"

It feels like I'm moving underwater as I start the car and back into the street enough to be clear of the scene. My nerves are clicking. I can hear them in my ears. Every muscle strains from head to toe. "I don't know what you're talking about."

"Yes, you do."

Her voice cracks and I think that's why I crack, too, honesty blasting out of me like water from a hole in a dam. "Jesus, maybe part of me was relieved I finally made a mistake. My whole life revolves around never making them. It finally happened and I . . . survived." I press a knuckle to my pounding right eye. "My fucking head was somewhere else. On Griffin. On you. And I hesitated because I'm just tired of seeing nothing but blood. He reached for his pocket, I saw black metal, and I'm trained to shoot to kill in that situation. And I didn't. I didn't want to kill him."

"You didn't," she whispers, her curious stare burning me alive. "But why did your first mistake have to be when a gun was pointed at you? It couldn't have been a freaking typo on an email or something?"

My half laugh, half scoff makes her eyes narrow. "This is coming from the girl who walked right into a robbery and didn't even think to call the police." My hand moves on its own, reaching out to capture her chin, lifting it. "You see now? You see how fast things can happen?"

"Yes." Time seems to wind down as we look

at one another. "I'm sorry I brought up Griffin. If that's why you made a mistake . . . I'm sorry."

"It never goes away. What happened to him is always there in the back of my head."

Her head tilts a little until my fingers leave her chin to cradle it, cradle her head in the palm of my hand. "When you're working or all the time?"

"All the time. All of it. I'm . . ." It's a good thing we're at a stoplight, because my eyelids grow heavier the longer she looks at me, the longer she compels me to talk, until they finally drop. "I can't close my eyes without seeing something ugly anymore, Danika. Griffin, the cases that come across my desk. I just didn't want to be responsible for it today."

"I understand."

Her voice is like ice on a burn. I sense the light has changed as the sound of traffic begins to flow around us, but no one honks at us for blocking one of the three lanes. They can either see I'm law enforcement, or they're just so used to people double-parking, they're resigned. For that reason and a hundred others all involving Danika, I keep my foot off the gas pedal. After the decision I made to keep our relationship strictly instructor-student, I shouldn't be cradling her head or confiding these secrets to her. Secrets I never imagined telling anyone. But it's like she already knows what I'm going to say before I manage to get it out. And she doesn't judge me for any of it. She understands me because she hates making mistakes, too. Maybe. I don't know, but I can't move for the fucking life of me.

Especially not when she reaches toward my chest and undoes the buttons of my shirt, all the way down to my belt. She pushes open the material, and I start breathing through my nose like a racehorse after the Derby. "Danika, I shouldn't have gone to your apartment last week. What we did was not only a violation of academy rules, but—"

The sound of Velcro being pried apart tells me she's removing my vest. I forgot I was even still wearing it. "But what?"

I grab her wrist to keep her from pulling off the vest. If she makes direct contact with my skin, I'll never be able to stop whatever is happening here. "I can't be with anyone, do you understand? Especially not a cop."

Comprehension tightens the corners of her mouth. "Because you could lose . . . that someone? The way you lost Griffin?"

"Yes." The very tip of her index finger grazes my bare neck and I jerk in the seat, moaning with a closed mouth. "I don't want to leave anyone, either. I could have caught that bullet in the throat or head, just as easily. I know what it's like to be left behind."

I must have loosened my grip on her wrist, because she slides the vest off and sucks in a breath. "Sounds like a good reason to celebrate being alive, doesn't it?" Her finger prods the spot where the bullet hit. I don't have to look down to know it's red and angry. Hell, I don't want to look away from the soft, brown comfort of her eyes or the swollen berry color of her lips. "This doesn't have to be a relationship, Lieutenant."

Danika

I hear the words coming out of my mouth. They could very well prove destructive, but I want this man, and I'm willing to be reckless for the chance. After the denial of seeing him on the ground passed, I was overcome with certainty. Certainty that might have come too late. He's supposed to be in my life, in some way, for much, much longer, I'd thought. It didn't seem fair or possible that I should be bombarded with that conviction at the exact moment he was taken away, but there it was. Maybe he's only meant to be a fellow cop or my friend's older brother. A mentor.

But I know he's supposed to be here.

Do I want him? Yes. I've been annoyingly attracted to him since day one, even when he's being a jerk. These things he's telling me, though? These insights into the man and these struggles he's been facing alone? They're making me ache to soothe him. I want that job. I want to be his break from the reality he's not handling very well right now. If someone else tried to take the responsibility from me, even in a casual capacity, I would throw down with them over it. So I know I have one option here if I want Greer to keep confiding in me. If I want him to touch me and let himself be touched. I have to be more than a friend, but less than a girlfriend. And for God's sake, I have to keep my heart out of it, because I won't be able to pry his away from him.

"What are you talking about?"

Greer bites off the question while staring at my mouth. I'm not sure how I missed the lieutenant's sexual interest in me, or at least the magnitude of it, but he might as well be wrestling with an alligator right now. If that alligator was his lust. "I'm saying . . ." I drop the vest in the backseat and let my mouth hover closer, closer to his. "Forget the academy rules for tonight. Go back to being the Grim Reaper tomorrow."

"One night," he rasps. "You think that's all this would be?"

"I don't know." I brush his mouth with mine. "How many nights do you need to get me out of your system?"

Something about my question upsets him. His eyebrows draw together, his grip tightening anew on my wrist. "Get back in your goddamn seat."

"No." Whew. I must be out of my mind. Anyone with working brain cells can see he's about to get tough with me. Reject me. Hurt my feelings out of necessity. But something tells me I'll never get another chance to see under his exterior if I don't rip it down right now. So before he can open his mouth and deliver whatever lie he's thinking, I kiss him.

And we go up in flames.

One of his hands winds up my hair, twisting, pulling my head back as he attacks from above. Growling must be his form of a password, because when he does it, my lips part automatically, letting his tongue inside where it works, works, works mine over in the rhythm of a swimmer's stroke. Only it gets faster and more about quantity, both of us trying to get the upper hand, and for the first time, I don't mind that I'm losing. And this is nothing like the first time he kissed me in my bedroom, because I'm not confused about the impulses he's woken up inside me. I'm embracing them. I'm not angry at him, either, unless you count the thirty hellish seconds he spent on the ground, staring up at the sky.

I can feel those thirty seconds in this kiss. The impact of the bullet, the way he shouted at me afterward, his apology and subsequent honesty. The ugliness he spoke about. He's telling me all about it with his mouth, so I let him communicate everything to me with hungry sweeps of his tongue, the occasional drag of his teeth down my lower lip, the hands in my hair pulling me closer, closer, until our foreheads grind together.

"Get back in your seat," he bites out when we finally pull apart.

My heart drops into my stomach and I jerk away, throwing myself across the car back into the passenger side. Staring down the avenue, I hesitate for a few seconds, too stunned by his rejection to move. My face is fevered, and my hands are still shaking from the force of his kiss, but I grab the door handle, intent on getting out of the car and away. But Greer hits the lock. "What are you doing?"

"Seat belt," he grits out, punching the gas.

We join the traffic on Second Avenue for several tense blocks before he hangs a left on Twentieth Street. My mouth drops open when he sails through a yellow light and turns into a closed parking lot beneath the FDR Drive. There is a loud rumble of traffic above, and in the distance, people run and bike along the East River, but we're the only car in the lot. He either brought me here to murder me or continue the kiss he'd cut short. And when the lieutenant shuts off the ignition, turning glittering eyes and a tensed jaw on me, I'm pretty sure it's the latter.

The steering wheel groans beneath his hands. "Tell me to drive you home."

"No." My heartbeat drowns out the traffic above our heads. He needs me. How have I not realized how lonely he is? Have I been just as lonely? Doing for everyone else, making people happy, then neglecting myself? Not tonight. "Forget the rules."

"I don't get like this with women. It's only you that makes me fucking crazy." A muscle leaps in his cheek. "I think. I reason. Look at me now, though. Back where I was that night at your apartment when the only way I could control myself was by taking control of you."

Oh my God. My windpipe is down to the size of a cocktail straw. I make him crazy? No, I make him *fucking crazy*. Does that worry me? It should. When the man I've been infatuated with says things like that, right on the heels of warning me he needs to stay casual? That's bad news. For me. Even worse news is I want him now more than ever. Because he's being honest, because he has valid reasons for not wanting anything serious. Because I need him back.

"You know that's what I want," I manage. "Tell me what you want me to do."

It's amazing, this shudder that goes through him and leaves authority in its wake. A change comes over me, too, and I'm not going to lie, it's still kind of a mind fuck because I'm the least submissive person I know. Or so I thought. When Greer is touching me, though, I need something else from him. All my energy goes into *doing* for the people in my life. Being right. Being the best and never failing. I want him to take away all my responsibilities and narrow my focus down to him. Just him.

So here I am, holding my breath and waiting for Greer to instruct me. Sort of like we're back at the academy, except I'm the only recruit and the rules don't exist. When his index finger taps the steering wheel once, twice, it might as well be the space shuttle blasting off. "Get in the backseat."

Air evacuates my lungs. I push open the door, climb out and take two steps on shaking legs. Greer exits the car at the same time and we lock eyes over the roof before we both slide into the backseat of his department vehicle, the night swallowing us as I straddle his powerful hips and our mouths come together.

CHAPTER 17
Greer

I must be out of my ever-loving mind.

So many rules are being broken right now, I would need two hands to count. Unfortunately, those hands are occupied right now, sliding down Danika's back to settle on her tight ass. I've been locked in a cage for so long, refusing to falter, commanding myself to meet everyone's expectations—and my own—that it's no longer satisfying. And Jesus, trying to be perfect has never been as satisfying as this.

I'm kissing the hell out of Danika.

Maybe letting a suspect fire on me and coming through it alive has given me permission to throw all manner of caution to the wind. But dammit. No. Danika feels like the furthest damn thing from a mistake, doesn't she?

I'm messed up over being shot, raw from telling her so much shit I never thought I would say out loud, and I just want to absorb her. Soak her right into my skin. She's letting me, too. Allowing me to set the pace, which is nothing short of desperate. Impossible to be anything else when her pussy is pressing down on my cock, her thighs shifting around like she wants to ride it, but needs my go-ahead. I'm going to give it to her, too. I'm going to give a giant middle finger to the rules and fuck this girl I've wanted to the point of stomach pains and sleepless nights. I've craved her for months.

Making my own rules in place of the ones I'm abandoning is giving me an anchor, too. One I need. Because I wasn't lying when I said Danika wrecks me. She's already doing it. Every time she whimpers or curls her fingers in the collar of my uniform, I fight a battle not to throw her down on the seat and take my release as fast as possible. My growing obsession with seeing to her needs is the only thing stopping me.

"Lift up your shirt," I growl into the hollow of her throat.

Her nod is dazed, but eager, although she casts a look over her shoulder through the windshield. "What if we get caught?"

Without a formal command from my brain, my teeth snap together, and I deliver a rough slap to her bottom. "Then you'll hide your pretty face in my neck while I show them my badge. And when they leave, you'll keep fucking moving. You want to break the rules, baby? Let's break them." Christ, there's lightning singing in my veins, her shallow breaths making me even hotter. Hungrier. "Once I'm inside you, that's where I'm staying. God himself couldn't drag me off. Are we clear?"

"Okay. Yes." Her brown eyes are half-hidden by heavy lids, teeth sinking into her bottom lip as she lifts her T-shirt. That lacy white bra is revealed and the purity of it makes me feel even more debauched. A man who can't keep his lust contained long enough for a girl to graduate. God, I never had a chance. She leaves the material bunched at her throat, watching me and waiting for what comes next. God, this is what it's like to have total control with none of the fear of failure. Danika has witnessed me losing my shit, my *restraint*, and still accepts me. More than accepts me. She trusts me enough to explore the corresponding part of herself that lets me be in command.

"You're beautiful. You know that?" I slide my hands around from her ass, lifting and closing them around her breasts. "Dressed in the same uniform as everyone else and I have to concentrate on not staring at you. Hours of it, Danika.

For months. So take your tits out and let me see them. I'm tired of suffering."

She blinks at me, then begins fumbling with the front snap of her bra. Her hands are shaking, her trim stomach shuddering in and out, but she finally parts the lace and shows off two firm breasts. The kind a man dreams about. The kind *I've* been dreaming about. They're on the small side and apparently that's just what I love, because the line around my restraint blurs along with my vision. Before I know what I'm doing, I'm whipping her shirt the rest of the way off and dragging her bra down her arms.

"Damn." Lust surges when I see Danika completely topless for the first time, and I wish fleetingly we were in a bed, so I could lay her down and lick every inch of her. But right now, I'm in fucking pain, my cock fighting to get free of my pants. I've never been this keyed up in my life, and she's right there with me, gazing at my mouth like it holds the secret to life. "You think you can stand to take your hot pussy off me long enough to unzip my pants?"

"M-maybe," she moans, giving in and writhing on my lap, earning her ass a slap. "Yes."

I'm not sure if she scrapes her fingernails down my chest and belly on purpose, but the rough, honest sensation of it rears my head back and rips a curse from my throat. Trying to preserve my sanity, I lift her by the waist and slide her back on my thighs. More of that smooth touch on my stomach has me panting, and when she reaches my belt, I watch her through a haze, growing more starved by the moment. Want. Need. "I like that you're clumsy taking me out," I rasp. "Means I've got you rattled, doesn't it?"

"I can't think straight." Her exhale catches. "Happy now?"

I drag lazy circles around her nipples with my thumbs, listening to the hitch in her breathing, the jerking of her thighs. "Good girl. That's how you've got me."

I'm not looking at her handiwork, but the second my zipper lowers, the release of pressure and rush of need between my legs is immense, impossible to ignore now. If I don't get inside her in the next minute, my fucking world is going to end. We speed to that end together when she wraps me in her hand and strokes my dick for the first time.

"Shit." Moisture seeps from my tip, hardening my balls even more because there's light at the end of the tunnel. "Again. Harder."

"Oh my God."

Her sob makes me focus on her face, but I have to look away just as fast. "You have to stop looking at it like that or I'll only make it one pump."

"Sorry, it's just . . . I didn't see it up close in the locker room—"

I cut her off by snagging her wrist, taking it away from my cock. In one quick move she isn't expecting, I slide one of her thighs over to join the other, then spin her around so she's facing the front windshield. Jerking her back against my chest, skin to skin, my free hand drags those taunting yoga pants down, down, over her ass to stop at her knees. "Don't talk about my dick again unless you're riding it."

With her pants down and her sweet ass curved into my lap, my hands are free to roam up and knead her breasts. She likes that. I know because her head falls back and lands on my shoulder with a throaty moan. "See? I don't mind you being bossy when the r-rules benefit me."

Danika turns her face slightly, our eyes lock, and she gives me a quick lift of her lips. My chest begins to ache, along with my erection, and for a moment, all I can do is stare. Goddammit, she's so pretty. How is it possible that I'm flying a thousand yards above my own body, but a few words out of her mouth and I'm grounded. What does that mean?

I decide to stop exploring it when she flicks her hips back, grinds back down. Does it again. Does it again. Until my fucking thighs and hands are shaking, my mouth open and growling at her neck. Every ounce of my focus goes into hunting a condom down in my pocket and covering myself, before reaching down between our bodies and guiding my cock to her heat. "Wet girl. Nice wet girl."

She arches her back and spreads her legs, allowing me to slip myself inside her inch by inch . . . and as she sinks down, I barely recognize the sensation because nothing that came before her compares. Made for me. I'm made just for her. All of the above.

"Oh God," we both moan at the same time.

How does she feel different from anything in my memory? Because I've waited so long? Or maybe it's the fact that she hasn't even moved yet and this is already the best fuck of my life by a thousand miles. Both? I don't know. Whatever the reason, I'm an animal as soon as she's fully seated, my cock tucked up inside that snug heat. Control? What control?

I tighten my ass muscles and thrust up—

"*Greer.*"

Pinpricks attack the base of my spine. "Shit, baby. Don't say my name until I get you closer."

"Sorry. Sorry." Again, she throws her head back on my shoulder and moans. "Oh my God. You feel so good."

"Me?" I draw back and push home again. "Any tighter and you're going to cut off my fucking circulation."

Her muscles clench around me, her body rolling and twisting in the sexiest move I've ever witnessed. It thrusts her tits up and exposes her smooth neck. "I'll do anything you want."

My chest begins to heave, my groin so full and heavy I'm almost dizzy. "You're going to kill me, aren't you?" I begin jerking her hips back so she can stroke me tight and fast. By the second slide of my cock into her heat, we have a rhythm, and God fucking damn, it's incredible.

My teeth are on edge to keep from shouting. She leans forward and props her hands on my knees, giving her enough balance to ruin me with little up and down bounces of her hips. Every strike of her ass on my thighs vibrates the taut flesh, making it impossible to keep my hands off. So I grip her there, guiding her up and down on my stiff arousal. It's everything I can do not to grind her down hard and give her my come, but I won't. I don't know what will happen tomorrow so I'm savoring her tonight.

The very idea of being separated from Danika sparks a denial in my head. Makes possessing her even more about now, now, now. "Tell me about what you're riding now." My hand gives her right ass cheek another slap, then slides around to tease her clit. "You like my cock up close, baby? You like it deep?"

Her pattern is staggered now, her little whimpers filling the car, filling my head and chest. "Yes, I love it. I love it . . . but your fingers, too . . . I'm not . . . I can't wait . . ."

I keep stroking her clit with one hand, but lift the other to her throat, circling it and urging her back against my chest. Fuck, the show she puts on from this vantage point fires me toward release like a bullet. Her slick body is highlighted by the distant streetlamp, shadows playing over her curves as she lifts and grinds, lifts and grinds. Her hips are my new best friend, twisting and scooting back, just enough to slip her pussy down to my base, squeeze, then ease back up to the tip. She's magic. There's no doubt in my mind. "That cock belongs to a man, Danika." I apply more pressure to her neck. Enough to make her suck in an excited breath, her body moving faster, my fingers blurring on her clit. "No more boys for you."

On my shoulder, she shakes her head no. "Greer, oh, I'm going to—" She breaks off on a closed mouth scream, her thighs trembling around my hand. "Greer."

I think I can hold it together long enough to give her another orgasm, but as soon as her pussy cinches around my dick like a belt, I know resisting the rush of pleasure is a pipe dream. "God-dammit, baby. Ripping it right out of me, aren't you?" There's a scraping feeling deep in my belly, then I'm shouting into her hair as the most phenomenal relief grips me. I'm coming inside her. Finally. Finally. It hurts, but it's happening . . . and then it doesn't hurt anymore, because the worst of the lust is leaving me, shooting up the stalk of my flesh. "You're killing me. Don't stop. Move. Move. Don't stop."

My body continues to ram up, up into her snug, clenching cunt until my fucking vision goes black. *Mine.* The word echoes in my head, but my teeth snap down on my lower lip to keep from saying it out loud.

When she falls back like a puppet with severed strings, I've gone boneless, too. Throughout my life, when I've given in to my needs and had sex, I've disconnected immediately afterward. Or maybe I never connected at all. This is vastly different. The sound of our shallow breaths in the car, the way her slight body heaves on my lap . . . the way my hand strokes up and down her fore-arm without any prompting. It's new.

It's scary how good it feels.

And when something feels this incredible, the pain of having it taken away would be even greater. My eyes close and I see things I don't want to see. Visions from this evening, from that afternoon so long ago. Christ, even the call I received mere days ago that Danika was a bystander at a robbery plays in my brain, reminding me why I don't form attachments to people. Why can't I follow my own rules with this girl?

I realize I've been quiet too long when Danika sits up and scoots off my lap. Without looking at me, she lifts her butt and pulls her pants back up. Reaches for her shirt and bra, beginning to don them. Watching her closely, I find a hand sanitizer wipe to wrap up the condom and zip myself back up. What do I say here? Please can we do this again? I got shot earlier and you still managed to make this the best night of my life? All of those things will lead to a commitment. One she deserves. But I can't give her that. I'm already in too deep.

When she sends me a sweeping look over her squared shoulder and begins to exit the car, I panic, though. Despite everything, I can't let her think it meant nothing.

My arm shoots out and wraps around her middle. A heavy beat of time passes as I draw her back against my chest, my heart booming like a cannon in my rib cage. "You're going to give me a kiss."

"It's over." She's back to being a smart-ass, but I know it's staged. Of course I do, with my cheek pressed to the racing pulse in her neck. "You're not in charge anymore."

"You want me to say please?"

She hesitates, but her flushed face turns, bringing our lips inches apart. "Yes."

"Kiss me, please."

Her tongue skates along her upper lip. "No."

"No?"

Brown eyes study me and I know that look. I've instructed her for months, so I know she's solving a problem or making a decision. Damn if I know what it is, though, so I stop breathing and wait. "If you want a kiss, find a way to see me again and get it."

With that, she climbs out of the car and closes herself in the front passenger seat. I sit there stunned for a full ten seconds before I move on autopilot to the driver's side, starting the car.

Five minutes later, when I drop her off outside her apartment building, she winks at me before climbing out of the car. No goodbye, no nothing. Still, by the time I reach the end of the block, I'm smiling. If I'm not mistaken, I've just had every rule in my book thrown in my face. I've been challenged. And I have no idea how to feel about it, but I know this.

I respect the hell out of this girl, she terrifies me . . .

And I'm now fucking obsessed with getting that kiss.

CHAPTER 18
—————— *Danika* ——————

Let it never be said that Danika Silva backs down from a challenge, huh?

It's Thursday evening—exactly twenty-four hours since my public sex-capades—and I'm dressed in my pajamas, hair wet from my shower. I'm on the edge of my bed with the door closed, muffled sounds from the television reaching me through the door. I'm flipping my cell phone up and down in my hand, working up the nerve to check in with the lieutenant. A.k.a. Greer. A.k.a. the Grim Reaper. A.k.a. the Orgasm Donor.

Underneath my nightshirt, goose bumps lift on every inch of my skin. God, I've been like this all day. As if I'm sharing a filthy secret with my panties. But I can't give in and do another mental replay of the backseat boogie, because I need to focus on the upcoming phone call. Not to mention, the gauntlet I threw down last night.

The lieutenant made the mistake of opening up to me about his ex-partner, about the fact that the job is getting to him, and now he's not just my instructor. Not just the badass with bazooka biceps and a scowl. He's real. He's a man who hesitates to fire on someone even though they're drawing a gun. He's a man who buys me stamps, mourns the loss of his friend, leads a book club and runs interference for my cousin with the department.

All these things have doubled my attraction to him.

And quadrupled my chances of getting hurt.

But there's something inside me that won't let Greer push me away. It would be the easy way out, wouldn't it? Sure, we could have a few more accidents where I trip and find myself impaled on his lap. We'd go our separate ways afterwards and call it a slipup.

Here's the thing, though. I don't want to do that. What we did under the rumbling shadow of the FDR Drive felt like the furthest thing from an accident. And I'm not going to pretend Greer is a waste of my time. He's not. The guy who bought me stamps, commended me in front of my parents and avoided taking a suspect's life at the risk of his own? If I don't try and convince him the world won't end if he's happy, I'll regret it.

Greer didn't sign on for more of me, but I can't shake the feeling he wants more. Even if he's afraid to admit it.

Flipping the phone one more time for good measure, I finally give in and hit CALL on the lieutenant's number, burying a nervous squeal in my throat. This is the guy I got naked for last night, and I totally, totally got the last word. Why am I nervous? Ahhhh.

One ring. "I am calm. I am cool. I am woman, hear me roar—"

"Good to know."

My heart shoots into my throat. When did he answer? "Come on. Don't you say hello?"

"My caller ID told me who it was."

I can gauge exactly nothing by his tone of voice. In the background, there's a lot of scraping chairs and crackling radios, so I know he's at the precinct. Not like he'd be baby talking me through the phone if he was somewhere more private. This is Greer we're talking about. Keeper of frowns and blower of piercing whistles. "I'm just checking in."

Silence passes. "How . . . are you?"

Oh my God, the way he asks the question. Like his mouth is right up against my ear and he's clearly, clearly asking about the state of my vagina, right? "It's fine," I breathe. Shit, he *was* asking about my vagina, right? I slap a hand over my eyes. "How has your day been?"

"A lot of meetings and paperwork. I discharged my weapon yesterday," he reminds me, like I could forget it for a single second.

"I know. I was there." I press my lips together and puff a laugh. "Both times."

"Jesus, Danika," he chokes out and it's priceless. It takes him a moment to speak again, and when he does, his voice is lower. It feels like he's sitting beside me. "The man I shot is under psych evaluation, but he's going to be fine."

The way he says it tells me he was worried. Knowing Greer was concerned for someone who tried to put a bullet in his chest makes me that much more positive he's got more to give. Maybe to me? "Did you go to see him?" I ask, my hand climbing my throat.

"Not inside the room, just to the desk." A pause. "I wouldn't know what to say."

Really? This man who can cut to the center of a recruit's bullshit from fifty yards away? "I'm sure they told him you were there. That's more than most cops would do after he fired on them." My fierce need to go find him and wrap him in a hug forces me to take a long, slow breath away from the receiver. "If you want to go into the room next time, I can . . . come with you."

He's quiet so long, I'm not sure he's going to respond. "Thanks for the offer, but they're probably transferring him to a different facility tomorrow."

"Okay. Just keep it in mind." I can almost hear the time ticking on this phone call. The longer we talk, the more intimate it becomes, and Greer doesn't think he wants that. Not the emotional kind of intimacy, anyway. I'm banking on the opposite, though, so I search for a way to keep him on the line longer. "Um. I've been thinking about something you said during our ride along." I wet my lips. "How will rubber gloves and nose plugs help me get stamps for my collection next time?"

He clears his throat. "Did I . . . say that?"

My cop-in-training sense tingles. "You know you did."

There's some shuffling of paperwork, followed by a sigh. "A woman got the last booklet, okay? I offered her cash and she wouldn't take it."

Feathers begin to whip around in my stomach, just imagining the lieutenant bartering for something I wanted. Being desperate enough to do it. "H-how much cash?"

"Not relevant."

A laugh puffs out of my mouth. "Spoken like someone who isn't existing on toast and leftover pizza."

"Is that all you eat?" A beat passes where I can almost feel his annoyed frown. Those whipping feathers blast into overdrive at the possibility he's concerned about the balance of my meals. "No . . . candy bars ever slip in there?"

"Sometimes." My eyes narrow when he gives a heavy exhale. "You're purposely trying to change the subject. How did you get the stamps if she didn't want your money?"

Is that the sound of his jaw grinding? "Do you have any idea what kind of upkeep it takes to own nine cats, Danika?"

"No."

"You don't want to."

I lie down on the floor and mimic making a snow angel on the hard wood. If he could see me, he would think I'm a lunatic, but there's no way to contain the champagne fizz popping off inside my belly, my chest. "You changed her litter boxes in exchange for the stamps. You actually did that."

"I'm late for a briefing."

"Liar." I turn my head and laugh into my shoulder before bringing the receiver to my mouth again. There's a blurry quality to my vision as I look up at the ceiling and try to picture him at his desk, all commanding and sharp in his uniform. "Thank you."

He grunts. Twice. "You have training in the morning. You better get some sleep."

"Yes, Lieutenant." *Take the leap.* If he's willing to scoop poop for stamps, I'm not imagining what's between us. "Listen. It's my mother's birthday tomorrow night. At their place. You know, where you had the chicken? Charlie and everyone are coming." Nothing. He gives me nothing. I die. "Don't give me an answer, okay? Just take the knowledge and do with it what you will."

"I'm on shift tomorrow night."

Disappointment weighs me down, but I manage to sound casual. "Okay." I swallow. "Good night, Greer."

His deep exhale wraps around me. "Good night, Danika."

I HAVEN'T HAD cause to get dressed up in a while, unless you count my foiled date. My mother never says out loud that she hates my yoga pants, but it's kind of a dead giveaway when she purses her lips and behaves like she's in excruciating pain when I show up in them. Thinking about the red dress hanging in my old bedroom closet, I smile to myself. She's going to hate the yoga pants even more after this, but it'll be worth it.

As soon as we were dismissed from the academy late this afternoon, I hit the ground running. I'd already been stocking up on decorations, so I hauled those, along with my change of clothes, across town. While my father occupies my mother with a movie, I set up the apartment and run to the store upwards of seven times, bringing back snacks, soda, beer and a hoagie taller than myself.

After tying the final balloon to the back of a dining room chair, I step back and survey my handiwork. Not bad. Beer is icing in the double sinks, more in the fridge. There's a snack bowl on every available surface, and there are almost enough balloons to carry the building away. Kind of like *Up* without the painful, heart-wrenching death. A quick check of the clock tells me guests will start arriving in half an hour, followed by my parents in approximately an hour, so I can't delay making myself presentable anymore.

Minutes later, I'm wrestling with the zipper of the dress a little and trying not to think what Greer's reaction would be seeing me in it. He's on shift so he isn't going to. I was probably jumping into the deep end inviting him in the first place, but I don't like the idea of him spending so much time alone after being shot. Sure, he has his book club, but I'm not sure a bunch of hard-nosed cops discussing murder mysteries is much of a break from daily police work. He needs friends.

I can be his friend and still want to see him without pants on, right?

I barely have a chance to fix my hair in a loose twist and sling on my heels before the downstairs buzzer starts to ring. Over the next little while, people begin to pile into the apartment. Women from my mother's church, their husbands, a few neighbors that have been living in the Kitchen since I can remember. Charlie arrives with an arm around Ever, Jack bringing up the rear with a blushing Katie. No wonder, since I'm pretty sure his tongue is in her ear.

Ever's whistle turns heads in the apartment. "Girl, you clean up nice."

That gets Jack's attention, and I know—I know—before he opens his mouth that my childhood best friend and Manhattan native will find a way to rib me. It's what we do. "What happened, D? Did you lose a bet?" Smiling, he reaches out and ruffles my hair, earning his hand a smack. "It's about time someone loses one besides me."

He's referring to the sucker's bet he lost to me, the terms of which landed him in the police academy. That's right. I play dirty pool and regret nothing. "I don't think it was a loss," I say, tilting my head at Katie.

"Hell, no." Jack pulls his girlfriend closer, laying a kiss on her forehead. "Biggest win of my life."

"You're welcome," I say, fluttering my eye-lashes. Turning to Charlie and Ever, I notice Charlie is more quiet than usual. He's always full of energy, looking for some way to be use-ful, but his expression is subdued. "Everything all right?"

"Yeah. Sorry." His tight smile is clearly meant to reassure. "You probably heard my asshole brother went and got himself shot yesterday."

Okay, so it's safe to say no one knows I was there. If Greer had some reason not to mention it to Charlie, I'm not going to create tension be-tween them by spilling the beans. Plus, Greer did me a solid by not telling anyone I was present during the almost-robbery at the yogurt shop or about the probation. Which is good, because both situations would have led to a lot of uncomfort-able questions. Like, *Are you insane?* And, *What does your probation entail?*

Oh nothing, just wild monkey sex.

"I heard something about it, yeah." Ever and I trade a solemn look. "He's going to be fine, though, right? Look at it this way, statistically he's more likely to be pecked to death by pea-cocks than to be shot again. Maybe it was a good thing."

Ever nods. "I take the word of anyone who uses 'statistically' in a sentence."

Charlie finally laughs and seems to relax. "Somehow that actually made me feel better."

"You might feel even better if you go see him." The suggestion is out there before I can stop it. Who am I to tell Charlie how to interact with his brother? It's none of my business, except Greer confided in me about getting burned out. If Charlie knew, he would probably make ten times the effort to be around Greer. So while I can't tell Charlie his brother isn't in a great place, surely a gentle nudge is acceptable? "He probably never takes a break, but he'd be forced to stop working if you did a flyby."

"Yeah." Charlie narrows perceptive eyes at me, clueing me in that I'm not as smooth as I think I am. "I might just do that."

Wanting to escape my roommate's scrutiny, I rub my hands together. "So . . . what can I get you guys to drink?"

As soon as I get one person their refill, another glass is empty until time begins to blur together. By the time my parents are supposed to arrive, the church ladies are tipsy, Robbie has commandeered the easy chair as his DJ booth—which is basically just him and his iPhone—and my feet are already starting to regret the heels. Thanks to the neighbor I position at the window as lookout, I manage to quiet everyone down enough to surprise my mother when she comes through the door. And I can see the woman totally knew about the party, even though she throws herself back against the wall and gasps dramatically.

Someone get Hollywood on the line.

"And my daughter, in a dress." She kisses her fingers. "Best gift of all."

"Don't get used to it," I say, handing her a glass of wine.

Jack wastes no time spinning my mother into a laughing dance, and the party gets back into the flow, although as more people arrive, I can see we're going to be short on supplies. I could probably send Charlie or Jack down to the bodega to get ice and another couple six-packs, but they're having such a good time. Plus Jack buying alcohol, even if he doesn't plan on drinking, doesn't sit right. So I decide to go grab it myself and be back before any of the chip bowls need to be refilled.

Palming my wallet, I open the front door—

And run into the brick wall that is Greer.

CHAPTER 19
—————— Greer ——————

Danika bounces off me, and I rush to grip her elbows, to keep her from going splat. I start to lecture her on being more careful, but then I *see* see her.

And damn. I wasn't expecting a dress. It's . . . red. Wait, what is her hair doing?

Good things. Great, actually. It's kind of loose on the sides, but still pulled away from her face. A piece of it is caught on her glossy bottom lip. Wait, there's lipstick involved here, too?

What have I walked into?

The softness of her skin distracts me from how different she looks, but only for a few seconds, because she straightens, and I'm back to gaping like a fucking jackass.

I flash back to academy orientation when she strolled in wearing sneakers, a T-shirt and jeans, her hair doing that flippy ponytail thing. She'd turned heads dressed like that. I'd been forced to refer to my notes when giving my standard new recruit speech, because she'd sat right in the front row with her big, brown eyes. I like that girl. The tough one who walks the walk. I'm not sure how I feel yet about this whole red dress business, except for one concrete fact.

If there are single men at this party, I'm going to escort them out. In handcuffs, if necessary. Am I being completely irrational? Yes. Not to mention selfish, considering I'm never going to be relationship material for Danika.

"I brought back your mother's Tupperware," I push past my tightening throat. "And the edge of your bra is showing."

Danika looks at me like I'm soft in the head. "So fix it."

Touch her in that dress? "I shouldn't have to. It should be underneath your clothes."

She does a two-finger press to her temple. "Let's start over, okay?"

"Great idea," I return, equally irritated. And out of place. And a little desperate to have this girl to myself—right now—when I know I shouldn't. "Take the Tupperware, please. It took me ten minutes to get the stupid top on, and I never want to look at it again."

"Tough day?" she asks, her eyes warming with amusement.

"Yeah," I answer honestly.

Her smile dims and she takes the Tupperware. A little frown forms between her brows when she feels the weight, but I try to appear busy checking my phone while she lifts the clear plastic and looks inside. "Is that a brownie?" She lowers the container. "A frosted one?"

"It's for your mother." People are starting to notice me standing out in the hallway, my brother being one of them, followed by Jack and the girls. Which leads to a fucking parade of raised eyebrows. Ignoring them, I do a quick scan of the room, but it doesn't yield any men of a marriageable age. Though I can't see the whole place where I'm standing. Is this why I came here? To make sure no one else can have her, including myself? "I can't stay."

Danika shakes her head, but she's still looking at the brownie. "You're staying."

"I'm on shift."

"Leave if you get a call." Her brown eyes hit me with the impact of a meteor. "Please?"

My stomach grows heavy. Has she ever spoken that word to me? Hearing it from her mouth makes me hot and anxious. It glues my feet to the floor and keeps me from leaving, simply because she asked me to stay. "Last time I asked you please, your answer was no."

The darkening of her cheeks tells me she knows what I'm talking about. "I'll change it to yes if you give this brownie to my mother yourself."

"That seems a little personal."

"So is the kiss I plan to let you take," she whispers.

Jesus. How have I managed not to drag her out of the apartment like King Kong on steroids yet? *Let you take.* She's speaking in our language. The kind we create more of every time we're together. "You drive a hard bargain," I say, moving closer, until she's forced to step to the side. As soon as I've moved from the dark hallway into the light, the craziest thing happens.

Someone is actually happy to see me.

Danika's mother comes swooping in like a perfumed bird, soaring through the guests with her wings out. "Lieutenant Burns, you came to my birthday!"

"Yes."

Before I can avoid it, I'm being hugged. Across the room, Charlie's eyeballs almost pop out of his skull, and if he doesn't stop staring, I might speed the process along. Everyone is looking at me wondering who the hell called the police, but apart from my brother, no one is making a huge deal out of me being hugged in public. Which lets me consider how I feel knowing I made a good impression on Danika's parents.

Good. Dangerously good.

Behind me, Danika is discreet about placing the Tupperware in my grip, but just like her daughter, this woman sees everything. She eases back and eyes the container with her hands clasped beneath her chin until I give it over. "I brought you a brownie."

"Oh, thank you. Thank you." I grimace as she pries off the impossible lid, takes a big whiff of the baked good, then reseals it with zero effort. "Come right in. What do you like to drink? Danika will take care of you."

Yes, she mentioned that. "Milk, please. I'm on duty."

Danika shakes her head at my choice, but skates off to fill my order, her mother in tow. I almost storm after them when I see Danika's dress doesn't have a goddamn back, but manage to hold myself in check, because there are still no bachelors skulking around. I'll have to check the bathroom and the fire escape when I get a chance.

Charlie, Jack, Ever and Katie approach like a foursome of marionettes. I picture them coming from a huddle, my brother as quarterback. Look casual. Ready? Break. And then they all do the exact opposite. It doesn't escape my notice that Jack doesn't look thrilled to see me. "Hey," starts Charlie, a cup of soda pressed to his bottom lip. "So, uh . . . when did you meet Danika's mother?"

"Yeah, you guys seem pretty chummy," Jack adds. "Meeting someone's mother isn't something you do unless you have honorable intentions, though."

Bolts tighten on either side of my neck. "Until a few weeks ago, you wouldn't have known an honorable intention if it bit you on the ass, Garrett."

Katie doesn't like what I have to say. "That's a load of bollocks. He was always very honorable with me. Except those few times." She purses her lips. "And a few times after that . . ."

"Let's not have a fight in the middle of the party," Ever murmurs, her smile tight. "I have it on good authority that church folks make the best eavesdroppers."

It's on the tip of my tongue to alert Jack to the fact that he isn't telling me something I don't already know. I berated myself on the way to the party for being too weak to stay away from Danika when there's nothing I can offer her but sex. My lack of honorable intentions has been at the forefront of my damn mind since Wednesday night. I'm well aware I'm behaving like a bastard, and it stings even more because I should be setting a better example for my recruits. For my brother.

My gaze seeks out the only girl who's ever succeeded in making me break the rules—

And after about twenty seconds, I really do not like what I'm seeing.

She's hobbling around in those heels, for chrissakes. My milk is in one hand, but she can't make it two feet in my direction before someone asks for a refill, or inquires about the cake or secures a favor for later in the week. For the first time since I arrived, I notice the balloons. There are a million colors, all tied in strategic spots. Out of the way, but still visible. There's a banner with her mother's name on it, streamers flowing out from either side. Chinese lanterns of various sizes are tacked to the ceiling, candles are bunched on several surfaces. "Who helped her with the party?" I bark the question at the foursome. "Did you guys help her do any of this?"

"No . . ." Jack looks around, as if he's just noticed the decorations, too. Slowly, everyone's gazes light on the beer icing in the sink, the food, the rearranged furniture. "She was gone by the time we got home. I would've helped if she'd asked."

"Me, too," Ever says. "She couldn't have done all this alone, right?"

Nobody has an answer, but I already have one. My stomach is starting to hurt watching her run the show, all nods and taking mental notes. How often does she do this? Constantly? Last time I was here, she'd just finished fixing the leaky sink and dropping off a prescription. Her cousin calls her about an impending robbery and she hops into a cab, no questions asked. She carries the world—her world—on her shoulders, and somehow I love that about her and hate it at the same time. Explain that one, Dr. Phil.

Have I been so wrapped up in Danika I forgot why I put her on probation in the first place? She's a cowgirl who wants to save the day all by herself, no matter the cost. But I'm not going to let that happen again on my watch.

After what seems like an hour, Danika breaks free and approaches us, extending the milk out for me to take. "Hey, sorry that took so long." She tucks a piece of stray hair behind her ear. "I just have to run out for more beer—"

"No, you don't!" everyone shouts at once.

CHAPTER 20
Danika

F or some reason, Greer insists on coming with me to the bodega. He seems more focused on my feet than anything else, but I'm so grateful for the respite from the party, I just switch off my brain and enjoy the cool night air on my bare arms.

When I glance over at Greer, his frown is now being directed at my back. "Do you want to tell me about your tough day?"

"No, I want you to tell me about yours."

What is up with his mood swings? He arrived in a black mood, but cooled off when I promised to kiss him. Now he's back to needing a nap. "You sound like a man trying very hard to remain calm."

"Good detective work." I merely raise a questioning eyebrow and wait for him to continue. "You could have asked someone to bring beer. Or help you organize the party. The people in your life would probably bend over backwards to help you out, but you never ask. It's a waste, Danika."

My blood feels light and tingly. All because he's taking time to make observations about me. It's silly, but I can't help it. "Maybe I'm just saving up for a really big favor."

"I'm not laughing."

"Do you know how to laugh?"

His scowl could send schoolchildren screaming for their mothers. "If I hadn't shown up, you'd be walking down Tenth Avenue right now by yourself, in the dark, looking hot enough to tempt a monk. You're exhausted, there're red marks on your ankles and your plan was to schlep a bunch of heavy beer four blocks and up two flights of stairs without any help. Why? And if you tell me people are thirsty, I will make your probation even worse."

Well. Things are certainly getting interesting. "How so?"

"You'll have to check in twice a day. Going forward."

Amateur. "People are thirsty."

I've just admitted I like talking to him, which basically shoots me up to a ten on the vulnerability scale. I mean, he could cut me off at the knees in so many ways here. He could tell me he wasn't serious, and I don't need to call him twice a day. Or he could tell me I'm pushing things to that serious level they were never meant to go. Unfortunately what he does instead only makes my heart knock in a masochistic rhythm. He stares over at me with a surprised expression, as if he can't believe I would want to speak to him more often.

"Um. Anyway." I blow out a breath into the silence. "Since you're so weirdly concerned . . . I'm not sure why I take everything on alone. I've been doing it so long." Pressing my lips together, I think back and search for a better answer. "When my father hurt his back, I started doing repairs and heavy lifting around the house. My mother might seem flighty, but she's actually a total badass, so she could probably pick up the slack my father left, but it's how we spend time together. It makes her happy. I like making people happy, even if I have to annoy them into it." We reach the bodega, and Greer follows me through the propped-open door. "Does that put a ding in my street cred?"

"No," Greer answers quietly. I can feel him watching me closely as I slide open the industrial fridge and lift out a case of Miller Lite. I hug it to my chest in preparation for waddling to the counter, but Greer stops me with a look and gestures for me to hand it over. "You'll survive watching me carry it."

I hesitate. "I'm not a martyr, you know."

He takes the case and throws it beneath one brawny arm. Lifting his free hand, he hesitates a second, then strokes the tips of his fingers down the side of my face, looking at me as if I'm a wonderfully complicated puzzle. One that maybe he doesn't feel capable of solving, but wishes like hell he could. Which I didn't realize until this moment is the exact way I—and maybe every woman on the planet—wants to be looked at. Right? Yes. Except for the whole part about him not thinking he can figure me out. I refuse to let him get rid of me—doesn't that solve any mysteries about what I want? *Him.* "Martyr, cowgirl, loyal friend, secret stamp collector." He shakes his head. "All those things and more. You don't belong to any one category."

And then he turns on a heel and walks toward the counter. As if he didn't just slay me.

Wow. Oh. This is bad. I'm falling for the lieutenant.

Hard.

I'm blown out of my stupor when Greer pulls out his wallet to pay. "No." I march forward, deftly ignoring the cashier's sigh. "You're not even drinking."

"I'll put one in the trunk for later if you can just take this tiny baby step."

"I didn't know probation included immersion therapy." I give a pained grin and make a sound like I'm dying. It's involuntary. But knowing the kiss I'm going to lay on him before the night is over, I guess I can justify letting him pay. "Fine."

He cracks a smile, and it has the effect of candle wax pooling between my legs. His bicep winks at me when he shoulders the case of beer and the overall effect is nothing short of mesmerizing. Just having him *with* me on this tedious errand is mesmerizing. On the heels of realizing I've taken a dive into the infatuation deep end, my brain is playing catch-up. I'm into Greer big-time, and I'm still pretty sure he's dead set against taking us any further. And this is the first time the possibility I could fail hits me. Hits me hard. "I—I should be getting back."

His frown blusters back in. "We're taking our time. People can fill their own fucking cups. It's a skill we learn in childhood."

It takes an effort, but I ignore the new ache in my belly. "Is it too late to hire you as entertainment for the party?"

"You can't afford me."

I don't realize we're having a smirk-off until the cashier starts tapping his fingers on the counter. In other words, get to stepping. We walk back out onto the sidewalk, the sounds of Hell's Kitchen swishing around us. A green light sends a fleet of cabs flying up the avenue, there's music coming from a parked car stereo, food sizzles on a halal cart. I've walked this path to the bodega a million times in my life, but it looks entirely different with Greer walking beside me. I'm trying to see it through his experienced cop eyes, wondering what his mind is registering. Wondering if this is the first and only time we'll walk this path together.

As if that thought has an outward effect, the wave of traffic dies down and suddenly the only sound is my heels clicking on the sidewalk. The pulse ticcing in my neck. I glance over at Greer, and he's staring, somehow encompassing me, head to toe, with rapt concentration. And I'm not even going to lie, independent woman or not, I don't mind this big, ripped, uniformed lieutenant carrying my beer for me. No, I do not.

He likes it, too, I realize. When we pass a group of people outside my building, he moves closer to me, pride flexing his jaw. That bicep flexes, too, and somewhere an angel gets its wings.

Inside the vestibule, Greer waits for me to head up the stairs first, but I still feel on the vulnerable end of the spectrum after having him pay for the beer. And also realizing my feelings for him run deeper than I thought. So I shake my head. "Age before beauty."

Looking a little confused, he nonetheless shrugs and takes the first few steps. But when he casts a glance over his shoulder, his eyebrows draw together. "Are you checking out my ass?"

I follow behind him slowly, trailing a finger along the bannister and admiring his firm butt without an ounce of shame. "Ten-four, lieutenant."

"Christ."

"Are you self-conscious?"

He lets out a harsh scoff. "No." We reach the first landing, and he rolls his shoulders. "Fine, a little."

My sides hurt from trying to hold in my laughter. "Okay, fine. My turn." I breeze past him, only vaguely registering my aching feet at this point. "Let me show you how it's done."

I can't remember a time I ever experienced this breathless, edgy excitement around a boy. Or man, as the case may be. But it's tripling the speed of my blood flow now. There's cotton candy and clouds weaving together in my stomach as I sway my hips, taking my hair out and shaking it as I climb. Knowing he's behind me watching is making me wet, making me crazy.

I'm not alone. The second we reach my parents' floor, Greer sets down the case of beer, spins me around and slams me against the wall. Yes, slams. It doesn't hurt either, because he leads with his hips. Pinning me. Instantly, I'm breathing like I just swam the Hudson.

His stubbled chin rasps against my smooth one. That's how close we are. Daylight would struggle to find space between our mouths. It's there, but just barely. "Are you finished with your fun now?"

"Feels like it's just starting," I gasp out, thanks to his belt pressing into my tummy. Hard. And I can feel what's contained just beneath it, too. "Oh."

"Give me my kiss," he demands.

Thank God for the wall or I'd be in a heap. "If you want it so bad, take it."

"Oh, I want it. I've been regretting not just taking it since the other night."

My legs are aching to wrap around his waist, but I force myself to remember our surroundings and potential nosy neighbors. Not to mention I'm curious about what he said. "Why didn't you take it?"

He seems to search for an answer. "There's a before and after to when I'm in charge with you. I need the boundaries."

"Why?"

"Because I like you both ways." His forehead pushes against mine so I can't see his eyes, but I feel his fast breath, the shuddering lift and fall of his chest. "I like how you are when I'm in control."

"And you like me when I refuse to take orders, too."

"Yes."

His confession affects me in two ways. One? I'm turned on like a nighttime skyscraper. Two, I'm kind of pissed. That's right, pissed. We're good for each other, and he's going to fight against us becoming something real, isn't he? Maybe hard enough for me to walk away at some point. But not right now. In this moment, I want to revel in the knowledge that this man likes me . . . for me. That we've argued, I've frustrated and disappointed him, and yet he showed up at my mother's birthday with a brownie. And he wants the kiss I promised. Lord, he wants it bad.

"You're in charge now," I whisper. Amazing how words coming from my own mouth make my muscles go slack, my neck loosen.

In response to my body's pliancy, Greer's hardens. Everywhere. His chest, stomach and thighs mold to my softness, flattening me to the wall slowly, in painstaking degrees while he studies my mouth like a scientist does with a glass slide. I can feel the full outline of his erection on my stomach, but I don't want to wrap my legs around him anymore. No, I want him to wrap them for me. Or command me to do it.

We breathe into one another's mouths for devastating moments before I feel Greer's hand wedge between our hips. It drags down, just to the right of my mound, then moves lower, lower, the pads of his fingers brushing my bare inner thigh, before continuing its climb beneath my dress. I'm whimpering, and he hasn't even kissed me yet, but the mere knowledge that his strong, capable hand is under my skirt is enough to dampen my panties. To create a moan in my throat.

That moan turns to a trapped scream when Greer wedges his hand between my thighs and grips my juncture. Hard. "Say it again."

"You're in charge now," I manage, my head falling back to hit the wall. Oh God, it's like everything inside me redirects and flies toward his touch, needing to be as close as possible.

"When you go back to the party, no more running around. No more going out for supplies or making yourself tired." He speaks with his mouth directly over my pulse, and the effect is a seismic tremor down the length of my body, ending where I'm tucked inside his palm. Pulsing. "If anyone or anything wears you out, baby, it's going to be me. Do you understand?"

"Yes. Yes."

"Good girl." His tongue finds my pulse, and

I jerk like I've been struck by lightning. I hang there, in that state of electrified heat, while his mouth moves on my neck, teeth scraping, tongue tasting. His lips move higher, trailing over my chin where our mouths finally meet. And then there's no more going slow. There's only fast and wild after that.

It's less of a kiss, more a devouring. His mouth opens sideways over mine, my jaw aches to match him, but oh God, it's so worth it. I've never been kissed like this, even by him. There's no holding back or even the idea of it. At first, it's a claim of ownership, his low growls and stroking tongue leaving me no choice but to sign on the dotted line. After that, after my responsive mouth and tipped-back head agree to whatever he wants, Greer becomes a man testing out what he now owns. He sucks each lip, razing them with bared teeth, dives in for deep tastes of my mouth. So deep and long and hungry, I forget what it's like to breathe.

That possessive hand never leaves my core, continuing to hold it tightly, but not moving his fingers or giving friction. It's like he wants my focus only on his mouth, so I give it to him. I have no choice. Everything inside me begs to do what he wants. My nipples are in tight points against his chest, and I can't help it, I twist a little in his hold, earning the rasp of his uniform shirt. I'm so worked up, so hot, the sensation makes me break away on a gasp.

"Fuck," Greer pants, tilting his hips against me. "I should have known kissing you wouldn't be enough."

"Definitely, definitely not enough."

He heaves a frustrated exhale, then my mouth seems to draw him back in. His pupils are dilated, sweat appearing in the hollow of his throat. Just as he's leaning toward me again, eyelids drooping, the phone goes off on his hip. "Shit."

We both take a moment to absorb what's going to be very difficult to explain to my body. That kiss wasn't foreplay. It was all that can reasonably happen tonight. I'm feeling pretty unreasonable, though. Every part of me is so ready for what should happen next, I think I sob a little when Greer removes his hand from between my thighs and steps back, answering the call.

"This is Burns." He listens for a moment, but doesn't take his eyes off me. "I'll be right over." He ends the call with a sigh, but makes no move to leave.

Don't cry. Don't cry. "You don't have to explain anything to me."

His forehead creases. "I actually believe you."

"You should. I'm going to be in your shoes someday, remember?"

That bothers him—the fact that I'm going to be a cop. That I'm going to have a dangerous job. The kind that could potentially lead to me ending up like his partner. Why? Why did I say that? We were just closer than two people can get. Now here we are one minute later, and there's a divide. Greer looks away, wheels turning behind his eyes, but they return to me after a moment. "Remember what I said about the party."

I'm back to being vulnerable, so I compensate by picking up the case of beer and heading for my parents' apartment. "You're not in charge anymore."

"Danika."

If he didn't sound kind of miserable, I wouldn't relent. But he does. "Fine."

I watch from outside the apartment door as he goes down a couple of steps, transforming back into the hard-ass lieutenant, instead of the man who told me he likes both sides of me. It's that reminder of what he said that propels me into calling out to him, unable to let him go out onto the streets without something positive between us.

"Hey, Grim Reaper."

He slows to a stop and waits.

"I'm not out of your system yet." Propping the beer on my hip, I turn my key in the lock and push open the apartment door. "Call you tomorrow."

He's still unmoving on the stairs when I disappear inside.

BY MIDNIGHT I'M alone in the kitchen of my parents' apartment. It's pretty clean considering the amount of people that were here. Not to mention, Charlie, Jack, Ever and Katie stayed after to help me clean up. At one point, I heard Charlie muttering something about not wanting to incur the wrath of his brother, making me curious if I'm not the only one to whom Greer attempted to teach a lesson tonight.

How do I feel about Greer looking out for me? I . . . love it. My head tells me it's unnecessary and he's being a bossy control freak, but the reminder that Greer didn't want me exhausting myself makes my chest feel light. At least until I recall that kiss in the hallway and every part of me goes tight and heavy. What am I going to do about this man?

I'm too tired to think about it tonight. I assured my roommates I wouldn't be traveling across town tonight alone, that I would crash on my parents' couch and come home in the morning. After one more task, that's exactly what I'm going to do. The snores coming from my parents' room bring a smile to my face as I pick up the final blue recycling bag full of bottles, intending to leave it outside in the fenced garbage area. I'm back in my yoga pants and rocking a pair of my mother's flip-flops, much to the relief of my aching feet.

Careful not to clink bottles together and wake the neighbors, I creep down to street level and exit the building, my keys tucked into my pocket. Quietly as possible, I ease the blue bag into the recycling bin and turn to let myself back inside. When I hear approaching voices behind me, though, I glance back over my shoulder.

I don't recognize the two males walking past on the sidewalk at first, because they have their hoodies up. But those hoodies are exactly what trip my memory. It's the kids from the yogurt shop. The ones who wanted to use Robbie to set up an inside job.

My keys are digging into my palm, blood whistling in my ears as I turn and unlock the door, doing my best to keep my face hidden. It's a glass door, however, and they might be able to see my reflection. I don't know. But this isn't good. They might have been stupid enough to post their robbery plans on Facebook—which is the reason the cops showed up—but I shouted at my cousin to come out with his hands up. They heard me. If they see me right now, I'm not sure how they're going to react. They're clearly not the most reasonable people on earth.

"Hey," one of them shouts at me. "Hold up."

I force my hands to cooperate and they do, allowing me to slide into the building and close the self-locking door behind me. Just before it clicks shut, though, I hear a couple of fast footfalls, and I turn around on instinct to face the threat. The blonde who I remember is right outside the door, another darker-haired kid just over his shoulder. Their eyes are bloodshot, like they've hit the pot a little too hard tonight, but even with glassy eyes, their expressions are hard. Intimidating. I can easily see how my cousin had a hard time denying them what they wanted.

"That's her," the dirty blonde shouts through the glass. "Fucking cop."

"Your little cousin with you?" says the other one. "He thinks we're going to forget he called his cop cousin on us? He thinks he can switch his classes around and hide forever? That's not how it works."

The blonde raps on the glass with his knuckles. "You hearing this, bitch? You and Robbie better watch your asses. It's a small neighborhood."

Which must be how they found out I'm training to be a cop. I haven't forgotten they had a gun that day in the yogurt shop. The cops might have confiscated it as evidence, but if these guys were motivated enough to procure one weapon, they could have another. With that in mind, I'm watching their body language and backing toward the stairs while they continue to taunt me. Pride won't let me run, plus I think they would be more inclined to come after me if I did.

Stay calm. Greer is in my ear, telling me to get my ass upstairs. For once, I listen, my throat burned raw as I move upward at a fast clip. They continue calling me names as I go, and when I reach the second floor, my parents' elderly neighbor is standing in his doorway, a television flickering behind him.

"Everything all right, Danika?"

"Yes, Mr. Leary," I reply, keeping my tone light. "Just some kids acting up, but I think they're moving on."

He gives a bleary wave, and we retreat into our apartments. Once inside my parents' place, I secure the dead bolt, the knob lock and the rusty chain. Then I lean back against the door, breathing until my pulse returns to normal.

First thing in the morning, I'm going to file a police report. I have to. I was stupid enough once to think I could handle these kids on my own, but I've learned my lesson, and I've learned it good. Calling the school and making sure they're aware of the threat to my cousin is added to my mental checklist. There's one more item that should go on the list—telling Greer what just happened—but I hesitate.

This is exactly what he's afraid of. If they'd done more than threaten me downstairs, if I hadn't made it into the building fast enough . . . I don't really want to imagine the possibilities. Plus, they told me to watch myself, implying they're not going to let the incident at the yogurt shop drop. Greer is already paranoid about people he considers his responsibility being hurt. Or worse. He's mega stressed with the daily toll of his job. So stressed he practically let himself get hit with gunfire.

The memory of him lying on the ground sends a shudder through me. We made progress tonight. He showed up. He's been opening up to me. If I go directly to Greer, what happened downstairs could be the equivalent of upending a checkers board. He'll flip. If I've made any progress in convincing him that something real in his life wouldn't be disastrous, it would be obliterated.

So I'll compromise. I'll file the report at my own Hell's Kitchen precinct. If Greer gets wind, so be it. I'm going to the police. I'm making up for my lack of foresight last time.

Aren't I?

Yes.

Blowing out a breath, I cross to the front window in the living room and look down at the street. There's no one near the door or on the sidewalk. They must have moved on. Swiping my phone off the coffee table, I make notes while the incident is fresh in my head, writing down their threat word for word. When I'm done, my fingers hover over Greer's speed dial. One phone call. One call could ruin everything.

I don't make it.

CHAPTER 21

Greer

I stare down at my phone and see the missed call from Danika. It came through ten minutes ago while I was at yet another briefing, this time about a homicide. A body was discovered in the trunk of a car parked at a construction site near the East River, the night I left Danika kiss-swollen in the building hallway. That was Friday night and it's now Monday. I've been home exactly once to shower, change and catch a few hours of sleep before returning to the buzzing precinct. In that time, five calls from Danika have gone unanswered.

I've never known myself to be such a fucking coward, but right on the heels of the reminder she's training to be a cop, I found myself looking down into a trunk at more loss. More horror. And it was like that walk to the bodega happened to someone else. Or took place somewhere else. Another dimension, maybe. One I don't belong in with this nonstop ugliness stuck to the insides of my head.

It would be so easy to answer, let her voice soothe me. She would ask me how my day is going, and I would actually tell her. Her lack of judgment, her seeming refusal to disregard me as an asshole, makes me feel like I'm on solid ground. I could show her my worst and she'd still be there.

Every hour that passes without speaking to her puts me a little more off center. Which is all the more reason to ignore the calls. I can already feel myself getting too reliant on those breaths of fresh air she provides. They could get taken away at any time. In a snap. I know this. Why can't I remember that lesson when she's right in front of me?

And why am I so disappointed she didn't leave a voice mail?

She left one Saturday morning, short and sweet. *Hey, it's me. You never took your caveat beer for the trunk. Um. Hope you have a good day. Bye.* I definitely haven't listened to it nineteen times. Or deduced that her scratchy, muffled voice meant she was still in bed when she left the message. Definitely not.

I'm considering playing the voice mail a twentieth time before I have to take a trip to the morgue for an autopsy report. It would give me that extra push to get through such an unpleasant task. But just as I'm hitting PLAY, my office door swings open and in walks Charlie. He's wearing his academy uniform and looks so well rested and happy, I want to shout at him to run far and fast from this place.

Once upon a time, law enforcement was decreed our family legacy, and I never wavered in my expectations for Charlie's career until recently. I wanted him driven. Following in our father's footsteps, like me. Until I saw how happy he could be when the pressure to be alone and focus only on the job was taken off. He decided to juggle police work and a personal life and he's sticking to it. He would stick to it forever, because he's determined. Unshakeable. Maybe because he was younger when our mother left and the aftermath wasn't as obvious to him, he was able to maintain some semblance of optimism. Positivity that only continues to grow.

As always, when I'm around Charlie, I encounter a swift charge of guilt. For not confiding in him what I know about our mother. It's for the best, I remind myself.

"Hey." He falls into the chair facing my desk. "Busy out there. What's going on?"

I bite back the urge to lie to him, to keep the shittiness to myself. This is going to be his job someday soon, and he'll have to deal with it. "There was a body found in a trunk at a construction site by the river. We're tracking down leads, speaking with CIs."

"Who's the car registered to?" Charlie asks without missing a beat.

"Stolen. Registered to a man in Brooklyn, but there's no connection to the vic." Despite my reluctance to share too much of this gruesome world with my brother, I'm more comfortable discussing case details with him than anything personal. I hate the reason why. Charlie is going to be a cop. A cop like me, like Griffin . . . like Danika. Holding myself back from him to avoid pain later is so natural, it's hard to fight against. "I have an appointment with the medical examiner in twenty. Aren't you training today?"

"Yeah, I'm on my lunch break." He untucks a brown bag from beneath his arm—which I somehow missed in my exhaustion—and settles it atop the mountain of paperwork on my desk. "Those are leftovers from Danika's mother's party. Danika saved them for you, and it's getting too depressing seeing them in the fridge."

My stomach climbs up into my mouth and refuses to go back down. She kept food in her fridge for me while I was ignoring her phone calls? "Please tell me you didn't come here to talk about girls."

"I didn't, actually, it just kind of popped out." One beat passes. Two. "But since I've already brought it up—"

"Jesus Christ."

Charlie holds up his hands. "Hey, I just thought you'd be interested to know that Levi asked Danika to reschedule their date this morning." He whistles long and low. "Before inspection, even. The guy is after it."

A bout of seasickness hits me like a battering ram. My right eye is going to twitch itself out of my head. I'm going to flip the desk. "What did she say?"

"Danika?" He draws out her name, scratching the side of his chin. "What did she say?"

My fist pounds down on the paperwork mountain. "Don't play dumb with me."

"She said . . ."

Eight seconds pass while he elongates the word *said*. I know, because the tic in my temple is keeping time. "You will live to regret this."

His grin is unacceptable. "She said no."

I don't realize I'm leaning across the desk until relief slumps me back in my chair. It's like having a bucket of warm water dumped on my head. "You've made your point."

"Yes, I have." He claps his hands together. "I

only have one more minute before I have to head back, so I'm going to spend it telling you how not fucking awful it is to have a girlfriend."

"I'm not in high school. I don't have girlfriends. And please wrap this up in thirty seconds."

"I'm going to channel Letterman and do this countdown style, sound good?" Charlie gives a loud *ahem*, like he's preparing to sing opera. "Number three best thing about girlfriends? The jig is up, bro. Men like to cuddle, too. Girlfriends are cuddle magnets. Ever is the best one—she's fucking taken—but there are others. Go forth and claim your cuddle magnet."

"Get out of my office."

"Number two," he continues, undeterred. "When a girl is your girlfriend, other guys don't ask her out. And if they do, you have permission to kick their ass."

"I'm not going to beat up a recruit."

"He won't be a recruit after graduation, and number one . . ." He waits for me to stop raking both hands down my face before continuing. "You like protecting people. I like protecting people. Imagine protecting someone who loves you." He's serious for a few seconds. "You want to protect the whole world when someone loves you, because they believe you can."

It's possible while I was avoiding my brother, he became one of the most intelligent people I know. Doesn't mean he's right in this case, but I'm . . . proud of him. For something besides his eventual law enforcement glory. Still annoyed as shit, but proud. "This has been mind blowing," I say, standing and slinging my jacket around my shoulders. "I'm late."

Charlie has already slid halfway out the door, but his smug face is still located inside my office. "Think about what I said. And whatever you do, don't impersonate someone else on a dating website just to find out what she's up to."

I pause in the middle of zipping my jacket. "What?"

"Forget I said that. Bye."

When he's gone, I stand there for a couple moments absorbing everything he said, lateness be damned. Despite my irritation, my brother's words are already sinking in and making me think. I don't want to think about anything but my job right now, because imagining Danika cuddled up on my lap will inevitably lead to a bad decision.

You want to protect the whole world when someone loves you, because they believe you can.

Goddammit, Charlie.

That was the worst thing he could have said to me. How will I ever be satisfied for even a second in this life unless Danika believes that about me?

The answer is: I won't. But I'm not meant to be satisfied. I'm meant to be a cop who wakes up every morning, performs his sworn duty and doesn't set himself up to become one of the tragedies he sees every day.

I know that. I know it. But before I leave the office, I still shuffle around some paperwork until I find the police report for Danika's mother's missing bike. Maybe I'm not cut out for cuddling, but it won't hurt to make a few phone calls between meetings.

CHAPTER 22
— *Danika* —

W e're not taking no for an answer."
I'm under attack. It's Tuesday at five-thirty. There's a blonde and a redhead in the doorway of my bedroom, and they've invited me on something called a girls' night out.

"Are you crazy?" I set down the NYPD recruit handbook I'm studying. "I can't drink tonight. I have training in the morning."

"I won't be drinking," says Katie. "We can ply Ever with booze and toast our sensible decision-making skills."

Ever nods. "See? It's a win for all parties involved."

I'm tempted to say yes for a couple reasons. One, Katie has only started getting comfortable setting foot inside a bar. She lost her brother to a drunk driver, and Jack is a recovering alcoholic, so alcohol is kind of her nemesis. But she's making an effort to have fun in spite of being around other people drinking, like her friends, so I want to support her in that. Especially because Jack's support can only go so far before he risks slipping. I can practically feel him Jedi mind tricking me from the living room, begging me to go keep an eye on his girl.

Number two reason I want to go out? To distract myself from the fact that Greer hasn't answered any of my phone calls in four days.

To be fair, I've been calling him at times when I predict he's busy. Such as the beginning and ends of a shift when briefings are taking place. So I guess we're both avoiding each other. I keep reminding myself I have nothing to feel guilty about. I went to Midtown Precinct North and filed an incident report about being threatened outside my parents' building. My cousin's school is taking precautions and holding a faculty meeting about student safety, in light of Robbie being harassed and threatened, through me. There is absolutely no reason why I should be relieved when Greer doesn't answer his phone. But I am. Because I'm positive my lie of omission is going to come through in my voice.

He's been so honest with me that the whole situation isn't sitting right. And now we're not talking at all. Pretty ironic, considering I kept Greer in the dark so we wouldn't erase the progress we'd made. I'm starting to wonder if I imagined that progress in the first place.

"See?" Ever drops onto the edge of the bed, totally unaware of the crater in my stomach. "She's thinking too hard. A change of scenery is definitely in order."

Katie crosses her arms. "I concur."

Maybe they're right. I've been staring at this textbook so long, the words are starting to blur together. My cell phone is like a time bomb sitting on my dresser, taunting me with every second it doesn't ring. I'm getting psyched out knowing Greer is scheduled as our instructor tomorrow. A non-cop-related diversion might be exactly what I need.

"Okay, fine." I hold up both hands when they start to happy dance. "But I need to be in bed by ten o'clock. No exceptions. Sprints and takedowns are hard enough without a sore head." I come to my feet. "And I want Thai food first."

Ever slaps a hand over her heart. "I want Thai food, too."

"SCREW IT." IT'S 10:29 when I hoist my fourth gin and tonic. "I'm pulling an all-nighter."

Katie giggles into her Sprite and if I didn't

know better, I would think the carbonation is making her tipsy. Or maybe being ridiculous is contagious. That's exactly what I'm being. Ri-damn-diculous. But it feels so good to misplace my common sense for one night. For months, I've been on the straight and narrow so I could be in top form at the academy. Furthermore, I weathered the storm of Charlie and Jack falling down the romance rabbit hole. I can't even remember the last time I drank too much and acted irresponsibly. What a shame.

I mean, we're only two blocks from the apartment and *The Late Show* isn't even on yet, so this isn't quite the rebellion of the century, but lately it's what I consider letting my hair down.

My hair is down, coincidentally, curling in all the right places. Ever tossed a short-ish pink T-shirt dress at me from Charlie's room, so I've thrown that on with some wedges. We're sitting at a high-top table, and I've noticed some fellas at the bar looking in my direction. I'm kind of enjoying the attention, too, to be honest. Possibly because four cocktails, not to mention that wine at dinner, have put me firmly in the camp of being annoyed at Greer. How dare he ignore my calls.

"No, no . . ." Ever leans in, a chunk of blonde hair landing in her drink. "An all-nighter is not a bad idea. If you don't go to sleep, you can't be hungover. It's science."

I lean in for a sip and poke myself in the eye with the cocktail straw. "That makes so much sense right now."

"Am I to be the voice of reason here?" Katie gives a sharp sigh. "I never get to be the bad influence. It reminds me of when I used to play Barbies with my neighbor growing up, she always made me be Ken."

"Let it out." Ever says, one eye squinted. "Purge that anger."

"I am bloody angry about it." Katie sniffs. "Made me talk in a man's voice and everything, she did. All I wanted to do was brush Barbie's hair."

"Wait." A laugh builds in my belly. "I can't tell anymore if we're drunk or Katie is drunk."

Ever snort giggles, followed by Katie.

"Okay . . ." I push my drink to the side. "I have to ask. Did the guys encourage you to take me out tonight? Because they're worried about my non-relationship with Greer?"

"Uh, no." No mistaking Ever's expression. She's miffed. "*We're* worried about your non-relationship. The guys are, too, but this is about us. Me and Katie love your ass, too, you know."

Katie nods. "It's true. I love your ass."

I lean over and take a sip of Katie's Sprite to make sure it isn't spiked. "I'm sorry, I can just feel everyone in the apartment wanting to know the story. But there is no story. Greer doesn't want a relationship. And every time I think he's changing his mind, he backs off."

"He's been so good to Jack lately. Pushing him harder, where he used to just write him off." Katie shakes her head slowly. "That's proof he can change."

Ever seems thoughtful. "Charlie says Greer has always been kind of a mystery. When his partner died, he closed up even more."

I sense she wants to keep going. This girl talk is making me feel better in a way I didn't expect, so I gesture for her to continue. "But . . . ?"

"But." Ever stirs her drink. "Charlie had to come to terms with his mother leaving—the why of it—before our relationship could work. I know Greer lost his partner and took it really hard, but Charlie has no idea how Greer feels about their mother taking off. Greer won't talk about it." She shrugs. "I'm just wondering if it's part of the reason he keeps backing off when he clearly has it bad for you."

"So bad," adds Katie, looking a little wistful. "If he was Ken and you were Barbie, he would throw himself in front of the pink convertible for you."

A laugh bursts out of me, but it fades fast. I thought I'd gotten to the middle of Greer's issues, but maybe I'm still on the surface. Maybe not answering my calls is his way of telling me I'll never get past his tough outer layer.

"I didn't mean to upset you," Ever says, her eyes concerned. "Should we do a shot?"

"You didn't upset me," I say too quickly. "And yes to a shot. But we better cut Katie off before she starts in on the Barbie Dreamhouse."

Katie sits up straighter. "There was enough room for Ken to live there, too. Quite comfortably."

Just as Ever signals the waitress to order shots, my phone goes off on the table. I have it flipped over so I can't see the screen, and for a second, my belly fills with helium thinking it could be Greer. But no. It's my mother. Because this is my life.

"Hey, Mom."

"Oh, you're awake. I was just going to leave a message. Danika, did your father tell you—" She breaks off. "Where are you?"

"I'm just out for a late dinner with Ever and Katie."

It's not a lie. We had dinner. My mother is old-school, though, and I'd like to avoid a speech about the dangers awaiting impressionable young ladies in drinking establishments. She'd be offering me up as next week's prayer request at church.

"Dinner. O-kay." She might be old-school, but she isn't dumb. I'll blame my forgetting that on the gin. "Well, I just wanted to let you know . . . my bike is back. Your lieutenant dropped it off himself a few hours ago. I was out shopping, but your father was here." My father shouts something in the background, but it's muffled. "Your father says the lieutenant has an honest handshake. Honestly, Danika, this man I married is crazy."

"No, I . . . yeah. He probably does have a good handshake," I murmur. My lips are having a hard time moving, because my brain is taking up all available energy. Oh, also my heart. There's a lasso tightening around it, squeezing, squeezing. "He's . . . Greer just showed up with your stolen bike?"

"Yes."

Ever and Katie lean toward me with dropped jaws.

"Did he say anything?"

My mother relays the question to my father at ninety decibels. After a pause and more muffled shouting from my father, she's back. "He told your father I need to stop propping open the door downstairs. I'm not so enamored of your lieutenant anymore."

Oh God. Now I'm thinking of Greer lecturing someone, all stone-faced and gruff. I'm tingly all the way down to my toes. My hand is wedged between my breasts and pressing down, trying to connect with my rapid-fire heartbeat. "He's not my lieutenant."

Ever and Katie snort. So does my mom. "You think the police give this kind of service to everyone? What kind of a stubborn girl did I raise?"

Properly chastised, I blow out a breath, already knowing where I'm going tonight. Spoiler: it's not my own apartment. "I'll talk to you later, Mom. Go out and start your rides again tomorrow."

"I'm planning on it. Good night."

"Night."

When I hang up the call, Katie is trying to subdue a smile and failing. Ever's fingers are flying across the keypad of her phone like her life depends on it. "Who are you texting?"

"Who do you think?" She blows a stray blonde hair out of her face. "I'm texting Charlie to get his brother's address for you. Unless you already have it?"

"No." She raises an eyebrow at me. I wave a hand at her phone. "Well, keep going."

CHAPTER 23
Greer

When my door buzzer goes off, I assume it's another addition to the book club meeting. We're almost finished with our discussion of *The Lost Order*, but since a lot of us are on cop schedules, it's not unusual for people to arrive late. There's a standing agreement that the meetings are casual and joining the conversation is not mandatory. But because the group counts as department-mandated therapy for a lot of the members, being present is necessary so I can sign off on their paperwork.

In the two years I've been running the book club, I've started to notice a cycle. Newcomers hate every fucking second of it, because they don't believe they need therapy. I've been there myself, after Griffin lost his life. Hell, I'm scheduled to meet again with a department therapist later this week about discharging my weapon. Not even running the book club can get me out of that appointment. Being one-on-one with a doctor makes cops edgy, but the group setting can be even more intimidating. It's one thing to admit weaknesses to someone you only have a temporary relationship with, but it's a whole other animal discussing it with colleagues.

It takes about two meetings for newbies to realize no one is watching them like a lab rat and no one is going to make them sing "Kumbaya." Frankly, I don't care if they join the discussion at all. As soon as they sense that, the truth comes out. And that truth is this: Every New Yorker has an opinion, and keeping it to themselves is the equivalent of Chinese water torture. Those opinions extend to books, too. Some of the most vocal members were quiet and skeptical in the beginning. Now I can't even wrap these meetings up by midnight sometimes, because everyone has to put in their two cents.

Being that a retired detective and a rookie cop are currently in a heated discussion about the protagonist's motivation, I deem it safe to get up and buzz up the late newcomer. I hold the button down and crack my apartment door, intending to return to the group of eleven cops . . . but instead of heavy male tread coming up the stairs, I hear a hollow clacking sound, so I decide to wait at the door and see if I buzzed in a trespasser by mistake.

Just like everything I've encountered since Friday night, the obvious fact that a woman is approaching makes me think of Danika. I've thought of her so much, I think I'm dreaming her when she appears at the end of my hallway. Imaginary or not, she looks like a goddamn meal coming toward me on a conveyor belt. No, not a conveyor belt. Those legs are bringing her my direction, and they're smooth, long and sexy. There's way too much of them showing, though, so it better not be Danika.

It's her.

No more denying it when she's ten yards away, striding like a runway model, jiggling her gorgeous tits all over the fucking place.

"Where's the rest of your clothes?" She sways to a stop in front of me, and I check the urge to tackle her. Just tackle her, get my mouth suctioned to a strategic spot on her body and ask questions later. My palms are sweating, my dick is getting chubby in my briefs. I'm about to demand again what the hell she's thinking walking around in a T-shirt, but the sharp, sweet smell of liquor hits my nose. "Have you been drinking?"

"Where are your clothes? Have you been drinking? I barely get past the shock of her mimicking my voice before she keeps going. "Oh no. Don't you pull this Grim Reaper act with me." She plants her index finger between my pecs. "I'm on to you, Lieutenant."

Yeah, she's had a few drinks. And I really want to demand an explanation. Who was she with? Did she use a safe method of transportation to get here? But I want to know what she means even more. So I'll save the third degree for later. But it's coming. "You're on to me?"

"Uh-huh. Look at you. Showing up and dropping bikes and brownies off all willy-nilly. Making me cancel my dates." Her hips are so loose, it looks like she's dancing every time she shifts side to side. "How did you find the bike, anyway?"

Just like the time she asked about my stamps escapade, I can't help but feel somewhat self-conscious revealing the lengths I'd go to to have her pleased with me. "It took me about two hours of searching the for-sale section on Craigslist."

Her lower lip pops out. "Why didn't I think of that?"

My gut knits tight. "Even if you had thought of it, Danika, you wouldn't have gone to reclaim the bike at the suspect's apartment alone. Right?"

She toes the hallway floor with those fancy shoes. "Did you go alone?"

Is she worried after the fact? About *me*? "No, not even I would go alone."

A silence passes where she seems to have a hard time looking at me. "We're getting off the subject." She ambles closer. Close enough that I could count her eyelashes. "I'm on to you, Greer. You can ignore my phone calls. You can ice me at the academy or refuse to stay over for pizza. But the proof is in the pudding. So."

Jesus, I missed her. "So."

"That's right." She looks left and right down the hallway as if it just occurred to her I might have curious neighbors. "Are you going to invite me inside or not?"

"That depends. Have you read *The Lost Order*?"

"*The Lost*—" Color drains from her face, and I take that as my cue to step aside. When I turn to look over my shoulder, I'm not surprised to see the meeting has ground to a halt in favor of listening to the half-drunk girl shouting at me in the hallway. Eleven sets of shrewd cop eyes are watching the scene unfold with nothing short of rapt interest and amusement. The rules dictate that I should send Danika home. She's one of my academy pupils, and while I doubt anyone here tonight would report me for having a relationship—physical or otherwise—with her, I've always acted above reproach. I set the example.

The rules mean nothing with Danika standing in front of me, though. I'm nervous I'll have
nothing she likes to eat—and that's about it.
When did I throw out the textbook I used to follow to the letter? I'm pretty damn certain the
reason is wobbling on a pair of fuck-me shoes
outside my door. And I know that because since
she appeared at the end of the hallway, the
tightness in my muscles that's been building for
days has turned to liquid. I'm standing inside
my home, but my home feels like it's in front of
me, not behind. Here she is. She comes back. I
can already feel my guard dropping, and shit,
it's such a relief.

Danika, on the other hand, is staring at my
living room full of cops looking like a nun who
just took a wrong turn into Burning Man. "I'm
sorry," she whispers. "I'll just go."

Go? She spins on a heel to leave, and my heart
slingshots up into my throat. "No." I reach out
and catch her arm. "No. Come in. Please."

"I—I can't." Her brown eyes are incredulous.
"You're my instructor. We're not supposed to be
together."

I know she's referring to the academy rules, but
her stringing those particular words together is
like a gut shot. I've been ignoring the proof that
there's something I can't bury going on between
me and Danika. But my outrage over her saying

out loud we can't be together seals it. I'm done avoiding her. I'm done burying what she makes me feel. Hell, it's not working anyway, is it? When I dropped off the bike to her father earlier tonight, I spied some family photo albums on the living room bookshelf and almost offered to make a trade. A picture of Danika's college graduation for the bike. How about it, Pops? I've got it bad. *Worse* than bad. I've been an asshole to this girl that I'm fucking nuts over, but she came over despite my attempts to shuffle her aside. I don't want to hurt her anymore.

The opposite of hurting her is trying to make her happy. As in, an ongoing project. Can I let go of my caution and do that? I won't know unless I try. Getting her inside is the first step.

"You're going to have to trust me on this." I sigh over her skeptical expression. "I've built enough of a reputation, Danika, that if I was called to the floor over an inappropriate relationship with a recruit, my superiors would know it was a special circumstance." I swallow a mallet. "You are a special circumstance. I'd take that slap on the wrist just to have you yell at me again that the proof is in the pudding."

She tugs her arm away. "I don't feel special when you ignore my calls."

"I'm sorry." I take her fisted hand and press it up against my heart. "'Hey, it's me. You never took your caveat beer for the trunk. Um. Hope you have a good day. Bye.'"

Her brows draw together. "What's that?"

"It's the voice mail you left me on Saturday morning. I've listened to it more than is considered healthy, all right?" I can't believe I just told her that. "A car alarm goes off outside toward the end, and I'm pretty sure it belongs to a late model Lincoln."

"That is such a weird way of trying to change the subject."

"Yeah." I uncurl her fingers one by one and lay them flat on my chest. "You hoped I had a good day, right? I didn't. Honestly, baby, I haven't had a good one since the last time I saw you." She still doesn't say anything, so I go for broke and let it all hang out. "Danika, you're . . ."

"What?"

"You're the best part of my days."

I don't know what reaction I expected, but it wasn't suspicion. "Okay, who are you and where did you stash the lieutenant?"

And that's what I get for trying to be romantic. Without waiting for more sass to come out of her mouth, I stoop down and throw her over my shoulder. Before I turn around, I make sure the dress is covering Danika's ass and a good portion of her thighs. "You—w-wait." She slaps the back of my leg. "Did you mean that?"

"You lost your chance to find out," I lie, nudging open the door to my apartment and marching inside with a sputtering Danika. A couple of the older group members stand up, obviously trapped between trusting me and wanting to provide Danika with assistance, but I sit them back down with a glare. My kitchen is located just off the living room, so they have a front row seat to me pulling out a stool for Danika and parking her caboose on it. "Don't move until I'm finished." She opens her mouth, clearly ready to launch a protest, but I open my drawer and retrieve a Snickers bar, hesitating a moment before placing it in her hand. "Here."

"Here?"

"Yes." I point at it, like we both don't already know what object I'm referring to. "I bought it in case you showed up."

"You bought me candy?"

Christ, she's actually in my kitchen. When I pictured this happening, she walked in of her own free will, but this is no time to split hairs. "Do you like candy?"

"Yes."

"Then, yes, I bought it for you."

She picks up the Snickers and examines it. "How drunk am I?"

Is this going terribly? I can't tell. I have nothing to judge it against. But I know I'm anxious for everyone to leave so I can focus on having her here. We might be snapping at each other, but I'd rather bicker with Danika than do damn near anything. "Can you just stay while I wrap up this meeting, please?"

It takes her a moment to nod. "Yes."

She's so flushed and wide-eyed—like she's seeing me for the first time—my need to kiss her turns fucking unbearable. "I want you here."

"I want to be here."

CHAPTER 24

Danika

Whoa. *Invasion of the Body Snatchers: Manhattan Edition*, much?

For the twenty minutes it takes Greer to end the book club meeting, I'm glued to the stool. Not because I'm riveted by the conversation, although it sounds like an entertaining book, but I'm mostly in awe of Greer. He has these guys on a string. It's incredible to watch. I'm not a cop yet, but I know abrasive law enforcement personalities. I can see how easily Greer could lose them. One too earnest question or encouragement could shut them down. But they never do because Greer is . . . brilliant. He maneuvers them into a discussion without them realizing, getting even the most closed-off men to share their opinions. I wonder what he's like in an interrogation room. Quietly dynamic, the way he is at everything else.

Seeing him in this superstar capacity is almost too much right now. I'm barely recovered from his repeating my voice mail back word for word. From him telling me I'm the best part of his day. I'm still not convinced I didn't dream him saying those things. At least until his eyes cut through the crowd of men and find me in the kitchen, making promises. Hot, hungry ones. Sweet ones. I don't know which I want more, but I'm greedy for both. All. I had no idea what to expect coming here, but it wasn't this new version of Greer.

Careful what you wish for, right? I made the decision to not bow out easily after Greer told me he doesn't do relationships. And the serious reason behind why. Now I'm being hit with the full force of the lieutenant when he wants something. Me. I'm almost scared to be pinned by the weight of that drive. Scared and anxious to find out how it feels.

There's a lot of curiosity thrown my way when the cops file out of the apartment, each of them stopping to have paperwork signed by Greer at the door. Don't mind me, I'm just the rapidly sobering girl munching on a candy bar, drooling over the flex of your book club leader's biceps. Nothing to see here.

Seriously, though, where else am I supposed to

look? I've never seen him dressed so casually, in jeans and a worn-in white T-shirt. He's wearing boots, but they're a buffed brown color, so different from the shiny, intimidating black of his uniform pair. When he props an officer's paperwork against the doorframe and lifts the pen to scribble something, his shirt lifts, and I see a hint of black hair, curling down the center of a ripped stomach. Mother of God. If I hadn't shown up, would he have stripped it off, unzipped his jeans and . . . rode his palm down that strip of hair, sliding it into his briefs?

It's a good thing I promised to stay on the stool, because if I tried to stand up, I'd faint at the imagery of Greer stroking himself in nothing but that touchable white shirt. *Keep chewing and think pure thoughts.* At least I've got one portion of that mental command covered. I've just popped the final bite of Snickers into my mouth when the door closes behind the last person, leaving me and Greer alone in the apartment.

Is this the part where we bang like bunnies? After the way he's been checking me out, I'm expecting him to take me right here on the stool, muttering filth in my ear while I try not to orgasm after a split second. Instead, he saunters into the kitchen like a king on vacation at the seaside, takes me by the hand and leads me to his bedroom. All without saying a word.

He flips the light on, revealing a pretty basic setup. White walls, wooden floors, one window, a ceiling fan. But it's not standard because that's the bed where Greer sleeps. It's been tucked and smoothed like an Army sergeant would be inspecting it. There's a softness to it, though. A blue flannel comforter, a gray sheet folded over at the top, white pillows. It's king-sized and comfortable-looking, despite how rigid his bed-making technique makes it seem. It's a lot like Greer, this bed.

I feel him watching me, but I'm not prepared for the intensity with which he's studying my reaction. "Do you ever sleep late on your days off?"

A slight head shake. "No."

My mouth feels dry and clumsy. "That's a shame. It looks comfortable."

"You'll sleep in it tonight with me."

A shiver snakes up my back. "Are you asking me or telling me?"

His jaw ticks. "You want the truth?"

"Yes."

"I'm telling you."

Dammit, I really shouldn't let him get away with that. I would normally hand a man his nuts in an envelope for presuming to tell me where I'm spending the night. Demands coming from this man are unlike anything else, though, because we've created this dynamic together. He's making them because he needs to. And he knows I want him in the lead, too. Still, there's a point at which he takes charge and we're not there yet. I need that distinction. We both do. "I'll reserve judgment," I say, finally. "Do you want to . . . turn in now?"

I can see the outline in his jeans, so I'm surprised when he shakes his head slowly. "Let's watch some TV." He turns and pulls a folded, navy blue shirt out of his dresser, handing it to me. "You can sleep in this."

I nod, thinking he's going to leave the room and let me change. But he doesn't. No, he strips off his own shirt and goes to work on his belt. Now that I'm under six-pack hypnosis, the shirt slips out of my fingers and plops on the floor. Rushing to pick it up, I vow to stop drooling over his brick shit-house body and fail. Fail so hard. He's smirking by the time he drops his jeans, leaving him in nothing but tight black boxer briefs. Oh my God, the leg holes are straining to contain his thighs. Don't even get me started on that dead center part of him. It's like he's smuggling a torpedo. "That's all you're wearing to watch television?" I croak.

He winks at me and leaves the room.

Forget *Invasion of the Body Snatchers*, this is *The Twilight Zone*.

Taking deep breaths to relax myself, I kick off my shoes and drape myself in soft, navy blue cotton, which ends just above my knees. After a quick check of my makeup in Greer's tiny bedside mirror, I go to join him in the living room. The television is already on, and he's watching the news. Of course. But I know when he senses me coming because his back muscles flex, and he changes the station to a late night talk show.

I slide between Greer and the coffee table, intending to park myself beside him on the couch, but he snags me by the waist and draws me down on his lap. There are a few charged seconds where neither one of us moves, but the pace of our breathing goes haywire. I struggle not to moan when he plants his open mouth against my ear and hums, the vibration going straight through me. "I figured we could find out what all this cuddle talk is about."

"Is there a lot of talk?" I wheeze the question, and I don't even blame myself. Who could think straight with the hot muscular flex of his thighs under their butt? "I haven't heard anything."

"Good." The fingers of his left hand thread into my hair and tug, just enough to ease my head back. "I don't want anyone talking to you about cuddling but me."

"Oh really?" Prickles plague the back of my neck. "Who was talking to you about it?"

He's quiet for a beat, his breath slowing at my ear. "Could you really get jealous over me?"

No sense in lying. The decorated lieutenant would see right through my deception, let alone the man beneath who I've already humbled myself in front of. A man who already knows I can be stubbornly independent, to my own detriment. But maybe I tell the truth simply because I want him to know. "Yeah. I could."

His tongue drags up the side of my neck, as if he's rewarding me, and I'm already so wet, it's embarrassing. "Since we're putting our jealousy out in the open," he begins in a low rumble. "Who were you with tonight?"

"Just Ever and Katie."

An approving sound, followed by another slow glide of his tongue, right up to my earlobe. "Did they try to talk you out of coming to see me?"

The note of worry in his voice makes me wish I could see his face. "Ever is the one who texted Charlie for your address. They were prepared to drag me here."

He pauses. "Really."

"Really. They know I wouldn't waste my time on you if there wasn't a good reason. Even if you irritate me sometimes." There's a warm sound in his chest, like a big lion purring, and I gasp as his teeth nip at my neck, his mouth tracing up into my hair and messing it around. "What I was . . . there was something I—I was going to say—"

My mouth is captured by his in a long, suctioning kiss, but it's too short. It's too short, but when I find myself tucked into his lap in nothing short of the world's most amazing cuddle, I find it very hard to complain. "What was it?" Greer prompts me, his thumb stroking my bottom lip.

"Um. My mother's bike. I bought it for her because she's used to a lot of sunshine. But she wasn't getting enough in the apartment, you know? I could see she was getting depressed, and her skin didn't look healthy. The doctor said she needed exercise, so I took a chance on the bike and it did wonders." Finally, we're face-to-face so I can look into his eyes, and I find them concentrating on my every word, analyzing, making notes. "So it was a really big deal that you found her bike and returned it. I don't know when I could have afforded another one, and it just really means a lot to me. Thank you." Concentration lines form between his eyebrows, his palm curves to my cheek, then slides back into my hair, like he's testing himself, experimenting with me and what certain new touches feel like. How I react to them. It's almost enough to distract me from what I'm saying. "I was going to come here and say that. Thank you. Just so you knew I meant it. I didn't want to leave it in a voice mail."

"I like when you leave voice mails."

"You're welcome. That's what you're supposed to say here."

He makes a sound in his throat. And I guess that is that.

I lay my head down on his shoulder and take a deep inhale of his skin. No-nonsense soap, sweat, spearmint gum. It doesn't feel like our first time cuddling in terms of how our bodies curve together. But the beating of his heart against my shoulder, the steady rise and fall of his bare chest, is so new. Up close, I can see all the individual hairs on his chest, the dark whorls of them that grow concentrated at his belly button and vanish below my hip. His erection is tucked between the cheeks of my ass, but he seems determined to pet every inch of me, and I'm totally content to let him. He's so warm.

A yawn catches me off guard, but I shake myself to keep my eyelids from drooping. "What's your verdict on cuddling?"

His sigh shifts my hair around. "I think I'm fucked."

I turn my face into his neck to hide my smile. We stay like that for a few minutes, Greer trying to covertly sniff my hair, his rough palms covering every inch of me in tender slides. There's a huge change happening here between us. My bones are resonating with that certainty. I know there are still obstacles to jump over, too, but surely if we've gotten to this point, we'll keep moving forward, right?

My eyes are half open, but a photograph across the room on Greer's bookshelf catches my attention. It's a family photo and while it's far away, I recognize a young Charlie and a middle-school-age Greer. There's no mistaking their legendary father, either, in his full police dress blues. The woman in the picture is unfamiliar to me, though. She's blonde and pretty. Petite. Each of her hands rests on her sons' shoulders.

"That's your mother in that picture?"

His hand slows on my thigh, for just a breath, before it keeps going. "Yes."

The mood between us is so easy, I should let the subject drop, but Ever's words from earlier tonight echo in my head. *Charlie has no idea how Greer feels about their mother taking off. Greer won't talk about it.* Would he talk to me, though? He's told me about his burnout, opened up about Griffin. And I'm beginning to understand this man. He left that picture out because deep down, he wants to talk about it. Even if he isn't aware of the need. I can't let the opportunity pass. "If she left, why do you keep the picture out? Isn't it painful?"

"That's the point." Against my shoulder, his heart speeds up. "It's a reminder of how easily people come and go."

That confession is like a gash in my side. This isn't about me, though. "I would never make an excuse for a mother leaving her children, but are you so sure it was easy for her?"

He's silent for so long, I don't think he's going to answer. "She had another family within five years. Kids and everything."

"What?" I straighten slowly, my chest filling with cement. "How do you know?"

"I went to see her when I turned eighteen." His eyes cut to the side, like he's seeing things I can't. Like he's trying to figure out how to explain the images to me. "My dad had been building a file on her. One night he got called in to work and left it out on his desk, instead of locking it in his safe. I copied down the address and . . ." He shrugs his big shoulders. "She was only down in Pennsylvania, so I got there in a few hours. I wanted her to give Charlie some closure, you know? Me? I'd found a way to ignore how I felt about her leaving. But you know my brother. He's different than me. He gets cut so deep."

"You're not different from him," I whisper, almost afraid for him to continue recounting the story. Intuition tells me it's going to be bad. "You just handle pain differently. That doesn't make your pain any less important."

It takes him a few seconds to absorb that. "She didn't recognize me." He laughs, but it doesn't contain any humor. "I was leaning against my car at the end of her driveway. She walked out of the house with a stroller and . . . she almost walked right past me. I'd grown a lot, but I never expected to explain who I was. And then she stared at me like I was a ghost. I just left." His chest lifts and falls on a heavy breath. "I've never told anyone."

My eyes ache from trying to keep my tears from falling. It feels like someone took a machete to my lungs. "I'm sorry." I look up at the ceiling and will myself to say the right thing. "There's no excuse for that. I can't imagine what that was like. I think . . . when people make huge mistakes or do things that they're ashamed of, their brains block it out. They want to outrun the fact that they're missing something inside themselves." I turn on his lap and frame his face with my hands. "You aren't missing anything. You were there to make a difference in your brother's life, which is a selflessness she'll never understand."

His voice is raw. "I didn't get the closure for him."

"No, but he got it for himself, I think. Maybe he needed to do it alone."

"Maybe," he says, his expression cautious.

"What about your closure?"

Before I have a chance to prepare, his gaze sears me like a brand. "I'm trying to get there, Danika. I want to get there for you."

I'm in love with Greer. Stupid, serious, might-spontaneously-levitate love. I know it without a doubt in that moment. My heart and mind are high-fiving in the vicinity of my throat. I can't get comfortable and forget about the obstacles—he's still wary of being with anyone, let alone a cop— but I think we're more capable of jumping over them every time we're together.

I hop off his lap and cross to the family photo, snatching it off the shelf. With Greer watching me like a broody, beautiful animal on the couch, I march to the kitchen and stow the framed shot in the freezer, closing the door with a resounding whap. Working my best runway walk, I make sure Greer has a good view of my body. Then I strip his shirt over my head, tossing it aside. As soon as I'm in reaching distance, I'm grabbed around the waist, the oxygen vacating my lungs as I'm thrown down on the couch beneath one very hungry lieutenant.

CHAPTER 25
Greer

F uck. I've never felt this light. Above the waist, at least. Everything south of my abs is heavy, heavy, heavy. I've got the beauty I never stop fantasizing about stretched out on the couch beneath me, nothing but a teal thong to protect her from what's coming. She's squirming around, arms thrown up above her head, tempting me. Turning my dick to stone. But I need a moment to savor her. Savor what she's done to me.

Christ, my chest. It's like someone took a shovel and scooped out all the ugly shit that's been dragging me down, taking any sense of gravity along with it. No, not someone. Her. Since the beginning, I've been compelled to tell Danika the secrets I carry around.

Was it my cop intuition or something deeper, more complex that shouted at me she would understand everything? That she would be the one who'd look at me without pity or judgment. Thank God for whatever sixth sense forced me to expose myself to this girl. She made it so easy. She makes . . . putting one foot in front of the other so easy. Even when I can't bring myself to answer her phone calls, the simple certainty that she would keep calling has been getting me out of bed since Saturday night. God, she's so persistent. So sure that I'm worthy of her effort, I think I'm starting to believe it. And covet my time with her, in return.

There's still that damning tug in my gut, telling me to safeguard myself. This thing I feel for Danika . . . it's turning into an all-out obsession. So much more than I've experienced in my life for anything. Or anyone. If she were taken away from me now . . . or God, down the road . . . I'd lose my mind. Literally. I don't know if I'd be capable of the day-to-day life I live now.

But I'm not giving those fears any goddamn consideration tonight. My body is demanding to be satisfied. My girl came here for pleasure, too, and I'm driven to provide it. Her gratitude for returning her mother's bike wasn't necessary, but it turned me into an instant addict. One who needs constant fixes of Danika's appreciation.

My mouth is already watering for the taste of her pussy, but when I create a trail with my tongue down her smooth belly, she stops me. "No, I want you . . . that way."

"What does that mean?" I bite her right hip, then kiss over to the opposite side. "You want to suck me off?"

Her back arches, mouth falling open on a moan. "Oh my God, just hearing you say things like that makes me—"

"Wet?" I glide my open mouth up to her tits, bathing one of her nipples with a warm breath. "Is your little clit getting swollen for me, baby?"

A shudder passes through her. "Yes."

"Sure you don't want me to lick it for you?"

She bites her lip and makes a frustrated sound. "No, I'm not sure, but I know I've been having some very inappropriate thoughts about . . ."

"You stormed my apartment and chewed me out in front of eleven cops tonight, Danika. I think you can manage to say it out loud."

Her nod is stilted, but there's nothing but determination in her fingertips as they slide down my chest, my stomach, before hooking in the waistband of my boxers. "I want you in my mouth, please."

I'm hit with a wave of hunger so intense, my teeth snap together. "There's a good girl." I lever myself up with a hand on the arm of the couch and ease forward on my knees. The move brings my cock an inch from her sweet, panting mouth. I'm straddling her face, my thigh hair catching on her dark curls. Now that her fucking me like this is a reality, I'm burning for it. The stroke of her tongue, the stretch of her lips. "Take it out."

Her palms travel up my thighs, her breath accelerating. I'm already groaning by the time she curls her fingers into the waistband of my boxers, tugging them down. My dick springs out as eagerly as I feel, coming to rest on her cheek before she grips it, leading my flesh toward her mouth. She's so wide-eyed and flushed when my tip sinks in, I can't keep pre-come from escaping, probably dripping down the back of her throat. And Jesus, the possibility of that makes me very aware we've crossed that line we drew in the sand. I'm calling the shots now.

With both of my hands planted on the couch's arm, I push my hips forward, growls rippling in my throat the deeper she lets me in. "That's what I need, baby. Suck my cock with your jealous mouth." A little flare goes off in her eyes when I hit resistance, so I stop, retreat and enter her warmth again, knowing how far I can go this time. Having those boundaries lets me move with fast, firm pushes until her mouth is treating me to a nice, hot fuck. "Fucking Christ, that's so good. You wanted this? Show me how bad."

She moans and circles the base of my dick in one hand, stroking me toward the suction of her lips. My balls are already hard as rocks, but when she closes her eyes, tugging on me with that greedy grip, I have to concentrate hard on not emptying them. She's the sexiest thing I've ever seen, sliding her lips up and down my inches, cheeks hollow when she drags up to the tip. When she lets me go with a pop and her tongue circles the head, my stomach starts to quake like it can't take the sustained pleasure, so I know, I know, I can't let her keep this up.

"Get that tiny fucking thong off," I growl, even though there's no way I can wait that long. No, as soon as I drag my dick out of her mouth, I'm yanking those panties sideways and thrusting into her soaked pussy. She screams in my ear, her nails sinking like razors into my back. My heart stutters at the possibility that I hurt her with my aggression, but I'm reassured when her knees dig into my sides. Like a rider spurring on a horse. Only I'm the one riding her. And I do it hard. "When you got into a cab and rattled off my address in your little, pink shirt dress, you knew this is what you were going to get, didn't you? A hard cock between your thighs. Didn't you, baby?"

"Yes. Oh my God. Yes."

"Feel it." I shove her legs wide and give a tight,

quick pound. "Tell me you love it. Tell me you walk around the academy in those tight pants wet for a fuck."

A tear streaks down her temple, eyes glazed over. "I do. I love it. Please, don't stop."

"I won't. I can't." Snug isn't an accurate description for Danika. She's got these tiny muscles that flex around my dick every time I punch forward, as if they're welcoming me. My sac is so full, I can hear the fat slap of it against her taut ass, and there's no comparing my fantasies to the real thing. I grow more and more crazed with each drive to release deep inside her. Mark her as mine so thoroughly, that claim can never be questioned or erased. That's when I realize I'm not wearing a condom. "Fuck," I grit out, my thrusts slowing but not stopping. I can't. I can't stop. "Didn't protect you."

She responds by taking two handfuls of my ass and jerking me close, a long groan breaking free of her wet mouth. I'm so unprepared for the mind-blowing sensation, the sight of her getting satisfaction, that more pre-come leaks from me, my entire body beginning to shudder with the effort of holding back every ounce of what I've got.

"Stop moving," I rasp, my stomach tightening. "I'm too goddamn close."

"It's okay," she whimpers, definitely pulling

me deep again and grinding her hips up, her heels finding a home at the small of my back. "I never miss my pill. Please."

Relief blinds me like two headlights, along with the impulse to fuck her until the pain is gone. "I'm clean."

"Me, too." She sobs, those nails burying in the flesh of my ass. "Greer."

"Hold on to me."

In the end, I can't tell who is holding on to whom. Our bodies are flush, sweaty and racing to the finish. I bury my face in the crook of her neck with a guttural groan, my hips pump hard, fast, almost angrily. I've never moved in such perfect rhythm with anyone. Not even myself. I'm better with her. We're better together. As if we're communicating in a way that's only native to us, our mouths fuse, our fingers twine together above her head and we go over the edge.

Her close-lipped scream is the sweetest sound I've ever heard. It's woven through with the relentless slap of my body finishing inside hers. Jesus, I'm shaking like a fucking leaf it's so intense. I'm choking on her name, over and over. "Danika is mine. This is mine. All fucking mine."

"You're mine, too," she says on an exhale moments later. Her fingers sift into my hair, her pulse hammers against my cheek and I take a moment to bask in those words. To bask in the fact that she's taking ownership of me. Can I let her have me completely?

Start with tonight.

Feeling her shift under my weight, I attempt to move and can't. I'm actually immobile.

"I think you finally killed me."

Her laugh is more like a purr. "You make it sound like I've been trying to kill you this whole time."

I think of her strutting past me in the gym, agreeing to dates with other boys and getting thrown into Central Booking. "Haven't you?"

"Maybe a little," she whispers. "I've decided to sleep in your bed with you tonight."

It's my turn to laugh. I'm getting more and more used to the sound.

Finally having regained my strength, I stand and lift Danika into my arms, carrying her to my bedroom. "However I get you there, baby, is fine with me."

CHAPTER 26
— *Danika* —

I was right about Greer's bed. Once he's inside the sheets, it turns into an extraordinary wonderland of warm skin, husky grunts and shoulder kisses. Falling asleep last night was almost as exciting as couch sex. Just kidding. But traveling to sleepy town with the lieutenant was . . . amazing. With two o'clock in the morning rolling around, he was adamant about me getting some sleep, so there was no more hanky-panky, but being soothed to sleep by the knock-knock-knock of his heart and a test drive of the spooning position could sustain me instead of oxygen. I'm convinced.

Okay, though. Okay. I need to slow my roll. There were no promises made last night. Yes, he went full caveman and called me his. Yes, he's apparently in the kitchen now making me break-fast if the smell of cinnamon is any indication. Very un-Greer-like activities all being performed for my benefit. That has to mean something. We . . . have to mean something.

Roll not slowed, Silva. Back it up.

I woke up in the middle of the night wrapped in a bear hug. My first reaction should have been euphoria. But the way he held me so trustingly made me panic. For a few ticks of the clock, I couldn't figure out why. Then it hit me. All the truth he laid on me last night and I haven't told him about those punks threatening me outside my parents' building. That makes me a deceptive idiot. After he confided in me about his mother, I don't want any secrets between us. So this morn-ing, it's all coming out in the wash.

I roll over and squint into the sunlight, begging my heart rate to chill. He's not going to push me away over keeping the incident to myself. He's not. For crying out loud, he ignored my phone calls for days. We've both done regretful things, right?

Sitting up, I stretch my arms up toward the ceiling and roll my neck, trying to shake off the stress. The clock says 7:49, meaning we have just over an hour before roll call at the academy. Just over an hour before Greer walks past me, scratching on his clipboard, and I have to pretend he didn't gift me an orgasm straight from heaven's gates? Holy God, my limbs turn to warm oil just thinking of the way he . . . used my mouth like he'd bought and paid for it. If he hadn't been cuddling me like a coveted treasure just minutes before, I might have been offended. I only wanted more, though. And what came after? I'm going to be running funny today. There's no help for it. I just have to pray nobody notices.

With a deep breath, I come to my feet in the sunlight and look for something to cover up with. Turning in a circle, I find his navy blue T-shirt from the night before laid out on the end of the bed, without a single wrinkle. He must have put it there while I was sleeping. The intimacy of that still has my toes tingling as I leave the bedroom and tiptoe into the bathroom. I take a quick shower and brush my teeth with a finger before creeping into the kitchen.

What I see makes me fall a little more in love with Greer Burns. He's shirtless, first of all. Sweatpants sit on his ass like they're in love with him, too, the soft material advertising both tight curves like a spotlighted billboard. He's got two hands poised over a pan on the stove, but he's leaning sideways to read his propped-up iPad screen. Are those cooking instructions? I scan the counters and, amid the mess, piece together ingredients for French toast. Oh my poor, pathetic heart. She's a goner.

Remember. You're coming clean this morning. No backing out.

"Morning," I murmur, glorying in the sight of his back muscles chasing after one another. "Need some help?"

He clears his throat like he's about to address the press in an official capacity. "When am I supposed to flip these over?"

"Hmm." I slide into the homey scene and take the spatula from his hand. "It's kind of a judgment thing. There's no correct answer."

His grunt is released just above my ear, but he's not touching me yet. "Excuse me while I break out in hives." My laugh turns to a shivering gasp when his lips meet my neck, followed by a tiny raze of his teeth. "How did you sleep?"

Apart from the twenty minutes of wide-awake worry that Greer would freak out over me keeping things from him? "Perfect."

Is that relief I sense in him? I don't have time to examine his reaction before a mighty arm snakes around my middle. It pulls me closer in degrees, our parts conforming one by one. And then we're standing at the stove like a smitten couple, cooking breakfast. Is this really happening? I'm afraid to breathe in case I dissipate the whole moment. "What about you?"

"I've never slept better." His arm tightens around me. "Is this good? Me holding you like this?"

"Better than good." I flip the French toast over, shocked to find it isn't burned to a crisp. Tell him. Tell him about the police report you filed. "Um. Greer—"

"I want to talk to you." His lips find my ear, kissing the hair that covers it, inhaling me like I'm a pie fresh from the oven. "I don't know how this works. If I'm supposed to ask you out on dates or piss a circle around you or what. But I want it to be a given that you're spending your free time with me. I don't want to lose my shit thinking another guy is going to claim your Saturday night. Or any night. I want it understood you're going to be with only me. And I'm only going to be with you."

I'm standing very still, trying to contain the rapture in my chest, but some of it escapes my mouth in a *hhhhuhhuum* sound. "What about when one of us is working?"

"Then we wait," he enunciates in his stern lieutenant voice, before sighing. "Look, I know it isn't fair. Asking you to go all in with me . . . when I'm still feeling my way in the dark. I could fuck this up. Being with you. There's going to come a time when you're in dangerous situations, baby, and I have no clue how I'm going to handle it." His lips move in my hair, his fingertips stroking my hips, across my belly. "I'm just asking you to be patient while I work through it. And while you're being patient, I'm going to be my usual impatient self, so you'll have to be patient with that, too."

My lips trip up into a smile. As bad as I want to be with Greer, I'm not starting down a path that isn't good for me. Thing is, I don't think he'd let me keep traveling down that path if it wasn't a healthy place to be. I have that confidence in Greer, and I want him to know that. I think he *needs* to know. "Sounds like a lot of compromising on my end," I murmur, sliding the French toast onto the waiting paper plates. "It's a good thing I get you out of the deal. That comes with a lot of perks."

Greer turns me in his arms, shining cautious amusement down on my upturned face. "Yeah? Like what?"

"Like you don't have to wait at stoplights, you just speed right through them. If I'm ever late for a hair appointment, that could come in handy."

His fingers dig into my ribs and I squeal. "Smart-ass."

The smile blooming around his mouth is killing me in the best way. "Okay, I guess it doesn't hurt that you do sweet things for my mom and help bail out my little cousin. You buy me candy and carry my beer." I think back to all the studying I did over the weekend. "And you let me win bets, even though I answer with the wrong radio code."

He tucks his tongue into his cheek. "Found out about that, did you?"

"Yup. Your secret is out." I loop my arms around his neck, which requires me to go up on my tiptoes. "You've got it bad, Grim Reaper."

"Wrong." He cups my bottom and kneads. "I've had it bad."

"My mistake," I breathe against his lips. "I agree to your terms."

I feel a breeze on my backside, then his hands are touching bare flesh. So much for breakfast. "Repeat the terms. I want to make sure you have them straight."

Between our stomachs, his erection waits like a reward, long and thick. If I was wearing panties, they would be soaked by now, but I'm not, leading to a slick slide of flesh at the apex of my thighs. "Um. My spare time belongs to you. If I'm asked on a date—"

Slap. A hard blow from his palm to my right butt cheek has me gasping for air. It's possessive. Just the right amount of chastising. A signal that Greer is the authority right here, in this moment. That he needs to be. And somehow it's exactly what I need, too. That definitive period at the end of our conversation. Before, when he took control, it was seeking. A test. Now that we've claimed each other, nothing feels wrong. Our positions are clear, and there's no time for doubt when pleasure is on the menu. "I don't want it to reach the point where other men feel comfortable asking you out. Shut it down before that happens."

I whimper as he rubs a circle over my skin to soothe the sting of his slap, but deep inside my belly, there are fireworks going off, sparks trickling down through my limbs. "What do you want me to do? Tattoo the words 'off-limits' on my forehead? No one is supposed to know we're together."

"I'm going to speak to my superior this morning about making an allowance."

My brain struggles to catch up with several things at once. The fact that being spanked gets better every time. And the revelation that he's serious enough about me to put his reputation in jeopardy. I'm quiet a little too long, though, because Greer dips his head to capture my glazed-over eyes. "Would it bother you if people at the academy knew? They might think you're getting special treatment."

"You better not give me special treatment."

"Thought you might say that." He tilts his hips, sliding his swollen arousal between my thighs, lifting until my feet are off the ground. Jeeezus. The stars winking behind my eyes must be visible, because he laughs. "I think you'll make an exception after hours."

"You bet," I pant, clinging to his bare shoulders. "Greer, can you—"

"Finish repeating back the terms." He rolls his body, grinding me into his lap at the same time. "The amended version."

Oxygen has almost completely deserted my brain. "My time belongs to you. Unless I want a girls' night—"

A withering sigh. "Fine."

"Or I'm spending time with my parents."

"Spending time without exhausting yourself."

"Fine."

"And I get to come with you when I can."

My heart squeezes. "I'd like that."

Greer walks us toward the kitchen table and sets me down on the surface, dipping his head to suck on a sensitive spot under my ear. "Continue," he rasps.

I heave a frustrated sob. "I somehow predict when boys will ask me on dates and run in the opposite direction. Happy?"

"Not as happy as you're going to be." His hands climb my thighs, taking hold of my T-shirt hem and lifting it over my head. "On your back."

After weeks of being instructed by him at the academy, my body is so conditioned to obey him that I find myself staring up at the ceiling before I know I've moved. My grumble is cut off, though, when his tongue travels in a long lick through my flesh.

"So damn wet, baby," he groans, pushing a finger into me. "You have my permission to forget your panties at breakfast whenever you want."

Oh God. Another wet slide of his tongue, his thumb rubbing my clit starts my thighs trembling. "I n-need your permission for that?"

His head comes up, eyes narrowed. "That's right." Before I can prepare myself, Greer hauls me off the table by the ankles, spins me and locks me facedown with a forearm. "You want permission for that. Don't you?"

"Yes," I admit, breathless, my internal temperature set to inferno. Maintaining focus is becoming impossible, but if this is where we set our course, I'm going to have a hand in deciding the direction. "But only if I give you permission for something in return."

A heartbeat ticks past. "I'm listening."

My brain pulls up the go-to image I've been daydreaming about most lately. "You can remember to wear your beanie at breakfast whenever you want."

His laugh is surprised, then pained. "I'm already annoyed at every man who'll take you down to the mat today. And you have the nerve to make me smile?"

Exhilaration pops along my nerve endings. Fast on its heels comes exasperation, love, need. "What if you . . ." I have to stop for breath. "Make me remember whose hands belong on me. Make me feel it then. And now."

My words. They make the Grim Reaper pant. "Yeah?"

I slide my ankles wider and lift my backside, my inhalations shallow. Being perceptive, making sacrifices, trying new things. That's what it's going to take to be with this man. I'm so game. No, I'm eager. "Please, Lieutenant?"

His low growl makes me shudder. "My girl." That open palm zings against my backside. "Mine." The next strike is harder, and he massages the spot afterward, his touch gentle, and the contradiction is so perfectly Greer, I hear myself asking for more. More Greer. "Show me some pussy," he rasps. "Before you go strutting what belongs to me around, give your man a nice look."

Lord. Oh Lord. My vision is a blur now, but my muscles are still functioning for the most part. Keeping my cheek pressed to the table, I loosen my back and angle my hips. And that most sensitive part of me gets the next slap. Whap. I'm so shocked, I release a cut-off scream that gets louder when his huge erection rams home inside of me. Pleasure explodes in my middle. My orgasm is an earthquake, sending cracks down the center of my foundation. Beneath me, the table vibrates, thanks to my juddering body.

And that's before Greer begins to pump. He doesn't take it easy, either, our thighs slapping together as he grunts and takes. I can't . . . I can't keep up with the euphoria. It's grabbing me by places deep in my belly I didn't know existed and tightening, tightening, like bolts. I don't think there's any way I can climax again, but the trunk of Greer's hard flesh is playing my clit like a violin, rubbing back and forth over the spot until I'm sobbing into the table.

"Please. Please."

His forehead presses into the crook of my neck. A sweet gesture so unlike the hands prying my bottom apart so he can thrust deeper. "I'm fucking yours, you know that?" He drops hot, panting kisses beneath my ear. "I just want to be yours, Danika."

"You are." I clench my teeth and sail over the edge again. "Greer."

"God, baby. Fuck."

I'm hurtling so fast and hard into pleasure, I'm barely aware of his mouth leaving my neck, but when I hear him shout a broken curse, when I feel heat inside me and that final, rough thrust, something primal comes alive inside me. Something I think Greer woke up.

Damn right I satisfy my man.

I love it. I love me with him. Us together.

But minutes later, with sweat cooling on our bodies, I remember the confession I was going to make about the police report. About the incident. And I definitely don't love myself for ignoring the voice in my head telling me to come clean.

Soon.

As soon as he gets a little more comfortable with me and realizes I'm not going anywhere. I'll tell him then.

CHAPTER 27

Greer

usually hate sunny days. Everyone else's good mood only amplifies my perpetually shitty one. Today, though? The light is beaming through the slats in my office blinds, probably turning the back of my neck red, and . . . it's not unpleasant at all. I'm kind of hoping I get called out of the station today so I can grab a little vitamin D. For the first hour of my shift, everyone who passed me in the hallway did a double take, confusing me until I realized I was smiling. Or my version of a smile, anyway. Kind of a suspicious lip slant.

What the hell is wrong with me?

More like, what the hell is right?

As if there's any question. Vitamins are not the

only thing that begin with D that I'm looking forward to soaking up today, either. Thanks to my grueling schedule and mandatory meeting with the department therapists, it's now Friday afternoon and I haven't seen Danika since Wednesday at the academy. It still wasn't easy watching her perform hand-to-hand maneuvers with other men, but it was significantly more tolerable since she'd bent over my kitchen table hours earlier.

It wasn't easier, however, keeping it to myself that she's mine. Once I do that, she'll probably have a hard time finding a volunteer to be her practice partner, but sue me if I don't cry a river. I'll help her practice if she needs it. In private.

My fingers still on the keyboard of my computer, heat sinking into my groin at the idea. Fuck, there are too many hours between now and when I see her. Is she out in the sun right now, taking her lunch break on the academy steps? Is she tipping her face up toward the light, sighing over how good it feels? If I was there, how would it feel to sit down beside her and pop a grape into her mouth?

Good. Too good.

We should keep our relationship undercover. There's only one week left of academy training before graduation. I'm anxious to make this thing between us legitimate now, though. I've never made a commitment like this before to anyone, but claiming Danika is important to me. No denying it. I'm possessive over this girl. I'm going to be uncomfortable until everyone knows I soothe her when she's hurt or sad now. I kiss that mouth. It opens for mine.

My superior emailed me this morning, informing me a decision had been made about me seeing a recruit with the department's blessing. We're in the clear. So there should be no weight on my chest or cold prickling along my spine.

There shouldn't be, but there is.

I keep thinking of her coming down my hallway during the book club meeting, intent on calling me on my shit. She was never more of a cowgirl than she was in that moment. Apparently it's possible to love a quality in someone and have it put you on edge at the same time. It's something I have to wrestle with—this fear of loss—but I'm not afraid to tell Danika what's worrying me and when. Not now, when I'm confident she'll understand. The words won't come out of my mouth sounding like Greek. And even if they do, she'll help me translate it. I trust her to do that. Just like she trusts me to tell her what's going on in my chaotic head.

Maybe being vulnerable to another person isn't so hard. Maybe it's really easy and I have to stop checking for potential flaws.

If I want to keep her, trying is the only way.

Ignoring the constant ripple of discomfort in my belly will get easier. I have to believe that.

The next few hours move slower than shit, my eyes straying to the clock when they should be on my work. But I can't help myself from mentally reciting Danika's schedule, imagining where she is. What she's doing. Of course, the day I need time to move faster, I'm stuck shoveling paperwork instead of working in the field. We brought in a suspect and got a full confession on our Jane Doe murder case this morning, leaving me to tie up loose ends and officially classify the homicide closed. Solving a case so quickly is satisfying, but someone still lost their life, the ugliness is still there. But the certainty that the ugliness will be replaced by beauty, by optimism, when I'm with Danika later is what keeps my fingers moving, my pen writing.

When I have an hour left of my shift, I know she's on the way to her parents' apartment, dropping off groceries and visiting her cousin's baby. I know because she left me a voice mail while I was in the morning briefing, telling me so. The way a girlfriend does. She even tacked on a little kissing noise at the end, which probably accounted for the smile I couldn't wipe off my face earlier. Eventually, her plans are going to include me. Often. I'm going to know Danika's heart, the thoughts in her head, more every day.

If I'm attached now, how will I be in a month? A year?

A knot of panic tightens in my gut, but I ignore it.

"Lieutenant." A hard knuckle rap on my door-frame. "Got a second?"

I don't look up from my work. "Come in."

The officer clomps into the room, rustling some papers. "This was sent over from Midtown North with your name on it, sir. Not for nothing, your name is on everything, because shit gets done faster that way—"

"Shit should get done at the same rate of speed, no matter whose name is on it." Finally, I look up and see I'm being addressed by one of the Ninth's freshest rookies and find myself softening, thinking of Danika. She's going to be a rookie soon, and God help anyone who's an asshole—like me—to her. Swallowing the sharp taste in my throat, I nod at him and attempt to gather some good karma. "Go on."

He shifts side to side, eyes glued to the papers in his hand. "Couple weeks back, you signed two people out of Central Booking. One of them was a . . . Danika Silva?"

I go as brittle as frozen tree bark. "Give me the papers."

"Sure." He slides the stapled documents across my desk and clears his throat, while the lines in front of me bleed together. "When the incident report was entered into records, her name dinged in the system. Along with yours." A small silence fills the room while chaos goes off like a cannon in my brain. "You've never signed anyone out of custody before, so Midtown North wanted to make sure you were informed."

Subjects made verbal threats to witness . . . subjects made an attempt to gain access to witness's building . . .

Threats. I zero in on that single word, and a storm begins to gather inside me. Big, dark thunderheads, ready to burst. The report is from six days ago. Six fucking days. Meaning she's been traipsing around the city all this time with *threats* hanging over her head. Without my protection or even knowledge that she needed it. If she'd confided in me, I would have intervened, but she didn't even give me that chance. Something could have *happened* to her, and I'd have been sitting in the fucking dark.

She'd had every opportunity to tell me. But that's not what bothers me the most, although it's a huge-ass sticking point. I told her everything, goddammit. Everything. She couldn't do me the same courtesy? On something this important?

"Midtown North made a visit to the homes of the subjects three days ago. Neither one of them were home at the time, and the supervision seemed pretty loose, on both counts." He pauses. "They haven't followed up since then, so I wanted to get your eyes on it."

My nod is so tight, I strain a muscle in my neck. What if she hadn't gotten away from these two kids? What if they'd harmed her? The last week never would have happened. I never would have held her, told her my secrets. Memories that never would have been made. And right now, with betrayal stabbing me in the gut, along with fear and anger, I wonder if I would have been better off. Not knowing what Danika feels like in my arms at night. Not knowing how she wiggles her toes after pulling on socks.

How many memories will I have to live with next time, if she's not so lucky?

"Everything okay, Lieutenant?"

In lieu of answering, I push back from my desk and snatch up my keys. My cop sense is chafing the back of my neck, but my gravity is so off-kilter, I can't tell if it's accurate. All I know is Danika is in Hell's Kitchen, where those kids who threatened her live—and she's alone. I could call her and confirm she's safe, but . . . she could lie. She has been for six days.

Six days. She could have already been gone for six fucking days.

CHAPTER 28
Danika

O h, this is going to be fun. My parents are out for an early dinner, so it's just me in their apartment. After stowing their groceries away in the fridge, I install some shiny, pink streamers on my mother's bicycle handles. I can't wait to get a laughing phone call from her later. I'll probably be occupied by Greer—pretty please, God?—but the voice mail will have to suffice.

Greer.

Waiting for Friday has *sucked*. Is it shameful that I'm pondering climbing into his car later wearing nothing but a trench coat and a smile? I mean, considering the warm weather, no one on the street would be fooled. But isn't that part of the thrill?

Like I need added thrills? I'm a walking hormone lately. I've been sleeping on my belly, because I'm constantly replaying the way Greer put me facedown over his kitchen table. Being in the position makes the fantasy that much hotter, and I've needed the fantasy to get through three days without him. Really not helping my oversexed imagination? The fact that my roommates could not be smugger about how often they're getting laid. Greer told me to invest in nose plugs, but earplugs are coming in way handier lately.

Jerks.

I'm anxious for more than sex tonight. I want to know how Greer's week has been. Want him to wrap me in those big arms and confide everything. I'm going to do the same. No more keeping what happened after my mother's party from him. God, he's going to lose his shit, but I'm ready. I'll let him rage, and then I'll promise never to lie by omission again. He'll have to understand. This thing between us is fragile, and I was trying not to break it before it could get stronger. That's all.

Look, I'll break out the waterworks if I have to. If that doesn't work, I'll cry while topless.

Bottom line is by tomorrow morning, there won't be any gray areas between us.

Blowing out a breath, I stand and run my fingers through the pink streamers. A small smile teases my mouth. A quick stop at my cousin's house to visit her baby, then I'm heading back to the East Side to meet Greer. My stomach is fluttering just thinking about the hug I'm going to give him. He's not going to expect it and—

There's a loud noise downstairs in the building. Like metal banging off cinderblock, followed by quick thumping. Footsteps? My gaze flies to the door of my parents' apartment, as if I can see through the old, painted wood. I've been living in New York City buildings all my life and slamming doors and people being inconsiderate of their noise level is just par for the course.

I'm probably still on edge over what happened with those punks, but a buzzing begins in my skull when I remember something. The building door was propped open when I arrived. By my mother's flip-flop. I know from experience how often she misplaces her keys—she probably wedged it in there so they could get back in after dinner. Dammit. That stupid flip-flop has become such a fixture, I barely noticed it when I opened the door, distracted by other things. Tonight, mostly. Anyone could be in the building right now.

Relax. The apartment door has an engaged dead bolt. It's fine.

"Aunt Maritza."

My heart picks up into a gallop. That's Robbie,

calling for my mother. Panic is sharp in his voice. He lives a few blocks away. Why is he here?

I'm already lunging for the door to let him in. "Robbie." I turn the dead bolt and open the door, reaching out to pull him inside. "What's—"

I only have a second to register Robbie's sweaty, disheveled appearance before I notice he's not alone in the hallway. He's running from someone.

The kids who tried to rob the yogurt shop. The ones who threatened us both. They're right on his heels. They're moving fast enough that I know instantly they've been chasing him.

"Shit." My pulse rumbles in my ears as I yank Robbie inside, attempting to close the door before the other two reach us. Is there another option? He's my cousin. I love him. I would sooner saw off my own arm than leave him out there to fend for himself. But bolting the door before those kids climb the stairs? My judgment is telling me it's a pipe dream when a booted foot shoves through the opening, preventing me from closing the door. "I've already called the police," I shout through tight lips. "You probably have less than a minute before they show up, so get moving."

Their laughter makes it obvious they don't believe me. "Fuck you. Open the door."

"Not happening," I say.

Over my shoulder, I see Robbie reach behind the couch and remove my father's baseball bat, which I'd forgotten was even there, since he's never needed it. I make a hasty motion for Robbie to get back over here and help me hold the door. Both of us are pushing on it now, and my feet are sliding, sliding on the wooden floor. Even when Robbie adds his strength, our opponents seem to have adrenaline and anger on their side. Maybe drugs. I don't know. But I can't hold it. They're coming in here, whether I like it or not, and I can barely breathe around the agony of that fact.

My parents. Thank God they're not here.

Greer is going to shit a stampede of bulls.

This timing is horrible. One more week and I'd have my police weapon on me. That's not the case, though, and I have to be as prepared as possible when they make it inside. Which they will. There's no holding them off.

Taking the bat from Robbie, I let go of the door without warning, hoping to make the intruders lose their balance. And it works. The dirty blonde one stumbles inside, going down on his knees. I lift the bat to bring it down on his back, but my swing pauses in midair when I see the gun. The one being pointed at me by his friend who's standing in the doorway.

"Please. Don't shoot." The words come out of my mouth sounding strangled. Is this real life? I was installing pink streamers two minutes ago. Now I could get shot?

Greer was right. Look how little it takes to die.

No. Irritation floods me. Fuck that. He wasn't right. I'm not going out like this. I can't. Tears blur in my eyes and clog my throat. My face is piping hot. I can't swallow.

"Look," I rasp. "I'm going to drop the bat and we're going to talk about this."

"There's nothing to talk about," the gun holder says back. "It wasn't enough that you called the police the first time. Then you called the fucking school and got us expelled."

"What? No. No, that wasn't supposed to happen." The conversation between me and the school administrator replays in my head, her telling me they would use discretion. These kids must have done something to force the school's hand, although would they have revealed my phone call? Don't they know the trouble it could cause? "I was only trying to keep Robbie safe."

The blonde one is back on his feet. "Well, you did a shitty job, didn't you?"

Gun Holder is angry, but his hand is shaking. He barely has the strength to keep the weapon up for an extended length of time. Should I keep him talking until someone else enters the building? I don't want anyone else to be in danger. If his arm gets tired, will he fire at us and get it over with? Or be embarrassed enough to bail and fight another day?

"Look, I'll come with you," Robbie says behind me. "Leave my cousin alone. She didn't do anything wrong."

"Robbie, no—"

"Oh wow," Gun Holder scoffs. "What a fucking gentleman."

"Nice try," adds his friend before turning around. "Get inside and shut the door, man, before someone sees us."

"Too late." I almost faint when I hear Greer's voice, but thank God I didn't or I would have missed what happened next. There's a blur in the doorway, Greer's hand moving at the speed of lightning to confiscate the weapon. Blondie tries to intervene, but Greer lifts both his weapon and theirs with ruthless efficiency, one trained on each intruder. "Down on your stomachs. Hands behind your heads. Do it now."

Their jaws are down by their ankles, probably a lot like mine, but they do as they're instructed. Sirens begin blaring outside, though, torpedoing me out of my stupor. My training kicks in, and I move on autopilot, retrieving the handcuffs from Greer's belt. Two sets. Neither one of the kids struggle as I cuff them, feeling Greer's eyes burning into me the whole time.

By the time I've finished my task, backup has

arrived, thundering up the stairs of the building like a cavalry. I comfort my cousin in the kitchen while the intruders are read their rights and Greer fills the officers in on what happened. I'm still soaring on adrenaline and residual fear, but not enough to stop dread from settling in. Greer looks like he's about to erupt. His eyes are bright, but clouded. His jaw and shoulders are bunched, the answers he gives clipped. I have the fight of my life ahead of me, and I deserve every second of it. How awful it must have been for him to climb the stairs and find the gun trained on me. Not as awful as losing his partner, surely, but terrible. Terrible enough for him to cut me loose?

A sharp pain invades my middle. I fight a battle to keep from doubling over as another officer takes my statement and Robbie's. Finally, the officers bring the perpetrators downstairs to load into their vehicles, thinning the herd down to me, Greer and Robbie.

"I'm going to head home," says my cousin, his face still pale as he turns to me. "I don't know what to say. I'm so sorry. I—I, they were chasing me, and I didn't know where else to run."

"You didn't do anything wrong." I pull him into a tight hug. "Text me when you get home, all right?"

He nods.

And then it's just me and Greer.

God, I must have some brass ones, because when he closes the door and turns that fury on me, I stand firm in the face of it. I don't look away, even though my stomach is in king-sized knots and I want to throw up. "Call your friends. Ask them to come pick you up in a cab." A deep groove appears between his eyebrows. "You shouldn't be alone right now."

Okay, so he's not wasting any time swinging for the fences. "I'm not alone. I have you."

His voice is hoarse when he responds. "No. You don't."

It's a sandbag dropping onto my chest. All the air rushes out of me. "I'm sorry. I should have told you. But—"

"You've learned nothing." Raw energy ripples through his frame as he strides toward me, taking me by the shoulders. Shaking me. "Being arrested. The probation. Everything I taught you, Danika. You didn't learn a fucking thing from any of it."

"Yes, I did." I'm frozen, head to toe, but somehow my mouth is working. Jesus, he's more furious than I could have ever imagined him. Furious and haunted. "I filed the report. I took it seriously. I just—I just—"

"You just what?"

"I knew you would drop me." I'm half screaming, half choking on my words, but I don't care. The only thing I care about is cracking the shell hardening around him. "I knew the second I reminded you I was a vulnerable human, you would freak out and drop me. And that's exactly what you're doing." I bat his chest with my hands. Once, twice. "You're so predictable."

Distress flares in the depths of his eyes, but it winks out just as fast. "Yeah? Well, so are you, baby. You want to carry the whole world on your shoulders?" He jerks his chin toward the door. "When the world turns against you, all you're holding is a bat and an ego."

"I have an ego?" Little red pinpricks float into my vision, my throat going tight. "You think people live or die just to hurt you?" I shake my head. "You're not just a coward, you're a self-centered idiot. I shouldn't have kept what happened from you, okay? I know it was stupid. Maybe I was even doing myself a favor, ending this now. Because sooner or later, the job would have put me in jeopardy, and you wouldn't have been able to handle it." I stomp a foot down on the floorboards. "Admit it. This was never going anywhere."

Greer flinches, some of the rage draining from his eyes. And his ringing silence is my answer, isn't it? I was a total fool thinking I could fix what was broken inside of him. The damage is too complete, and I'm clearly the worst person to patch it up.

"Thank you for saving me and my cousin again," I whisper up at him. "But please get out. Get out. It hurts to look at you."

Disbelief and panic battle it out in his expression. "You're throwing *me* out?"

The look I give him is full of meaning. "You were leaving anyway."

His hands tighten on my shoulders, as if he's trying to decide if he should pull me close instead of kicking me out of his life, but the decision has already been made. By me. Him. Both of us, in very different ways.

So I wedge a hand between us and shove myself away. Greer stands there and stares at me for heavy, breathless seconds. Those big fists clench and unclench at his sides, before he turns on a heel and strides for the door. As it closes behind him, I hear him on the phone with Charlie, telling his brother to come escort me home.

I flop down cross-legged right where I'm standing, the pain of loss and waning of adrenaline leaving me in the form of big, sloppy tears.

Game over.

CHAPTER 29

Greer

I'm drunk.

Just not drunk enough to blur the images in my head.

So I keep pouring. And pouring.

But the image only doubles, so the joke is on me.

When Griffin died, I only saw the aftermath. I was spared the fear on his face. I didn't have to participate in those precious seconds where he watched his life hang in the balance. But I witnessed both of those things with Danika today. Oh, she'd still had her temper. That refusal to give up. She'd been on shaky ground, though. And watching as she ran through her final options will haunt me for the rest of my life.

I'm so goddamn angry at her. So why am I sick without her in front of me? I don't understand. I've never wanted to shout at someone and hug them at the same time. She took a decade off my life today, but if she walked into the apartment right now, I would throw myself at her feet like I'm the asshole.

Jesus Christ, I am a mess.

I throw back a shot of tequila, my eyes squeezing shut in deference to the burn. Closing them is a mistake, though, because there's Danika, gorgeous and fierce, baseball bat raised above her head. Pulse hammering in her neck—I can hear it all the way out on the landing. Gleaming steel reflects in her brown eyes. If I make one mistake, or hell, a single sound, this kid is going to get spooked and pull the trigger. After being shot last week, I've never been less confident. With my girl on the line, I could make a fatal error. I could watch her die. My worst fear. It's my worst fear, waiting to unfold.

That realization is the last thing I can remember before my body sprung into action, refusing—refusing—to fail with Danika on the line. Thank God.

Failure is all I feel right now, though. My body feels like hollow, lead armor.

She needed me today. She was shaken up after

having a gun pointed at her. I could have held her and whispered comfort into her neck, but I left. That was my privilege as of a few hours ago. Not anymore, though. I'm choosing solitude over having myself flayed open every time Danika tries to be big and brave. No matter that . . . I love those things about her. Those traits are a damn liability, and she flaunts them without thinking of the consequences.

God, I wish I was still shaking her.

I wish she was underneath me, too. Touching my face while I stroke my tongue up the side of her neck. I could scold her while she's under me, in between kisses. Flip her over and spank her, soothe her, drive into her. All while telling her she almost killed me. Afterward, I'd make her apologize again. Then I'd apologize, too, for being predictable. For reacting exactly the way she knew I would.

Would those things have made me feel better?

I'll never get the chance to try. The decision is made.

This wound in my chest is going to scab over eventually. It has to. I can't survive like this. What's the phrase? Can't live with women, can't live without them? Truer words were never spoken. I can't be with Danika. But I can't fucking imagine my world without her. After such a short time, I'm already missing a limb with her gone. Imagine if the worst happened.

I just have to keep imagining. What if, what if, what—

There's a knock at my door.

And whoosh. All my resolve drains out through my ears. If it's Danika on the other side of the door, I'm going to make a fool out of myself. I should be praying it's someone else. But my heart is in control, and Danika is at the switch. So I stand and force myself to walk with an even gait, feat though it is. With my guts in my throat, I open the door—

And catch a mean right hook across the face.

There's a crunch, followed by pain, and then I'm staring at blood spray across my entry table, where I catch myself. My left eye throbs, my nose feels like it was stepped on by an elephant. Sticky cobwebs lace in patterns on my brain, muddling my thoughts, but I finally command my body to straighten and confront my attacker.

"Jack." Blood drips down to slur my words. "I was expecting you."

The recruit is looking at me with nothing short of disgust. The way I probably used to look at him. Amazing how fast tables can turn. "I told her. Told Charlie, too. You were going to chew her up and spit her out. No one listened."

Who the hell does this prick think he is? Coming here and spitting in the eye of my misery? In Danika's name, no less, which is something I'm supposed to do. I'm the one who makes people pay for hurting her.

No, I *was*.

Agony swarms in my ears. "It's not your job to defend her honor."

"Whose job is it? Yours?" Jack's eyebrows lift when I can't answer. Because I don't know who to listen to—my head or my heart. "Oh, you don't realize you lost her forever yet?" His scoff starts a pounding in my temples. "She's long gone, man. You might still be in limbo, but she's not hanging out for more of this bullshit. Danika might have taken a chance on you, but she's too smart to take two."

"I'm not in limbo. I'm doing . . . I did what needs to be done," I manage, staggered. The way we parted today seemed final, but we've been in so many arguments, I'm not sure I processed the difference until now. Jack's right. She's done. She gave up on me. "You've thrown your punch," I rasp. "Now go."

He stares at me in silence. "I think I'll stay awhile." Ignoring my dark look, Jack swaggers into my apartment, but he's brought up short when he sees the open tequila bottle on my kitchen table. His hands slide into his pockets, and he breathes in and out, before turning around and ignoring the tequila. "Look, before I met my Katie, I would have bloodied your nose and walked away whistling." I've never seen Jack serious, but he's deadly serious now. "I can't do that anymore. She forced me to deal with the shit in my head . . . and I'm thinking maybe it's my turn to pay it forward."

A scoff scrapes up my throat. "I've had enough forced therapy for the week, Garrett."

"Because you discharged your weapon."

Did Danika tell him? No, she wouldn't. Must have been my brother. "Yes."

Jack tilts his head. "So you've been completely open during those sessions?"

"What is this?" My hands shove through my hair. Had I been honest during the mandated therapy? No. I hadn't. I'd given the standard answers that would get my paperwork through and an early dismissal. Feeling jumpy, I go to the tequila bottle, cap it and shove it in my freezer. When I see the framed family photo among the frozen vegetables, placed there by Danika, I swallow a lump in my throat. "You go to a couple weeks' worth of AA meetings and now you're ready to diagnose me?"

He sighs. "Let me ask you a question."

"Go ahead. Blow me away."

I get the feeling he's bracing himself and realize too late there's a good reason. "What if

you'd died that day? Instead of your partner."
He pauses. "What would you have missed in the
years that came after?"

This punch is twice as powerful as the one he
delivered at my door. I'm staggering while standing still, trying to catch my breath in the middle
of my kitchen. My mind searches for an answer,
flipping back through almost three years and
coming up with nothing. Nothing since Danika
walked into the academy for orientation and
my heart started hammering. There are a few
snatches of moments with my brother, those
rare occasions I let myself spend time with him.
One memory of my father squeezing my shoulder
and telling me I'm living up to expectations.
Between those snippets of time, there's a gray
void. All those days spent going through the
motions, keeping a buffer between me and the
world.

I haven't been living at all.

"You can punch me now if you want," Jack
says, scratching the back of his neck. "I didn't
like asking you that, but hell if the hardest questions don't pull a head out of someone's ass the
fastest. I know it worked for me."

I'm stripped so bare, I can no longer keep myself from demanding what I've wanted to know
since he arrived. "Is she okay?"

He's back to looking like he wants to sock me.

"No. But she's the master at pretending she's fine. We're all taking turns keeping her company, which is annoying the shit out of her. Katie and Ever are on shift right now. Me and Charlie take over in the morning. Unless she murders us in our sleep."

She's pretending to be okay. That's so Danika, my ribs crank open another inch. "Thank you."

Jack nods. "I've got my redhead waiting for me, so I'll leave you alone."

"Good."

"After I say one more thing." He ignores my growl. "When the love of a lifetime gets dropped in your lap, you can either strap in for the ride or hit the brakes like a pussy. But if you decide to man up, you better be ready to work. Danika sets her mind to something, she accomplishes it. And right now, her mind is set on getting over you."

Hearing that, I'm done. I'm the boxer swaying in the ring with bloodshot eyes and a fractured jaw. A stiff wind could knock me out. "I'm ready for you to leave."

He makes a crackling radio noise into his fist. "Ten-four."

When the door closes behind Jack, the silence is piercing. It has been like this for years, and I never noticed it until . . . her. Before Danika swaggered into my life, I would have gone on like this indefinitely, assuming it was the better, safer route. And it is. I'm one hundred percent safe right now. Alone. I have the lowest chance of having someone I love being ripped away.

I do love her, don't I?

Jesus, yes. I think I loved her the first time she hit the training mat, squared her shoulders and got back up to do it all over again. She's mine. I claimed her. She let me. Then I shoved her away. All because she made a decision to prevent me from shutting her out.

I hear wheezing and realize it's me. Reaching toward the kitchen counter, I snag a dish towel and wipe the blood off my face. With the slight improvement of my vision comes the first slice of clarity I've felt since this afternoon.

Griffin lost his life, along with all the experiences he might have had. But I might as well have died with him. Unless I do something to change it. In three more years when I look back, what do I want to see, instead of gray fog where memories should have been made?

Danika. Me and her. In this kitchen. Walking along the sidewalk carrying beer. Sitting at her mother's kitchen table. In the grocery store. On vacation. Christ, I could take her places.

Hiding from potential loss is stopping me from being happy. More importantly, making her happy. There's nothing stopping me from trying, except me.

And the fact that she's already moving on.

Panic clashes with determination in my gut. I have to get her back.

I'm going to get her back.

I need her so much.

CHAPTER 30

Danika

When is the last time I rode a bike?

They say once you know how, you never forget, right? Too bad my legs feel like Popsicle sticks trying to turn the wheels, all graceless and wooden, as my mother and I pedal along the Hudson. Wooden is the state of my whole body, actually. I'm a square trying to fit through a bunch of circles. Eating, walking and carrying on conversations takes an effort. All I want to do is crawl under my bed and remain there until the passage of time stops this torture inside me.

Instead, I walked crosstown to my parents' place, as is my Sunday tradition. Not wanting to go upstairs where memories of Greer leaving me crying like a baby on the floor would hit me like a hundred-pound mallet, I rented a Citi Bike, instead. Since my heartbroken butt wants to hide from the world, I'm giving it the finger by taking a bike ride, instead. Stubborn dies hard.

I pictured myself with Greer today, one of us convincing the other to finally crawl out of bed and go out for breakfast. It would be awkward at first, making eye contact with the lieutenant across a legit table in a restaurant, but those tongue-tied moments—the swarm of butterflies in my belly—would be part of the fun, wouldn't they? I'd tease him, he'd grunt back, we'd quiz each other on favorite movies and foods. Maybe he would reach across the table and brush a curl out of my eye.

That was never going to happen. Not any of it.

Sunshine glints off the water, my vision making the whole scene blur. My mother's laugh floats back over her shoulder, tempting a smile from my mouth, but it collapses almost immediately. Oh man, he did a number on me, didn't he? I'm not so stubborn to believe I was faultless. I made a bad decision—one that locked Greer out. But was it so dumb of me to think our feelings for each other would stand that test? I'm ten million miles from perfect, but he already knew that. Wasn't he supposed to want me in spite of my faults?

Yes. So I'm going to put my head down, push

through the final week of the academy, barrel through graduation without making direct eye contact with the lieutenant . . . and put the Grim Reaper behind me. Keeping myself intact along the way is going to be a mega challenge. I'm in love with someone who dropped me like a bad habit.

Here's the thing, though. I'm stronger now than I was the day Greer bailed me out of Central Booking. I've learned a lot about myself. What I will and won't accept, how to let go of my need to control everything and most important of all, I'm not invincible. I have limitations. And I'm not going to forget those lessons, just because the man responsible for teaching them no longer wants me. That would be the ultimate act of stubbornness, and it's apparently where I'm going to draw the line.

My mother coasts to a stop, putting her right foot on the ground to stabilize herself. She lifts her face to the sun, closing her eyes to soak it in. I do the same for a while, but move us toward a bench when passing joggers start to grumble over us blocking the path.

"Are you ready to talk yet?" My mother snaps off her helmet and sets it on her lap. Carefully, she crosses her hands on top of the shiny, black surface. "That man hurt you, didn't he?"

I keep my face lifted to the sun. "Yes."

When my parents came home after the near-fatal invasion of their apartment, the cops were long gone, and I was lying on the couch. I explained to them what happened, leaving out the part about my breakup with Greer—hell, they hadn't even known we were together—but my perceptive mother continued to prod for more. I haven't been forthcoming until now. Maybe it's the change of scenery or I'm just willing to try anything to scab over my wounds, but keeping the hurt inside is beginning to be excruciating.

"Talk to me, Danika."

"There's not a lot to say." I plant my hands behind me on the stone bench. "I made the classic mistake of trying to fix a man. It didn't take. And now it's over."

She's quiet a moment. "It's not like you to give in."

"It's a losing battle," I blurt, before taking a deep breath. "Greer is . . . afraid to feel. Afraid if he lets someone in, he'll lose them. It wasn't an intentional test, but I threw the possibility of losing me at him way too soon. He didn't pass it. He wouldn't have passed it in five years, either. So maybe I just lucked out getting it over with early."

My mother turns to me on the bench. "So let me get this straight. Greer is staying away from you because he likes you too much." Misery clamps down on my vocal cords, so I can't answer, but she interprets my silence as a yes. Even though it's way more complicated than that. Fear, control and trust hang in the balance. "Lord, but youth is wasted on the young."

"Yeah. Maybe." I bend forward and brace my elbows on my knees. "It's not just him with the problem, Mom."

"Oh no?"

Her sarcasm isn't lost on me, but I ignore it, in favor of the pressure building in my chest. "No. I think . . . maybe it was wrong of me to expect so much out of Greer. I was holding back, too, right?" Finally, I take off my own helmet and sling it over the handlebars of my rented bike. "I hold back a lot. From everyone. When I'm stressed out or have too many responsibilities, I just keep my mouth shut. And I don't think I realized until now that suffering in silence hurts, instead of helps. I don't want to feel obligated toward the people I love. I just want to love them. You know?"

Her hand strokes the back of my hair, causing my throat to clog. "We're not just talking about Greer anymore."

I shake my head and look out over the water. There's already a loosening of the strings inside of me. Strings that have been tied and knotted in so many different locations, they've gotten tangled. Since I can remember, I've considered everyone else's problems my own. Mine to fix. It was my privilege to be counted on. Somewhere along the line, though, I pushed myself too far down the list of important things. While I was trying to be invincible, I started to believe it and I let others think I was, too.

But I'm not. *No one* is. If I want to be a successful cop, daughter and friend, it's time I start letting people in on my secrets. Stop pretending I don't have a breaking point. Because I do. Maybe I didn't hit it completely until Greer walked away from me. Is losing him the final lesson that's going to change things inside me? If so, as much as I want to ride twice as hard on my stubbornness to combat my heartbreak, I can't let what I've learned about myself go to waste. I won't.

"Do you think, maybe we could just do things like this once in a while? Do things together without any other commitments?"

My mother pulls me sideways, into an embrace. "I thought you'd never ask."

"What?" I ask, confused. "Ask to spend time together?"

She sighs. "Since you were a little girl, you've always needed a purpose. Something to focus on. Something to fix." Her body moves in a shrug. "I thought if I asked you to come over and do nothing, just talk or go for a bike ride, you'd tell me you were busy. To call back when I had a real problem." She shifts on the bench. "Don't kill me, but I broke that dining room chair on purpose, just so you'd have to come over. We like having you around. If I'd known my requests were making you unhappy, I would have stopped."

Oh, now this is incredible. Only my mother.

Only me, too. Because I totally understand her logic.

"I like being depended on," I murmur. "But it's okay for me to depend on someone else once in a while. Or just go ride a bike."

My mother hugs me tighter. "Good. Now we can do this every week."

"Don't push it."

Our bodies shake as we laugh together, but it's not long before what I've gained today reminds me of what I lost in order to learn something valuable about myself. How long will this lesson haunt me? If my heart feeling like it's being pulverized in a blender is any indication, there's not going to be a quick end to this pain. Here's hoping that being honest with myself, with others, will start to make it more manageable soon. So I can move forward feeling whole again, with some sense of closure.

As we ride back toward the Kitchen, Greer's voice floats into my ear.

I'm fucking yours, you know that? I just want to be yours, Danika.

This closure I'm hoping for? Yeah. Not likely.

Greer

Here's the reason I don't watch television crime shows. A case almost never wraps up as fast as they portray. There's about a thousand hours of detective work and dead-end leads that don't make it onto the screen. It's grueling and it requires patience.

Right now, while I'm standing outside Danika's building with a hangover to beat the band, I'd love to try and solve this case. The case of us. Every muscle in my body is screaming at me to climb the goddamn fire escape and bang on her window, where I would beg her to take me back. But I have to put in my hours first. She deserves the extra time I'm going to put in, because she's not getting half-ass from me again. No way. I'm coming in strong.

After Jack left the other night, I drank more tequila. And when I woke up, my brain was trying to squeeze out through my left eye socket, so I slept some more. The second time I woke up—this morning—I had to deal with a hard truth.

I'm not good enough to win her back yet.

There are things in my life I've neglected, besides her. My brother is one of them, and doing something about it is long past due.

There will never stop being a chance that I could lose him. But—as galling as this is to admit—Jack kicked my ball of common sense and got it rolling in a new direction. If I lost my brother tomorrow, I would still have all of the pain . . . but not enough good memories. In fact, the only recent ones I have are him showing up unannounced and forcing me to acknowledge how much I care about him.

Now it's my turn.

Unfortunately, I've just lost the love of my life, and I'm in a downward tailspin, so the memory my brother and I will make today isn't going to be sunshine and roses. Actually, it's going to be pretty damn smelly. But this is where I'm at right now. This is where I'm at. And even though I've pushed Charlie away, I have every confidence he's going to be onboard. Because he's a good man and I could learn a lot from him. We could learn a lot from each other. And starting today, I'm going to do my best to make that happen.

If I'm going to be what Danika needs, my will

to be *better* needs to extend to every corner of my life. So I'm taking a page from her book and repairing what needs fixing for my family. Unlike a television show, this isn't going to be a fast fix. I need her to know I mean it. That I'm going to be a good man who's not afraid to change.

I called Charlie three minutes ago to let him know I was outside. He's still pulling on a wrinkled T-shirt when he walks out of the building. I don't comment on the red claw marks all over his shoulders and chest, but it's pretty obvious how he was spending his Sunday.

"Hey." With a yawn, he scrubs a hand over his hair. "What's up?"

"Do you own rubber gloves?"

He's awake now. And looking at me like I'm crazy. "Er . . . like the cleaning kind? I don't think so. Why?"

"I need your help."

Christ. He reacts like I just asked him to be my best man, and hell, something sharp sticks in my side. After clearing his throat several times, he's still gathering a response. It hits me hard that I'm no better than Danika at letting people in my life know I need them. I haven't even admitted to myself until now that I *do*. Sure, I understand things like following protocol, safety procedures and calling for backup, but when it comes to real life—right here and now—I've been living in solitude and relying only on myself for anything non-work-related. At least Danika lets those around her know she loves them. I give nothing.

"There's a ninety-nine cent store around the corner," Charlie says, finally. "We could grab some gloves there."

"Aren't you going to ask me what they're for?"

He shakes his head. "If you need my help, you're going to get it."

Now I'm clearing my throat. "You should say no. I've been a shitty brother, and you should tell me to go to hell, so you can get back to your Sunday."

I've shocked him. Maybe I've even shocked myself a little, but my shoulders already feel lighter, saying the truth out loud. Making myself own it. "Is that what you want me to do?"

My swallow gets caught. "No. I want you to get used to me showing up."

Charlie rolls his eyes, but I can see the sheen in them. The smile he's battling. "As long as it doesn't involve rubber gloves every time, I think I can get used to that."

"Deal."

We're turning toward the corner, in a silent agreement to go buy gloves at the ninety-nine cent store, when I see Danika. She doesn't spot us at first and maybe that's a good thing. My features aren't schooled, and it's probably nothing but naked agony at having her so close, knowing I don't have the option to hold her.

I'm not alone. I have you.

No you don't.

When the world turns against you, all you're left holding is a bat and an ego.

My gut burns with regret. No, touching her is not an option until I've restored the confidence I ripped out of her on Friday. In us, in herself. I won't allow myself the chance to win her back until there's not a shadow of doubt that I want her, exactly as she is. And that I will *never* walk away from her again, no matter what kind of danger she faces.

Danika's steps falter when she sees us, her brown eyes shooting wide. There are earbuds in her ears, and she fumbles, trying to remove one. What is she listening to? God, I want to go back to the night she slept in my bed and start over, knowing what I know now. That I love her and I might as well already be dead without her in my life. That fact is so obvious right now, when my pulse is going haywire at the sight of her. My mouth is a desert, and I can't stop staring. Staring at this loyal, beautiful, courageous girl who let me in, but I fucked it all up.

"Hey, D," Charlie says into the charged silence. "Where've you been? Everyone thinks you're still in bed."

It only occurs to me now that she's coming home from the night before, and my head starts to fucking melt, a bellow of denial building in my throat at the very notion she could have been with someone else. Until she answers and I'm dropped from the sky down into an ice bath. "I went on a bike ride with my mom." She edges past us, as far away from me as she can get. "Um, hope you left me some coffee."

She's not even going to say hi to me. It's the worst possible torture. Her cheeks are a little sunburned, and she's got on a loose sweatshirt I've never seen. I'm holding myself back from pouncing on her . . . and no hello. Nothing. This is what I get. I totally earned her silence. I *left*.

In my periphery, I notice Charlie split a look between us. "D, can you let Ever know I'll be out with my brother for a while?"

"Sure." Finally, she gives me some eye contact, and just for a split second, I see everything there. Anger, sadness, frustration. She misses me and thank God for that. It might get me through the next couple days. "Where are you going?"

"To buy some rubber gloves," I answer in a raw voice, gratified when she freezes in the act of unlocking the door. "Maybe a couple of nose plugs."

"Whoa," Charlie says. "This is the first I'm hearing about nose plugs."

Danika pushes through the front door of the building. But not before she glances back over her shoulder and something passes between us. It's more than a hint that there's more to come. It's a promise.

CHAPTER 31

Danika

The women's locker room is my only refuge.

Seriously, I get a gun pulled on me one time, and my friends turn into psychotic babysitters. Last night, I woke up in the middle of the night to go pee, and when I came out, Ever was waiting for me with a glass of water and a smile. My efforts to convince them I'm fine are not working. Probably because I'm full of shit. I'm not fine.

Especially because Greer is on the academy schedule for the day.

I bend forward on the bench and stick my head between my knees, breathing hard, trying to calm my nerves. Yes, I saw him outside my building over the weekend, but I didn't have time to psych myself out for that encounter. I've had *more* than enough time to get nervous about seeing him again at the academy. Especially because seeing him post-breakup was like a kick to the solar plexus. Seriously. He couldn't have waited to break my heart until after graduation?

Charlie came home from being out with Greer, happy but tight-lipped. Why did he need rubber gloves and nose plugs? Did he return to the stamps lady's apartment? Why?

Doesn't matter. He's running drills twice this week, then he'll be at the commencement ceremony. After Saturday, forgetting about the lieutenant will get easier. I'll only see him on the off chance he stops by the apartment to see Charlie. Making myself scarce won't be difficult when that happens. I've got this. I'm on the road to heartbreak recovery.

Pay no attention to the girl hyperventilating in row three.

When I hear the locker room door open and shut, followed by the voices of some female recruits, I sit up straight and shake myself. "For the love of God. Pull yourself together, Silva."

I stand up on rubbery legs and run in place, ignoring strange looks from the new arrivals. A check of the clock tells me inspection is in eight minutes, so I can't put off changing anymore. Taking deep breaths, I open my locker . . . . and around a million books of stamps perform an avalanche, piling up around my feet.

"Damn, Silva. Are you some kind of hoarder?"

I'm too busy trying to swallow my heart to respond to the barb. There are so many stamps and at a glance, my expert eye tells me they're not normal, run-of-the-mill ones. No, there are collector's editions I've only ever seen on the Internet. Some foreign ones. There are more Elvis booklets, like the one Greer brought me before. And there's no doubt Greer left these.

Did all of these come from the cat lady? No. Not all of them are available at the post office. At least not currently. He might have gotten some from her, but the majority would have had to be purchased on the Internet. After *a lot* of research.

But what does it mean?

Does he want me back?

No time to think about it now. Or ever. He thinks he can fix the situation with hundreds of . . . incredible, breathtaking stamps that I'm dying to add to my collection books? He's got another think coming. I'm not hanging around for more pain. I have to remember what it felt like. When he turned and walked away while I was shaking from needing him.

I'm not alone. I have you.

No. You don't.

The echo of those words propels me into a crouch. Jaw tight, I scoop the books of stamps into the locker before dressing at warp speed. Moments later, I'm walking into the gym, Charlie on one side of me, Jack on the other, like a couple of demented sentries.

"Brought you a water," Jack says, dropping an ice-cold bottle of Poland Spring into my hand. "Make sure you hydrate."

"Ever is making chocolate cream pie tonight," Charlie chimes in. "Guess who's getting the biggest slice?" He pokes me in the side. "This girl right here."

"Guys." I pull my right leg up into a stretch. "If you keep this up, I'm assuming a new identity and moving to Siberia."

"We can FaceTime," Jack points out.

"Sorry, I'll be going off the grid."

Charlie winks. "Smoke signals."

I'm considering knocking their thick heads together, but I stop when I realize they've taken my mind off seeing Greer. For a full sixty seconds. Which is no small accomplishment since I've been thinking of him nonstop. Also every hour prior to that, since I met him. What an asshole. It must have taken him days to round up all those stamps.

Asshole.

A familiar whistle blows and we line up, everything moving on autopilot, except my stomach, which buries itself under the gymnasium floorboards.

I force myself to look straight ahead as Greer moves down the line, his pencil scratching on his clipboard. My head is like a cave, though, making his approaching footsteps sound hollow, a lot like my belly. "Silva," he says when he's right in front of me. I lift my chin and stare at some imaginary spot beyond his shoulder. But that same chin drops at what he says next. Still making notes on his clipboard, he murmurs, "As goddamn beautiful as ever."

Whoa. What?

In my peripheral vision, heads are turning. During inspection, the gym is silent except for the lights buzzing overhead, so everyone heard that. Everyone.

Doesn't he care? I know he went to his supervisor about a special exception being made for our relationship while I'm still a recruit, but I assumed the request was withdrawn after we went our separate ways. Does this mean his request was approved?

I snap my jaw up off the floor. It doesn't matter. There is no relationship.

But my blood is humming like a generator as Greer continues down the line.

Greer

S imply fucking put, I'm going out of my mind without her.

Having her in front of me, lined up for inspection, sends me through a flashback of all the times we've been in this same position, making the magnitude of what I could lose even more real. My electric mix of scrappy girl and gorgeous woman. My woman. It wasn't my plan to call her beautiful this morning, but the words wouldn't stay trapped inside. It felt so good surprising her that I'm dying to make a hobby out of it.

Starting now.

I haven't touched Danika since I shook her and spoke to her so cruelly, before walking out of her parents' place. I was only beginning to realize how miserable I could be without her when she passed me outside Charlie's apartment. Now? I go back and forth between feeling like my insides have been slashed to ribbons, and being completely numb. Staying away from her has been utter hell, but taking the time to plan was necessary. There are two ways I could blow getting her back. Being impulsive and screwing up. Again. Or proving her right and being my by-the-book, predictable self.

I have two things going for me now—the element of surprise and the knowledge that she's still attracted to me. Not just my body. Me. Us together. That belief is mostly a play to keep my sanity while I'm getting back into her good graces, but I'm running with it like a mother-fucker.

The first two hours of the day are spent in one of the lecture halls. Try talking about community relations with romance on the brain—it's not easy. After lunch, I blow my whistle to bring the recruits running, along with Danika. They start breaking up into groups, assuming we're going to start conditioning exercises, but on top of charming a certain cat lady out of stamps and scouring the internet for other, more coveted booklets, I've spent the last handful of miserable days planning something else.

"Everyone head to the locker rooms and grab your things. There's a bus waiting outside to take us to a training facility in Queens. We're going to work on your tactical skills." I pause for dramatic effect—proving I'm delirious with exhaustion. "In the maze."

There's a hush before every recruit begins speaking at once, their excitement obvious. Except for Danika, who's watching me with curious eyes. The maze is exactly what it sounds like, but it wasn't created for recreation. It was built to train officers on how to take corners and provide cover when navigating a potentially active crime scene. Recruits are usually trained in empty houses, veteran cops posing as perps, and these recruits have already completed that portion of the curriculum. The maze is far more advanced, used mostly by the Emergency Services Unit and occasionally the military. Sometimes I join them when I'm looking to blow off steam, but I've never brought recruits along for the ride.

I've called in some favors to get these near-graduates a lesson in what's to come. They're going to fail the first time—it's just a given at the maze. Even I failed my first time going through the narrow, weaving passages with smoke in my eyes. It's designed to hammer into an officer's head that he's not invincible.

Which means it's going to be a test I have to pass, too. One I can't fail. Am I an instructor today? Yes. Am I also a man trying to prove something to his woman?

Better believe it.

CHAPTER 32

—————— *Danika* ——————

This place is nasty.

Not garbage dump nasty. It doesn't smell like sewage or anything. No, it's formidable. High, gray concrete walls form a perimeter around the maze. Brittle vines climb the sides, disappearing into cracks. The overcast sky above does nothing to lessen the worry that we're going to find a fire-breathing dragon inside.

When we walk through the wide entrance, a bunch of badasses in ESU gear smirk at us from a very basic, unmanned reception area. They huddle closer together and laugh amongst themselves, taking our measure with quick sweeps of intuitive eyes. Translation: We're about to hand you your butts on a silver platter. Funny, I believe them. Meanwhile, Jack and Charlie are posturing at the smirkers like they're getting ready to call out the biggest one. Lord. This is what happens when their girlfriends aren't around to keep them from turning into Neanderthals.

Greer approaches the recruits, and my pulse begins to gallop. Am I crazy thinking this impromptu trip to the maze has something to do with me? I'm not a self-centered person—mostly—but the timing makes me wonder. I was almost shot on Friday. Greer broke up with me over it. Now he's throwing me into an intense simulation while he watches from the sidelines?

"Listen up."

My blood jumps along with my body at the sound of Greer's voice. We fall into an inspection line without hesitation, as if we're back in the gymnasium. In twenty years, we'll all probably still react on instinct to Greer's commands—he's that grippingly confident and in charge. Only . . . I know him well enough now to see the chink in his armor. There's a thin sheen of sweat on his forehead, and his knuckles are white on the clipboard.

"This is a more amplified scenario than the ones you've been trained to handle," Greer continues. "Your flight or fight instinct will be stronger. Your ability to focus will be diminished. Control the fear. Don't let it overpower you."

Another ESU officer saunters out of the reception area and stands beside Greer, grim-faced. "You're going through the maze in entry teams of four first. Your job is to clear the building and retrieve the hostage. Say hello to your hostage," says Greer. The ESU officer does a pinky wave, earning him a grudging laugh from the recruits. "The officers who've agreed to assist us today will be using rubber bullets to deter you. That shit stings, so keep your goggles and vest on at all times. No exceptions. If you make it through the group session without getting tagged, you can come back to the beginning and go through solo. If you *do* get tagged in the group session, go sit in the grass and call your mommies for moral support." He gives an uncharacteristic wink. "And if you tag one of these assholes, you can call their mommies and gloat."

That gets a laugh out of the three remaining ESU officers who are sauntering into the maze like a faction of gods, weapons tucked under their arms. Charlie's goals include moving through the ranks and retiring in a million years as a bureau chief, like his father, but Jack's shooting skills could land him among ESU ranks in the future. Glancing over at my best friend, I can totally see his big, cocky ass making it there for the first time, scaring recruits out of their minds someday.

Greer calls out names, putting us in groups of four. I'm with Charlie, Nick and a girl named Raquel who has spent the last few months working herself to the bone, like me. I've got a good crew. We go into the reception area and gear up, deciding among our group that Charlie will run point, since he has some after-hours experience training with ESU and knows their procedures, even if he isn't an expert. Yet.

Over the next half hour, we watch teams go in through the front entrance and walk out the back one, lights on their vests illuminated like billboards of shame. Out of the twenty recruits who enter the maze, only two walk out untagged. I'm relieved to see Jack is one of them.

"There's more than one entry point to the maze," I whisper to my crew. "If two of us come in through the exit, they might be distracted by the two of us at the front. We'll cut the ground we have to cover in half."

"Good point." Charlie checks his weapon, which is also loaded with rubber bullets. "We might screw ourselves if the hostage is located up front and they take out the two of us coming in from the main entry. The other two would have to do double the work to retrieve him."

"So let's send you in through the front," Raquel says to Charlie. "That gives the front entry team the best chance of survival."

Charlie laughs. "I'm the sacrifice, huh? Fine." He slaps a hand over his heart and throws me a deadpan look. "Tell Ever I loved her."

I snort. "Will do."

Greer appears in the doorway of the reception area, his heavy gaze resting on me for a few beats. "You're up."

We're heading for the maze when I realize Nick isn't with us. I turn in a circle, surprised to find him ten feet behind, his gaze locked on Levi, who's just come through the obstacle. Levi's hunched shoulders and wry expression tell me he must have failed. He grimaces at Nick, slashing a finger across his throat, and Nick smiles back. And even when Levi passes, Nick continues to just stand there, watching his friend head for the grass.

I give a not-so-subtle cough. "Nick, are you coming?"

"What?" His head jerks around, and he jogs to catch up. "Yeah. Sorry."

Training exercise or not, my pulse is hammering in my ears as the four of us approach the maze. My weapon feels foreign in my grip. Sweat rolls down my spine. It's ridiculous, but I have the added burden of unfinished business. As if I'm a soldier going off to war while in the middle of a fight with her sweetheart. Stupid. But when Greer catches my eye, a knot forms in my throat.

There are so many things we haven't said. I don't even know what the stamps in my locker mean yet. That chink in his armor is bigger than before, too, his jaw locked like the door to a safe.

"Ready?" Nick asks, giving me a discreet elbow in the side. "Let's head around back."

I tear my attention off Greer. "Let's go."

Charlie and Raquel take their position at the front entry point, while Nick and I jog around toward the rear. The recruits waiting in line for their turn make interested noises over our strategy, but there's no time to process that or psych myself out. Because it's time. There's no whistle signaling we should begin—that would tip off our opponents—but a neutral observer from the control area opens the doors.

And it's on.

Nick and I move in a buttonhook, him going to the right of the door, me stepping left and finding the wall with my back. Weapon raised, I assess the layout as quickly as possible, seeing the maze is a series of rooms. Okay. Okay, we've done this before.

We've just never done it with music blaring and gunshots firing in the distance. The music is so loud, I have to scream to be heard. And boom. My legs are anxious to run, my mind calling for me to find a solution to the chaos. For a few seconds, Nick ceases to exist, and it's just me. But it's *not* only me in the maze. I'm part of a team. It's alarming how quickly my impulse kicks in to forget our strategy and go after the hostage alone. Just rely on *my* instincts, instead of trusting my partner. Can't do that. *Can't.* That's how people get killed.

Follow your training.

At first, it's Greer's voice saying those words in my ear, but eventually it becomes mine. My own voice repeating what I've learned and keeping me focused.

Nick and I clear each room, one of us opening the door, the other hooking in and clearing the space. We've only been inside the maze about thirty seconds when our rhythm falters, though. One of the doors is locked.

That's when the lights flicker and go out.

"Oh, come on," I groan, my words swallowed up by the pounding bass. If I was wearing a police belt, there would be a flashlight attached, but we've got nothing. Except phones. Without consulting each other, Nick and I whip them out and open flashlight apps, holding them above our weapons as we try to recapture our equilibrium in the dark. We need to get inside that locked room. My instincts tell me that's where the hostage is located.

Nick and I trade nods, like he's already figured out the same thing. Because he's my teammate and we have the same goal. It's that easy. I'm not doing this alone. Hoping Charlie and Raquel can manage to hold off the ESU badasses a little longer, I step aside, train my gun on the doorway and give Nick the signal to kick in the door. He does.

Gunfire rings out and Nick's vest lights up. I'm so stunned, it takes me a split second to register the shot came from inside the room, so I raise my weapon and fire. From inside the room, another vest lights up, belonging to an ESU officer. There's no time to gloat over that small victory— although, I'm planning on it later—because the hostage is sitting cross-legged at the officer's feet. Playing Candy Crush.

Greer

When Danika stumbles out of the exit, I'm caught between three emotions. Pride, first and foremost. Christ, there's so much pride I can't decide if I want to laugh or squeeze her to death. She did it. My girl fucking did it. Second, I'm relieved as hell. She was safe inside the maze, but ask if my heart cares. It's a thousand pounds right now and living in my stomach just imagining her in a scenario where she could feel fear or loss of control.

My third and final response is irritation because the "hostage" is pretending to be incapacitated, tongue lolling out like an idiot, forcing Danika—who's half his size—to carry his weight.

"Enough," I bark. "You've got two legs. Use them."

The jerk-off comes back to life and smirks at me.

Well. Apparently news has made it around the department that I'm seeing Danika. Or was seeing her, as the case may be.

If I want to be with her again, I have to get used to my heart living in my stomach. That's how it's going to be, if I want to have a heart at all. Because she owns it. Every beat. And as I watch her smile light up her face over the victory, I have zero doubts that it'll be worth the worry to have happiness with her. To make a life with her. To let her warmth and beauty push out the cold ugliness that's dominated my life for so long.

God, I want that so much, it must be right there in my eyes when she finally looks over at me, because her smiling lips wobble, and she stops walking.

We're not done yet, though. There's more to come, and I want her focused. Later. Later I'll tell her how proud I am of her and erase all the ugly shit I said last Friday. "Okay, Silva. Head back to the front with the other winners." I refocus on my clipboard, even though I'm still seeing her. "Nick, go call your mom."

After the rest of the teams brave the maze, there are a total of four recruits who've earned the right to face it alone. Am I surprised Jack, Charlie and Danika are three of them? Not really. Charlie and Danika have been my strongest recruits since the beginning, and Jack is making up for lost time. I would be concerned their three egos aren't going to fit into one apartment after today, except for one fact.

The ESU guys only operated at half speed during the group exercise.

My brother, Jack and the other recruit emerge looking like someone put their head in a trash can and banged on it for an hour. Pretty much the same way I looked the first time I went through the maze. Maybe I'll tell them that later and save their delicate feelings. Maybe not.

My own delicate fucking feelings are hanging in the balance right now.

Danika is the final recruit to go through solo, and her confidence has slipped in the face of her friends' failures. The need to say something encouraging to her is intense, but the door to the building bangs open, and in she goes, weapon raised.

When I hear the hollow sound of bullets being fired, my vision grows hazy, the lunch I ate threatening to come up. I'm so focused on getting through the next few minutes and proving to Danika that I can, that I believe in her, I forget about the earpiece in my ear.

Until it crackles with static and my blood goes cold.

"Lieutenant Burns. You might want to get in here."

Danika

Pain throbs in my ankle, hot and sharp. Is it twisted? Sprained? I don't know.

I need to get up off the ground where I tripped hard and fell, but I can't see. There's smoke everywhere. Somewhere in the back of my head, I know it's meant to look like tear gas. It's not actually tear gas. But that knowledge doesn't help me see anything, does it? I manage to crawl on my elbows behind an alcove wall so I can get my bearings.

Ha. Bearings? I don't even know which direction to head for the exit. I've already been hit by more than one rubber bullet. I'm the maze equivalent of DOA, but I still have to make it out.

I can't stay in here forever. This is what it's like to be alone. Without a partner to cover me or call for backup. Now that I'm incapacitated, my options are whittled down to nothing. If this was a real life situation, I'd be well and truly screwed, but the consequences would be far worse.

Christ. My ankle hurts. The pain is flooding my eyes with tears, but I can't take off my goggles to wipe them away. Dammit. I get it now. How important it is to trust a team, in addition to my own gut. In the future, I won't find myself in a situation like this alone. Right now, though, I need to get my shit together. *Come on, Silva.*

I try to stand and fire shoots down to my toes, stealing my breath. My butt lands on the ground, and I release a choked gasp. Another round of smoke goes off, rubber bullets hit the wall above my head. Whap, whap, whap. Where's the exit? Which way did I come in?

"Danika."

Greer. Is here? His silhouette appears in the smoke, and I swear I see bullets bouncing off his shoulders before he's down on the ground beside me, his powerful back against the same wall as mine. Amazing that even in a smoky battle zone, my breath holds itself in his presence, my spine straightening. Inside my chest, though, that's where the real chaos happens.

It wants to leap out through my mouth and let him take custody.

His eyes are more than a little wild as he looks me over, attention landing on my swollen ankle. That giant chest lifts and falls on a shudder, and he blows out a slow breath up toward the ceiling. When he leans toward me, I'm not prepared for what he says in my ear. "Get up."

Just like that, I want to kill him. "You don't think I'm trying?"

"Try harder." He lifts my chin in a cold hand, seeming to gather his words. "God knows I want to carry you out of here, baby. No one would fault you with that ankle. But I need you to understand something. I know you can do it. I have faith in you." His swallow shifts the muscles in his throat. "And next time you face something dangerous, you're going to have faith that I'll be there, waiting for you, when it's over. Do you understand?"

Well, if I thought I was crying before, it's nothing compared to now. My goggles are going to look like a fish tank by the time I make it out of here. Damn this man. I knew deep down what this exercise was about. I knew, didn't I? Stupid, glorious idiot. He did this for us, and I'm not going to miss the chance to build the bridge to something real, something amazing, he's offering us. "I love you," I blurt. "And . . . in a way, you *will* be carrying me out, because I'll be feeling and hearing you the whole way. I do the same for you, right?"

"*Yes.*"

I hold out my hand and he takes it, squeezing. "Partners?"

I'm not asking to be professional partners, and he's well aware of it. With my eyes, I'm promising to trust him, to believe in him and requesting the same in return. I'm promising to be more trustful, period. A vow I know I can keep now. "Partners," he rasps, his expression fierce in the near darkness.

"Good." I take a deep breath. "Now get out."

He makes a sound and looks away, but that gaze thunders back to mine right away. Bullets ping the wall above his head. "Jesus, Danika. You just made it a lot harder to walk out of here without you."

"You love me, too," I whisper in his ear. "That's why you'll be able to do it."

Greer's mouth finds mine in a single, hard kiss, and I hear a few howls out in the darkness. His fingers push through my hair, his lips landing on my forehead, lingering there a moment. Then he's gone and it's just me inside the smoke.

It's not easy and I get shot twice more, but I find a way to walk on my ankle that doesn't make me want to scream. Keeping my weapon raised and returning fire when I can, I slide my back along the walls, wincing as I go. Finally, I recognize the series of rooms Nick and I swept during the group drill and limp toward the exit, bursting out into the muted sunlight.

Everyone is there waiting. Jack and Charlie look ready to murder me. I only have eyes for Greer, though. He's white as a sheet, and his clipboard is snapped in half, but he's here. And he's waiting for me, letting me know that's how he'll stay. With his words inside the maze echoing in my ears, I believe him.

Every fiber of my being is demanding I go to Greer, so I do exactly that. I manage to take three more limping steps before he lunges forward, drops the broken clipboard and scoops me into his arms. "You can't stop me from putting ice on that ankle and acting like an asshole when you try and run on it too soon. So don't even try."

"No." I laugh the word into his neck. "I won't."

"I fucking love you," he breathes, tightening his grip on me. "I love you, I'm proud of you and I need you. Come be with me."

Happiness turns me weightless. "Yes."

Danika

When I was a kid, my father brought me to a Knicks game at Madison Square Garden. It was the biggest, brightest place I could imagine. As a grown woman, it doesn't seem quite as huge, but my heart races nonetheless as I prepare to walk onstage and accept my diploma, beneath the massive lights and flashing cameras. No way in hell was I going to graduate with a crutch, so I've spent the last few days keeping my ankle rested. I've got a limp, but thankfully I should be fully recovered in a couple of weeks. In time to join the force.

Where have I been resting my ankle? At my apartment during the day. But as soon as Greer's shift ends, I can set a clock on him striding into my bedroom, sweeping me up into his arms and carrying me out to his waiting patrol car.

"I'm making up for not being able to carry you out of the maze," he grumbled the first time. Each day after that, though, he only smiled and took me home.

Home.

Crazy enough, his apartment already feels like . . . ours somehow. Maybe it's the way he stuffed every kitchen drawer full of Snickers bars and bought flowery throw pillows for his bed. Imagine *that* trip to Bed, Bath & Beyond. Or maybe I feel welcome because he never stops looking at me like he can't believe I'm there. Or how he whispers in my ear while I'm sleeping that he never wants me to leave. Yeah, I think that's it.

God, he looks incredible up onstage in his dress blues, shaking hands and handing out diplomas. In this entire arena, I'm the only one that knows he wears nothing but briefs and a smile when we're at home. Home. There's that incredible word again. I've been lucky enough to have three of them in my lifetime. My parents' apartment, which will always hold millions of treasured memories. The three-bedroom where my roommates and I dwelled while succumbing to the L word. Now, Greer's place. Considering he put a key to the apartment on my ring last night while I was sleeping, I don't think he minds me calling it home, either.

Jack must hear my dreamy sigh from his spot ahead of me in line, because he turns and winks at me. I flip him off and we both smile.

The line moves and I hobble forward. One would think my confidence would be shaken after getting injured in the maze, but it's stronger than ever. I don't mind saying Greer had something to do with it, because I know I restored his confidence, too. In the universe. In fate. How to live with knowledge that no one controls either of those things. We have to grab on to happiness when we're lucky enough to have it offered. We did. And we'll keep doing it.

It's Charlie's turn to accept his diploma, and I strain my vocal cords cheering. He blows a kiss to Ever in the audience—he didn't earn the nickname Romeo for nothing—and shakes hands with Greer. Tears cloud my vision seeing them there together, two courageous men that have changed the course of my life in different ways. In the next few decades, that course will change again and again—they'll be with me when it happens. My friend. My Greer.

They pose for a picture, and Greer hands over the diploma, but before Charlie can walk off stage, Greer does something that steals my breath. He calls back his brother and pulls him into a bear hug. At first, Charlie is clearly stunned, but he responds quickly, hugging his brother back. Finally, it descends into macho back slapping, which makes me laugh through my tears. Something tells me their relationship is going to be different from now on.

A few minutes later, a thrill slides over me when Jack shakes hands with Greer and accepts his diploma. I can hear Katie whistling in the audience where she sits beside Jack's mother, both of them beaming up at the new man he's become in such a short time. One of the best. I'm so proud of him, I think I could float up into the Garden rafters. Even better, he's proud of himself. It's right there on the too-handsome face I've known since childhood.

Before I know it, Greer says my name into the microphone. Navigating the stairs is a joy—not really—and I can see Greer is biting the inside of his cheek, wanting to come assist me. In the end, though, I make it on my own, my gait as even as possible as I move toward him on the stage. Call me a lovesick puppy, but I couldn't stop walking to him if I wanted to. The love in his eyes is like an invisible conveyer belt, drawing me closer to the place I'm happiest.

"Hi," I mouth at him.

"Hi, baby," he says back.

Directly into the microphone.

My mother's cackle cuts right through the eruption of audience laughter.

I'm compelled to kiss him once we're standing in front of each other—especially after that—because I'm getting used to greeting him that way. It would be so easy to make this moment about us. But Greer doesn't do that. He shakes my hand and gives me the diploma like I'm someone who's just gone through months of difficult training to achieve something. And I have.

I'm a cop now.

I look out at the audience and find my parents, taking a moment to savor the accomplishment. The pride radiating from Greer only makes it sweeter.

Greer

It's a strange thing, letting go of control.

Well. Let's not get crazy, I'm still Lieutenant Hard-Ass, and Danika can attest that I call the shots when we're making each other moan. As for shutting myself off from experiences life has to offer so I won't face another loss? I'm done with that. When I lost Danika, I had no option but to let go of the past, and Christ, I feel light and heavy all at once. Light with relief. Heavy with love for my girl.

There's still ugliness. There always will be because of the nature of my job. Now, though? I'm feeling more beauty than ugliness because I stopped trying to block it from coming in.

Now it's everywhere. Across from me in the pillows every morning. Crying out underneath me at night. Danika. Beauty is her. It's in the way she tucks her face into my neck as I carry her up the stairs to our apartment right now.

Yeah, our apartment. As soon as we find out where she'll be stationed, I'm going to ask her to move in with me. Depending on how far she has to travel, it might be more convenient to live in a different neighborhood, so I'm waiting to find out. I like the idea of starting from scratch and seeing what we create together.

She doesn't eat as many Snickers bars as I thought. She seems to be happier with yogurt. At least, I thought she was, until I bought forty varieties of the stuff, then she promptly switched to cereal. Really, she doesn't have any discernible pattern when it comes to food. But I'm going to keep watching her and trying to nail one down.

Slowly, I ease her down outside the door and let us in. "Are you hungry?"

Her sleepy hum wraps around me. "I'll make us grilled cheeses."

This is what I'm talking about. How am I supposed to shop for her when she doesn't require a set menu? "We don't have the stuff for that."

"We have cheese, butter and bread."

"We do?"

God, her smile is sexy. "We do."

This is a game we've been playing, seeing who can use the words *our, we* or *us* the most times in a sentence. It's a fun game, okay? I never want to stop playing it. Also, I win most of the time, which leads to her fake pouting. Which leads to kissing and eventually hot, sweaty fucking.

See? Great game. "Do you want to sit at our table or our couch?"

She slides toward the kitchen, giving me a seductive look over her shoulder. "Either one is fine for us." Bending forward, she opens a cabinet and removes the skillet, giving me a nice look at her tight ass in those uniform pants she wore for graduation. I've never wanted to kiss her more than I did on that stage tonight, but it was damn fulfilling watching her shine. I'll never stop being grateful I had the privilege of witnessing her setbacks and triumphs along the way. I love this girl. I loved her the day I saw her, but that love is so deep now, no one will ever find the bottom of it.

As if she can sense the sudden seriousness of my thoughts, Danika sets down the skillet on the stove and turns. That restraint I used onstage is colliding with the hunger she always makes me feel . . . and I just want us skin to skin. I'll never get enough of her, and I can't seem to stop proving myself right.

"We . . . should eat later," I rasp.

She's already limping toward the bedroom. "Race you to our bed."

I scoop her into my arms with a growl. "Don't you dare."

Seconds later, I lay Danika down on the bed and start to undress her, but she frames my face with her hands, drawing my forehead down to meet hers. Everything narrows down to her. This. It's like she waves a magic wand and relieves me of any grief or worry I've ever felt, leaving nothing but us in the present. "I won the game this time. You're slipping."

"Am I?" I slide my tongue into her mouth, working both of us up with a slow, wet kiss. "Feels like I won pretty huge. Feels like it every second of the day now."

"I won, too," she whispers, capturing me with a look. "Let's call it an indefinite tie."

My smile feels more natural than ever. "It's a deal."

"I love you, Grim Reaper."

"God, I love you, too." My fingers travel into her panties and find their mark, shooting her hips off the bed. "Let me show you how much."

Is this your first time reading
The Academy series?
If so, you won't want to miss the first
two books in the series . . .

DISORDERLY CONDUCT

Charlie and Ever's story

INDECENT EXPOSURE

Jack and Katie's story

Available now from Avon Books!